MW00884092

The
UNEXPECTED
REQUEST

Rebekah A. Morris

DEDICATION

To Meleah Ellen Jones
Who made me write more than the first thousand words.

CONTENTS

FOREWORD

I didn't intend to write a Western. I had never dreamed of writing one, but to my surprise, I found myself doing that very thing.

It all began when I was looking at a calendar. I came across a picture, which intrigued me. There was something about the mountains, the tawny grass and the low clouds that pulled at my imagination, urging me, calling me to write. I could almost hear the crunching of the frozen grass and the jingle of horses' bridles as they came up the slope.

A few nights later I sat down determined to write a thousand words about that picture. It wasn't long before they were written. Curiously I reread my work. It was rather interesting but that was all I really thought. I posted it on my blog to see what my readers would say about it.

Several weeks later at church, my friend, Meleah asked, "So, what happens next?"

I looked puzzled. "In what?"

"That story on your blog. The one about the two men on horseback."

Laughing a little, I shrugged. "I don't know."

"Well, finish it," she instructed.

I didn't write any more on it for weeks as I had no idea what did happen next. But almost every Sunday, Meleah would ask if I had written any more. Finally, over lunch, I asked her, "Okay, what do you want to know?"

She was ready with her questions. "Who are they? How are they related? Why did the younger one have his gun out? Why were they in a hurry to get to the cabin? Who is Sally?"

I was astonished! I hadn't expected my thousand words to create such interest. So, I set to work. Writing only in thousand word segments, "Meleah's Western," as the story was known to my readers, began to grow. Each time I posted another part on my blog, Meleah would have more questions until the main plot was worked out in my mind. It was slow going at first, with weeks and sometimes months between parts, but at last I really set to work and the story sequence began to flow from my fingers. Once a week my readers were treated to the next thousand words, which, more often than not, left them in tight or exciting places. Soon they were begging me to hurry with the next part!

If it hadn't been for Meleah's interest in that first thousand words (half of the first chapter), I never would have written "The Unexpected Request." I hope you enjoy reading it and find it as interesting and intriguing as my blog readers have.

Rebekah
August, 2011

CHAPTER ONE

A bitter wind struck the two riders full in the face as they crested the ridge. The view of the mountain range was partly obscured by the low clouds, which had moved in after dawn. The towering peaks were still visible, the white of their snow etched against the deep blue sky. Ignoring the frigid bite of the wind, the riders reined in to take in the scene. The valley lay before them in the shadow of the clouds while the ridge they were on was in full sunlight. Stamping with impatience, the horses tossed their heads, each breath a frosty white cloud in the clear air, and the saddles jingled. The older rider pulled his hat lower over his face to try to block the wind and glanced back over his shoulder at the way they had just come.

"Let's ride," he said, noting the impatience of his companion.

No need to urge the horses, for only a slight hint was needed to set them both off at a brisk canter. The sound of the frozen grasses under the horses' hooves was almost the only sound to be heard for miles. Scarcely a word was spoken between the two riders who had been up long before dawn. For over an hour they rode, the younger rider paying no attention to either the scene around them or the clouds above. It was the older rider who kept alert, first glancing around and behind them as they rode and then looking with growing anxiety at the fast gathering clouds that blotted out the towering mountain peaks above them. On they rode, ever on, scarcely slackening their horses brisk pace for anything.

The wind was growing in bitterness with each passing moment, and the older rider sensed a storm was on its way.

"There's a cabin ain't too far from here," he announced, speaking loudly to be heard through the wind. "We can rest the horses an' have a bite to eat."

His companion made no answer save for a slight inclination of the head.

The horses were blowing hard when the two riders pulled them to a halt in front of a ramshackle cabin. No smoke came from the chimney and the latchstring of the door was out. A tiny shed built onto the cabin was just large enough for the two horses. Taking the saddles off the horses, the younger rider quickly rubbed them down with a handful of straw found on the floor and gave them something to eat.

The older man soon had a fire blazing in the fireplace and pulled out some cold meat from his pack.

"Come on," he called to his comrade. "Set yerself down here an' get a bite or two. This fire ought ta thaw ya out 'fore long."

The friend thus urged removed his hat and took a seat on a three-legged stool near the fire. He was a dark haired man, rugged in looks with a full dark beard and the build of a man who had spent most of his life out in the wilds. He ate rapidly and in silence, every now and then turning to glance out the one window.

The wind shook the old cabin and whistled and roared around the chimney. The younger man suddenly sprang to his feet knocking over the stool and strode to the door saying,

"I'll go saddle up."

"Ain't no use, Ty," called out his companion. "We'd never make it. That storm is bound ta hit 'fore too long. I been watchin' it all morning. It'd be a sight better ta jest stay here the night an' strike out first thing in the mornin'. We'd never make it tonight," he said again.

Ty turned, and his voice was almost harsh as he said, "You can stay if'n ya want, Carson. I can't. We don't know how long that letter took ta reach us. Anythin' could a happened by now. I'm goin'. Come or stay as ya please." The wind slammed the door back against the side of the cabin as Ty strode out to the shed.

For a moment Carson sat where he was, staring at the open door. Then with a sigh he stood, picked up his pack and put out the fire. He could understand his companion's impatience to be off, though it seemed rather foolish to leave the cabin in weather like this.

Several hours later, after traveling with what speed they could through the bitterly cold wind, blowing snow and growing darkness, Ty suddenly reined in his horse.

"I know the trail. Follow me," was all he said, or shouted rather, and turning his horse to the left, he set off with Carson right behind. Soon they reached a wooded area and were somewhat sheltered from the fierce winds and driving snow. The trail twisted and turned, now going up the side of the mountain and now back down. At last a light glimmered through the trees in front of them. Both men, more from long habit than anything else, pulled up their horses and in silence looked searchingly at the light, listening all the while. Then, still in silence, they slowly approached. A cabin made of roughly hued logs stood in a little clearing, sheltered behind by a towering cliff which somewhat blocked the fierceness of the winter storm. Light streamed through two small windows as the riders approached. Ty dismounted, and with one hand on his gun, called out,

"Sally!"

The door flew open, and a young girl stood in the doorway peering into the dark. In another moment Ty was beside her and had her in his arms, while she hung, laughing and crying to his neck.

"I'm back, Sally. Everything'll be all right now," Ty soothed.

Carson, without a word, took his horse as well as Ty's, and disappeared in the direction of the small barn he had noticed. Ty, with Sally still clinging to him, entered the cabin, and the door closed behind them.

The cabin had only one room, lighted on one side by a glowing fire and a few candles. The other side was shrouded in darkness and a rough bed was to be seen in the corner, a still form lying under the bed clothes.

The wind was heard whistling outside around the cabin, and Sally shivered a moment in Ty's arms.

"I thought ya'd never come," she whispered. "Oh Ty, it's been so very long."

Ty released himself gently from the girl's hands and returned the gun to its holster before saying anything, and then his tones were low,

"I ain't intended for it ta be this way. How's Pa?" He glanced over at the bed as he spoke.

"Very weak."

Ty moved slowly over to the bed and gazed in silence at the thin, rough face of the man who was his father. It had been two years. Two long years since he had left that cabin and joined Carson in an adventurous trek farther west into the Colorado territory. Little did he dream at that time how long it would be before he saw either his father or sister.

The man stirred and called feebly, "Sally."

"Yes, Pa," the girl answered quickly, "I'm here. An' Pa, Ty's home."

Slowly the sick, old man opened his eyes. His gaze wandered around the room, coming at last to rest on the rugged, bearded face of his son. "Ty, that you?"

"Yes sir. I've come home."

"Sally told me you'd come, an' I didn't doubt it . . . The Good Lord has been right kind . . . to me an' I . . . prayed you'd make it home in time . . . to hear . . ." the older man's feeble voice faded, and his eyes closed once more as he fell asleep, worn out after only a few words.

"That's how he's been for days now," whispered Sally. "He hasn't the strength ta talk for more'n a few sentences 'fore he goes ta sleep once more."

The brother and sister moved softly away from the bed. The girl, struggling to keep the tears from her eyes, stirred the pot over the fire and then sank drearily onto an old log hewn bench.

Ty, taking off his coat and hat, hung them on a peg near the door. His movements were quiet yet an alertness not seen in his earlier riding, was visible. His keen gaze swept the cabin from one rough log side to the other taking in each small detail. His quick ear was the first to catch the sound of his companion's footsteps in the snow before they reached the cabin. With the opening of the door, a blast of frigid, snow laden wind entered nearly blowing Carson into the room and snuffing the candles' flickering flames. Ty hurriedly pushed the door shut, slipping the latch over it to secure it from the wind.

"Ain't much feed fer the horses, but I reckon the storm ain't gonna last too long." Carson spoke with a softer voice than usual for he too had noticed the bed with its quiet occupant.

Sally filled a small tin cup with broth before motioning the two travelers to eat. This they obeyed at once, for such a long, hard ride had stirred up quite an appetite in them.

Nothing was said in that dim cabin. The whistling of the wind round the chimney sounded as though it would gladly tear the old cabin down to get at those within its walls. Anyone who had not been used to the roaring and sighing would have been quite fearful. As it was, no one so much as noticed it save for an occasional glance now and then at some particularly strong gust.

"Sally," the sick man's voice sounded from the bed.

Ty arose, followed his sister to the bed, and lifted with gentle hand the gray head of the father as Sally spooned some warm broth into his mouth.

"Ty, get the . . . pouch . . . hangin' by my gun," the voice was low but insistent.

Ty strode across the room to the door over which the rifle was hanging and lifted the old leather pouch. Placing it in his father's hand he waited in silence.

"Get the Good Book, Child."

Sally stumbled to a shelf and brought back the Family Bible, laying it gently on the bed at her father's side.

It was several minutes before the old man spoke again.

"All these years . . . find her. You must!" In his excitement the father raised himself up and grasped Ty's hand with a vise like grip. "Ty, promise me you'll find her! Promise . . . promise . . ."

"I promise," Ty assured quickly, trying to ease the old man back onto the pillow. "I'll find her."

The hold relaxed and the tired eyes closed. The face was white, and the breaths came in gasps from colorless lips for a few minutes then steadied into the slow breathing of the sleeping.

The young man turned at last with set face. "Who am I ta look for?"

Sally shook her head. "I don't know," she choked over a sob. "I sometimes think his mind ain't right. He's never told me 'bout any person needin' found. In fact he never talked of anyone 'cept you since he took sick."

The night wore on. The storm raged with unabated fury through the woods and around the little cabin. Inside all was still. Carson slept, rolled in a blanket on one side of the darkened room. Sally sat on her little bench near the fire. Sat and thought, cried a little when she thought of her father and slept, then awakened and thanked God that Ty was home. As for that young man, he didn't sleep. He spent most of the time sitting beside his father's bed in silence. It was good to be back home again.

CHAPTER TWO

"Find her! Find her!"

The words echoed over and over in Carson's mind making him stir restlessly. Wearily he opened his eyes making them focus on the walls, the fire, Ty over by the bed, anything. It was no use. The words kept repeating themselves. They would not be silenced. At last Carson gave up and, closing his eyes once more, let his thoughts drift back to a time long since past.

"Jake, that you?"

"Yep," was the response as Jake drew up rein before a small cabin and sprang from the saddle.

"Why boy it's been ages since I laid eyes on you. How've you been?" The speaker was a middle-aged woman with locks beginning to show grey yet with rosy cheeks and bright eyes.

"Been right fine, Mrs. Lacks. Yep, been a while, but I ain't had callin' time now days. Say, Bob round here by any chance?"

"Not at present, but I reckon if you care to wait a spell, he'll be comin' back right soon. Supposin' you just sit under that shade tree an' I'll bring you some buttermilk."

Jake nodded and strode over to the tree. He wasn't much given to talking when he could get by without it.

Mrs. Lacks soon returned with the buttermilk, remarking how warm it was for this time of year. Jake drained the cup without a word. Indeed it would have been difficult to get a word in, for Mrs. Lacks took advantage of her rare visitor and talked on and on. At last, just as Jake, who had noticeably been growing restless, was about to mount and ride off, the sound of a horse was heard, and in another minute Bob rode up.

"Howdy, Jake."

"Howdy."

"I'll be leavin' you boys now as I've got a heap of things to do," Mrs. Lacks informed her visitor and Bob, noticing the silence between them, and realizing in her own good heart that she was not wanted then, she retired to the cabin.

Bob spoke first, "What news?"

"She'll come out."

"When?"

"Soon's I can get ta her."

"When'll that be?"

"Leavin' first light."

"That soon?"

"Yep."

"That all ya come ta tell me?" Bob was used to cross questioning his level-headed but rather closed-mouth friend. It was the only way to get the whole story from him.

"How 'bout ya comin' too?"

"Me?" Bob didn't sound too surprised. "I'd jest be in the way."

Jake grinned. "Ya might fine yerself that wife yer aunt's always tellin' ya 'bout."

"Then I reckon I oughter go. Aunt Kate's been after me ta find that there wife this very mornin'."

"Meet me at the Big Rock Trail, first light."

Bob nodded. "Will do."

And Jake mounted and rode off, disappearing around the bend in the trail.

The birds sang in the trees and high up an eagle soared in the blue sky. A warm summer breeze blew up from the valley, and everywhere flowers turned bright heads up toward the sun. Bob was silent as he unsaddled and took care of his horse. He paid no attention to the small commonplace things around him. His thoughts were mixed.

"I reckon it'll be a good thing fer Jake ta be gettin' hitched, but I jest can't quite believe I'll ever be doin' it. Course I'll go along, but I ain't expectin' much pleasure outter the ride back. Then 'gain, I reckon Jake'll be that turned in his head, he'd ride straight into an ambush an' not know. It jest might be a right good thing ta go 'long. Aunt Kate though, 'll have her hopes set right smart on me gettin' hitched, an' it'll be powerful disappointin' to her when I don't. Can't say's I blame her over much. What with not havin' women folk as neighbors an' no girl in the house. Must get mighty lonesome. I jest ain't ready ta settle down ta house an' family. Maybe never will. But I aim ta go with Jake an' bring his girl home."

It was almost a month later that Jake and his bride Ellen were established in a small log cabin in a clearing made by Jake's strong young arms. They were a happy couple. Ellen never complained despite the hardships of living in the West. When Jake and Bob were off on hunting and trapping trips together, Ellen found the time weighing heavily on her hands. It was Mrs. Lacks who became her companion. Together they would sew or knit in the colder winter months. During the spring and summer, Mrs. Lacks taught the young bride all about gardening. Ellen was a delightful pupil, always eager to learn and improve herself and her surrounding to show the deep love she felt for Jake. Ellen felt at times that she would do anything for him. He was her pride. Always on his returns, no matter how short a time he had been gone, his wife would come running out to meet him, full of joy to have him at home once more.

Thus it was that his trips became shorter and less frequent. When God blessed their home with children, they ceased all together. Those were some of the happiest years of Jake's life. What mattered that the cabin was small and rough and they didn't have fancy clothes nor china dishes? What mattered that their closest neighbors were a good twenty minute walk away and no schools were nearby to send their children to? What mattered it that the only books they owned were the Bible and the alminac? The Bible was the book from which Jake had learned to read, and Ellen had been a school teacher.

"Who knows," Jake would say to his fair Ellen, "Perhaps this land'll be more settled in a few years an' there'll be a school." Whereupon Ellen would laugh gaily and say it didn't matter.

When tragedy hit, it was like a bolt of lightning out of the clear blue sky.

"Where da ya think ya'll be headin' fer, Jake?" The sun was shining from a cloudless sky. All around the signs of summer were to be seen, from the glowing flowers along the road where bees buzzed busily, to the full leafy branches of the trees arching high overhead.

"West."

"Ya aim ta go far?"

Jake shrugged his shoulders. His face looked worn and haggard. His eyes rested not on the beauties around him but on the low mound of earth near the now empty cabin and the little cross, which marked the last resting place of his beloved Ellen. "I got ta get away, Bob," his voice was dull. "Me an' the young'uns jest got ta get away," he repeated. "Too many memories of . . . her." Jake's voice grew husky.

"Well, I reckon ya ought ta." Bob nodded in agreement. "Jest send me word when ya's settled down, an' I'll be seein' ya." Bob held out his hand. After a wrenching grasp, Jake turned from the friend of his boyhood toward the wagon and spoke to the horses. With a lurch, the wagon began to move off down the trail. The trees waved their green branches as though in farewell while unseen birds sang their goodbyes and a squirrel chattered from a fence post.

Bob stood silently beside his horse in front of the cabin and watched. Two young faces looked out the back of the wagon. Bob lifted his hand in farewell. The children returned the wave until they could no longer see the man who had been as an uncle to them. Bob saw the older one place a protective arm around the smaller form beside him. He swallowed the lump that rose suddenly in his throat. It was always hard to say goodbye.

"May the good Lord go with ya, Jake, an' help ya ta bear it." Bob's murmured words were the prayer of his heart as he mounted and turned his horse's head homeward, leaving behind the lonely log cabin with its forsaken, but never to be forgotten, grave.

In the fireplace, a log broke, sending a shower of sparks up the chimney. Carson rolled stiffly over. The storm had spent itself, and all was quiet save for the heavy breathing of the sick man in the corner bed. Sally slept on, spent from many sleepless nights of watching, her head leaning against the wall and an old shawl around her shoulders. Ty, still at his post by the bed, never looked less like sleep, Carson thought looking at the young man as he watched with those keen eyes of his, the deep slumber of the man who was his father. For a long while Carson lay there in silence.

The old family Bible lay still on the bed where Sally had placed it. Reverently, carefully Ty picked it up. It was too dim in the corner to read, but he opened it just the same. Would there be any clue in this old Book as to whom he had promised to find? Or was his father, as Sally thought, not right in his mind? Turning quietly, so as to have what dim light the fire could cast on the Book, Ty opened its pages. There was an inscription on the first page, but the writing was so faint that in the dim light it was unreadable. Ty knew the Bible had belonged to his mother. For several moments

Ty sat unmoving, his thoughts on the mother who had gone away from them all so many years ago. His father had scarcely ever spoken of her. What had she been like? Why wouldn't his father talk of her? What had happened to her? It was all so perplexing. Ty realized that he didn't know for sure if his mother had died or not. He had for years assumed that it was so, but after careful thought, he began to wonder. Every time he or Sally had asked, the father would change the subject and look so old and tired that it was a long time before either child asked again.

Ty turned from these disturbing thoughts to the business at hand. Softly he turned the leaves of the old Book, noticing a pressed flower here and there, an underlined verse now and again, but nothing he could call a clue. Glancing from time to time at the face on the pillow, he kept up his search.

Carson rose after a while to put a new log on the fire and then lay down again. Ty glanced up at the movement and noticed the wind had died and all was still. Sally slept on undisturbed. What had she had to endure, with him gone and the father so sick? In the morning Ty would have a talk with her. Right now he would continue his vigil and his search for something, anything, that might lead to this missing person. At last his patience was rewarded by a small, delicate piece of folded paper. With hands that trembled slightly, the paper was opened revealing a tiny photograph. The face that looked back at him was that of a young woman. The hat and clothes were enough for Ty to know that the woman was from a city, but which city and who it was, he couldn't say for sure. Ty bent over it, trying in the dim light to study the face.

So absorbed had he become that he didn't notice Carson raise himself up suddenly on one elbow and listen.

"Hist!"

Ty jerked his head up, and his hand went instinctively to his holstered gun. Carson had quietly picked up his rifle and held it cocked and ready in his hand.

Silence everywhere. Ty strained his ears as he placed the family Bible hastily but with caution, making no noise, back on the bed then rose from his seat. A slight rustle outside and the silence was shattered by a sudden sharp crack as of a rifle.

CHAPTER THREE

Ty was across the room in an instant, gun in readiness as Carson, with his rifle in his hands cautiously approached the door.

"Ty!" Sally gasped out in terror. "Don't go out there! Don't!" She had sprung up from her seat and now gripped her brother's arm tightly with all the strength she had. "They said they'd be back. Oh, Ty!" Though her voice was low, it was full of fear, and she trembled.

Ty glanced down at her then back to the bed. The sick man slept on undisturbed.

"Stay with Pa," he ordered softly. "I'll be careful—"

"Ty," Carson answered the pleading look Sally had given him before she turned slowly toward the bed, quivering in every limb. "If'n it were them, I reckon we'd 'ave heard more'n jest one shot. Ya jest wait on guard right here, an' I'll check things out."

"Carson, I can't let ya do that. It's me they're after. They must'a known I'd be back with Pa so sick. I'll go out an' you can wait here."

The younger man moved a step toward the door, but Carson stepped in front of him.

"Ain't no use, Ty. My mind's made up. Ya stay here. I'll give the usual signal if'n I want ya." And before Ty could protest or argue, he had pulled back the latch and slipped silently out.

For several minutes Ty stood in the deep silence listening. He couldn't hear Carson's steps out in the snow. Why had he allowed him to go out? What would he find? Would he even be able to give the signal if he wanted to? Just when Ty could stand the strain of inaction no longer, the door opened noiselessly, and Carson glided back in.

"What'd ya see?" Ty questioned.

Carson shook his head with a slight smile. "I reckon we're as jumpy as a rabbit in a fox's den. That weren't more'n a branch snappin' under the weight a snow. Large branch too. Recon it'll make right good firewood."

Ty let his breath out in a long sigh. "I reckon I am nervous. Ain't been back here since the trouble. If'n they catch wind I'm back--" he shook his head, leaving his sentence unfinished, and holstered his gun once more.

A stifled sob reached his ears, and he turned quickly. Sally, kneeling by the bed with her face buried in the bedclothes, was crying. With soft steps Ty moved to her side.

"Sally," he whispered, "ain't nothin' ta be 'fraid a now. Carson found it were jest an old branch broke." He stroked her hair awkwardly.

"I ain't cryin' for that," came the muffled response.

"Then what are ya cryin' for?"

"I . . . I reckon its jest, oh jest for everything. Ya know I ain't one ta cry much." She lifted her face wet with tears and looked at him. "I don't know what's the matter with me, but Ty," her eyes showed the panic she tried to hide. "Promise me you'll be mighty careful. They'll find out you're here an' then . . ."

Ty nodded. "I'll be careful. I promise ya that. I aim ta keep's quiet as possible. No use askin' for more trouble when we got enough on our hands."

All fell silent. Sally allowed Ty to help her to her feet and then to the chair by the bed. Carson sat before the fire with his back to the brother and sister, and though he could hear every word exchanged, he tried not to intrude more than he could help.

"Sally." The sick man roused from his sleep once more and opened his eyes.

"Yes, Pa."

"Is that my son? Is that Ty?"

"Yes, Pa."

A smile lit the old man's face. "She told me you'd be comin'. Ty . . ."

Ty sat down on the bed. "Yes, Pa."

"Ya will find her, won't ya?"

Ty nodded but before he could ask any of the many questions that burned on the tip of his tongue, his father spoke again.

"I knew ya wouldn't . . . fail me." The voice was feeble and low. "In . . . the pouch . . . on my watch guard. Son, get it."

Ty opened the pouch and poured the contents into his hand. His father's watch gleamed in the dim light. On the watch guard Ty found a small gold heart. It appeared to be part of a locket, a broken one. There was no picture. He held it in his hand.

"Is this it, sir?"

The father looked. "Yes, Ty. It was . . . her's . . . but I . . . kept this. It . . . should help . . . Ty."

"Yes, Pa?"

"You never knew her . . . but . . . in the Good Book . . ." The sick man closed his eyes. His breath was scarcely discernible.

"Pa!" Ty's voice was insistent. "What is in the Good Book?"

"The picture . . ." His lips moved, but no sound was heard.

Ty bent over him, his ear almost touching his lips and heard the words, "Take care . . . of . . . yer . . . sisters."

Ty sat up with a start. He glanced at Sally. She seemed not to notice his sudden agitation, for all her attention was focused on her father.

For a full minute no one stirred. Then with one great apparent effort, the father's eyes opened once more, and his voice sounded with a sudden strength.

"Ty will do what I couldn't. I'm goin' home!" There was an exultant ring to his voice as he uttered the last word, and a smile broke full across his face. His gaze was on something unseen by human eyes.

Ty and Sally sat in awed silence staring at the transformed and now lifeless face on the pillow. Neither of them spoke. It seemed a sacrilege to break the silence.

All was quiet. The branches of the trees were heavy with their load of snow. Occasionally the snow would slip off with a soft sound leaving the branch to spring lightly up into the air. Here and there birds with feathers ruffled to keep out the cold could be seen searching for seeds. Most of the forest animals, however, were snugly settled in their warm nests. The only sound heard was the faint hammering from the barn where Carson was busy at work building a rough pine coffin. Smoke spiraled skyward from the nearby cabin chimney, yet though the sun was rapidly approaching the center of the sky, no one inside had so much as thought of eating.

The brother and sister were sitting on either side of a small table near the fireplace. Before them lay the broken locket, the small picture and the family Bible. They had been sitting thus for some time talking and puzzling over the events of the preceding night.

"I still can't see who it is yer ta look for," Sally sighed. "If we have a sister, why ain't we heard a her before? An' why didn't Pa tell us even her name?"

Ty shrugged. "I jest don't rightly know. I'm wishin' I did though." His brows drew together in a frown as he gazed at the table.

"Are ya sure there isn't anything else in the Bible that would help?"

"I didn't see nothin'."

"Ty, are ya sure he said 'sisters' an' not jest sister?"

"An' if'n he didn't, then who would I be supposed ta find?"

It was Sally's turn to frown. They had been over this ground before, and yet she just couldn't quite believe she had a sister. Looking up slowly, she almost timidly began to speak. "What if Ma really isn't dead an' that is . . ." She didn't finish her sentence.

"I've been wonderin' that very thing myself if'n ya want ta know the truth. Only I don't see how that can be."

"Perhaps there is a record in the Bible."

Ty opened the Book and saw the faint inscription again. After a moment of careful study, he read it aloud. "For my darling daughter on her wedding day 18__ from Mother." Ty looked up. "That's all that inscription says. Ain't much help."

Sally said nothing only reached for the Bible to see for herself. After reading the same words, she turned a page or two. "Look, Ty. There is a record of some sort in here. See there is Pa's name, Jonathan Andrew Keith Elliot. Why'd he have so many names, I wonder? There's his birth date written. Below his name is Ma's, Eleanor Mary Crook Elliot an' her birth date. Ty, there is no date a death here."

"I know. I looked years ago an' always wondered why. If'n she did die, why ain't her death recorded?"

Sally didn't answer. She was busy reading the rest of the writing on the page. "Our names an' births are recorded here, an' there is no other name anywhere." She looked up. "I jest don't see how there could be a sister an' it not be recorded."

"Sally," Ty almost groaned, "I don't see either, but it don't change the fact that I have ta find someone."

No more was said for a while as Sally turned page after page looking for anything that might be called a clue. Ty sat thoughtful. Slowly he picked up the small picture and looked at it. As he gazed, vague memories stirred from some forgotten recess of his brain. In a dazed and perplexed voice he began to speak. His low voice had a faraway feeling to it. Sally ceased turning pages and listened, staring in wide-eyed wonder at her brother.

"She was there . . . an' Pa. It was a cabin. Small, but weren't like this . . . Flowers in . . . a pitcher, seems like. There were others there. We went away . . . you an' me . . . She was gone when we got back . . . No sign a her. Her bonnet was gone. I looked for it . . . Pa said . . . she was gone away. Never said where . . . Pa cried. I heard him . . ." His voice trailed off and all was quiet.

Sally hardly dared breathe. Was Ty remembering some clue to these puzzling questions?

"Sally," Ty spoke firmly. "This is Ma's picture. I'm sure."

Sally nodded.

"An' I wonder . . ." There was obvious hesitancy in the brother's voice. "I'm jest guessin' ya know, but could Ma 'ave left Pa an' gone back ta the city?"

Sally gasped. "Left him! Why?"

"Think. Pa was livin' out here in the wilds long 'fore he got married. Could be Ma didn't like it an' went back."

"Why? I mean, what would she do an' how would she live? Ya don't think a sister could've been born after she . . . left?"

Ty shook his head. "Else how'd Pa know. I'm mighty certain he ain't never got no mail. No, I reckon perhaps there was—" here Ty stopped.

Sally finished the sentence in horror stricken tones. "An illegitimate sister."

Ty nodded grimly. "Maybe Ma never told Pa 'bout her 'til she were leavin'. That'd explain why she ain't in the Bible."

"Ty, could it be?"

"I jest don't know, Sally, I jest don't know. How else would ya explain the missin' name an' no date a death?"

For a long time they sat there in silence. Each busy with his own thoughts. Surely that couldn't be right, and yet, how else could it all be explained?

"Why'd Pa say ya could do what he couldn't?" Sally wondered.

Ty was several minutes in answering. "I reckon," he began at last, "he might not a knowd where they lived, an' I'm ta find out."

"Well, I can tell ya one thing Ty Elliot, ya ain't goin' nowheres without me.

CHAPTER FOUR

Both fell silent as crunching footsteps were heard on the snow approaching the cabin. Though Sally started, Ty didn't move, for he recognized the steps of Carson.

On the treshold, Carson paused.

"Is all ready?" Ty questioned quietly.

Carson nodded.

Ty rose from the table. The time had come to place his father's body in its final resting place.

Sally tried to stay her tears, but they wouldn't be held back. They flowed down her cheeks as the three stood by the newly made grave deep in the mountain forests, where no human eye would be likely to see. Carson and Ty spread snow over the mound of earth before all three turned silently back to the cabin. Sally clung to Ty, the one known earthly tie that was left to her. Never in all her eighteen years of life had she felt so forlorn. Pa was gone. Pa, the one who had been everything to her since Ty had left so suddenly two years before.

As the trio slowly neared the cabin, Sally stumbled. The struggles, hardships, and endless anxiety of the past months had taken their toll on her young body. Without a word, Ty picked up his sister and entered the cabin. Placing her gently on the bed, he brought her a bowl of stew. After she had eaten, he sat by her side without a word until he saw her fall into the first real sound sleep she had had in a long time.

The afternoon waned. The sun dropped lower and lower in the western sky. The two friends sat in the gathering dusk. Ty's thoughts were mixed; memories of the past came back to mingle with the perplexing and bewildering puzzle of the present. Could anything be more complex than the task he had promised to do? How was he to fulfill his father's wishes? With a sigh he at last arose and stepped over to a pallet on the floor. This was where he used to sleep. Perhaps all he needed was a good night's rest. He realized with a start that only the day before he and Carson had ridden the last of their arduous journey. Was it any wonder that he felt so exhausted and his eyes refused to stay open? He had hardly slept since they had set out. Ty's body relaxed, and in another minute he was sleeping as deeply as his sister.

Carson too had been thinking that quiet afternoon and evening. He had sat before the fire gazing into the dancing flames. His quick ears caught the sounds of Ty's bedding down; he smiled to himself. "The boy needs it. Ain't used ta this sorta thin'. He ain't learnt ta take his sleep where an' when he can git it an' trust ta Providence ta wake him when he needs it. That'll come in time, I reckon." After a few more minutes Carson too stretched out, rolled in his blanket Indian style, and closed his eyes.

Stumbling toward the door, the old woman gasped for breath. Her hand went to her head, and she swayed a moment. Sheer willpower kept her on her feet as she opened the door of the cabin.

"Aunt Kate! Yer sick!"

"Just a might dizzy, Bob. Don't go off gettin' excited."

Bob frowned. "Aunt Kate, yer workin' too hard. Ya got ta have rest. Ya ought ta be in bed this minute."

Aunt Kate shook her head. "Ya know I don't have time fer that. There's work ta do."

Bob shook his head, and before his aunt could protest, he had picked her up and carried her to her bed. "Yer goin' ta rest," he ordered firmly. "I reckon I can take care a the house an' her." Glancing out a window as he spoke, he smiled involuntarily at sight of a little sprite of a child playing in the grass with her doll.

The child couldn't have been more than three years old. Her hair was light and hung loosely about her fair face in little curls and waves. The sunshine played about her through the shady tree branches and turned her hair into locks of pure spun gold. Bob called her his little sunshine.

"The sun don't usually like ta share its brightness with anyone else, but I reckon the good Lord told it ta share a might with the child, jest ta brighten others' lives," he was wont to say to his aunt after the child had gone to her trundle bed and was fast asleep.

"I reckon you're right, Bob, but to think—"

"Now, Auntie, don't ya go an' spoil the evenin' with thinkin'. I jest ain't goin' ta do no thinkin'."

His aunt would smile indulgently and change the subject.

Now as she lay in her bed, she wondered how Bob could do all that needed to be done. She tried to rise but fell back on the pillow as the room whirled around her. "I'll be all right in a day or two," she told herself. But the days passed, and she was no better.

"Bob, suppose you let me take the young one to stay with my girls until Kate gets back on her feet?" The speaker was a gentle looking woman who had come over nearly every day to help out.

Bob hesitated. He knew the Westlins were kindly people with three daughters of their own. They lived a mile or so away, and their latchstring was always out. He knew the child would be taken good care of, but . . . how could he let his little sunshine go to the house of a stranger?

Mrs. Westlin noticed his hesitation. "You sleep on it. I just thought I'd offer. Talk to Kate about it if you want."

Bob nodded.

That evening after he had told Aunt Kate about the offer, he sighed and looked down at the little face so innocent and sweet, sleeping quietly in her little bed. "No matter what happens, Aunt Kate, or where she is, she will always be my little girl."

Sleep was long in coming to Bob that night. For hours he lay on his pallet staring into the darkness of the cabin and listening to the breathing of the two who made this cabin home. Could he let Sunshine go? It wouldn't be forever, for if anything happened to Aunt Kate . . . no, nothing was going to happen unless she didn't get the rest she needed. Yet, how could she rest with the little one about? Bob moaned softly in the dark. Why did it have to come to this? He knew his Sunshine would have to go. But never, since the day she first came into the world, had she been away from the cabin. Never had she been parted from Aunt Kate. And only when Bob was away hunting and trapping was she separated from him. Bob moved restlessly. He just couldn't bring himself to say with certainty the thing that his heart knew must be. At last as dawn began to steal across the sky, Bob arose from his sleepless bed and began to gather Sunshine's things.

"Now, ya be a good girl 'til Aunt Kate gits better."

The little child dimpled into her sweetest smile as she leaned down from the horse where she sat before Mrs. Westlin and kissed Bob on the nose.

"I be dood," came the response from the baby lips, and another kiss was given.

Bob stood in front of the cabin and watched the horse walk off down the trail. "God forgive me if I'm breakin' my trust, but I reckon I'm doin' the right thing."

Aunt Kate did grow stronger, and though she wasn't quite the same, she could once again take care of the house, chickens and a little mite of a child. The day was never to be forgotten in the minds of these two when Bob brought his sunshine girl home again. She had been sadly missed; her childish ways and words once more filled the little cabin with brightness though outside the day was chilly and cloudy. Autumn was fast approaching, and Aunt Kate had gathered a handful of late blooming flowers to grace the table.

For two weeks the joy of being together remained. Then one morning,

"Aunt Kate, I reckon I ought ta go out trappin' once 'fore the cold weather hits. Ain't gonna be gone more'n a week if'n the trappin's as good as usual. I knowd I should'a gone an' done it some time 'fore this, but . . ." Bob's voice trailed off.

"I go too," came the sweet little voice on his knee.

"Well, I reckon when ya is a mite bigger, I'll take ya ta mind my campfire an' cook my food. Ya'd like that?"

The golden head nodded vigorously and the small hands clapped in glee.

Aunt Kate spoke then. "Ya can't go this time, honey, I need ya here, an' he won't be gone long."

All was silent. Bob looked at the fair young face before him. So like her mother, he thought.

"Oo promise oo tum bat soon?"

"I promise I ain't gonna be gone more'n ten days. If'n I leave this mornin' I'll come back the quicker."

And so it was that later that morning Bob rode off on his horse for a few days of trapping and hunting. Before he mounted he took the child in his arms once more and held her close as he whispered, "The Good Lord take care a ya an' I'll be comin' back. Don't ya ferget." He strained the little one to his chest while she clung to his neck. A strange ache began to press on Bob's heart as he set the child down and turned toward his waiting horse. A feeling almost akin to fear tugged and pulled at him as he rode off. He felt an urge to turn around and not go.

"I'm jest gettin' sentimental," he muttered to himself.

Six months passed before Bob again rode back down that trail towards his cabin. Six months of hardship and delay. Six months of catastrophe and trouble. He mused on all that had taken place since he had set out. Now at last he was almost home. His arms ached to hold his little girl once more and to taste someone's cooking besides his own. He rounded the bend and suddenly reined in his horse. Something was wrong. He could feel it. There was the cabin before him; however, no smoke came from the chimney. No welcoming light lit the window. No chickens cackled in the yard. In fact, there was no sign of life anywhere. Bob sat there motionless, scarcely breathing as he took in the scene before him. What had happened? Indians? It couldn't be. Everything was in too much order for that. Slowly he dismounted, and leading his horse off the trail, he left him in some underbrush. Quietly, stealthily he made his way to the cabin. The latchstring was out! Could Aunt Kate and Sunshine be gone for the day? No, the thought was absurd. With sudden force he kicked the door open. There was nothing inside. It was bare except for the table and benches. The old bedstead against the wall was there but no bedding. Dust lay on the mantelpiece and the ashes were cold. Icy fingers of dread began to twist about his heart. Where were they? His breath was growing more rapid, and his eyes darted here and there over the bare and forsaken cabin.

"Aunt Kate!" his shout brought back only the echo of his own words. With rapid strides he left the cabin and entered the barn. No sign that any animals had wintered there. As his eyes roved the surrounding clearing, they came to rest on a little wooden cross near the border of trees. With a cry of anguish he raced towards it only to read the words,

Mrs. Kate Lacks. Died 23, September 18—. Rest in peace.

CHAPTER FIVE

Carson rolled over stiffly and opened his eyes. The faint light entering the cabin through the windows indicated the arrival of the sun in the eastern sky. For a moment he lay there gathering his thoughts. At last, silently, he arose and built up the fire.

Ty stirred restlessly on his pallet. The habit of early rising was still upon him and in very few minutes more he had risen and joined Carson before the fire.

"Did ya sleep well?" Ty queried of his companion.

Carson shrugged. "Didn't stay awake ta find out. How 'bout you?"

A slight hint of a smile flickered across Ty's face. "Like a bear in hibernation."

For several minutes not another word was said. Each man was busy with his own thoughts. Now and then Ty would turn and look at the bed where Sally still lay wrapped in the heavy sleep of the exhausted. At last he spoke.

"Carson," his voice was low and there was a hint of trouble in it. "Sally an' me, we got a problem."

Carson nodded but said not a word.

Ty continued. "'Fore Pa died he made me promise ta find someone, but he never told me who it were, only ta find 'her'. All I got ta go by is this here broken locket an' this

29

picture." With almost reverent care he laid the items on his knee.

When Carson made no reply, Ty glanced up to see his face grow pale as he stared at the objects. With trembling hand he reached out and picked up the locket.

"Carson?" Ty queried, "Ya all right?" When he received no answer, he fell silent, knowing that the older man was not listening.

After a silence, which lasted for some time, Carson spoke as one waking from a daze. "What was ya sayin'? I reckon I weren't listenin'."

Once again, Ty told of his problem of finding the missing person. Of how he and Sally thought it might be an illegitimate sister and that the locket and photo were the only clues they had.

Carson sat and watched Ty's face closely. He could read the perplexity mingled with pain in his expressions. When Ty ceased to speak, Carson laid a hand on his shoulder.

"Son," he began, "I can't tell ya where she is, but I reckon I can tell ya somethin' ta help. It might jest relieve yer mind some too. It's a long story, but I reckon ya ain't wantin' ta light out today."

Ty shook his head and glanced again toward the bed where his sister still lay. After putting another log on the fire, he resumed his seat and prepared himself to listen.

"Yer pa an' me, we growed up together farther east. It weren't settled land then, but I reckon it is now, though I ain't been back there fer well nigh on ta a dozen years. When yer pa got hitched, he brought yer ma out ta his cabin far from anyone. This here picture is a right good likeness a yer ma. She sure was purty." Carson fell silent as he looked again at the tiny picture.

Ty made no move and remained silent.

"Ye pa loved her more'n anyone knew. An' when you an' Sally come 'long, he was so proud I thought fer sure his buttons were gonna bust. But then yer little sister came. She looked jest like yer ma, an'. . . well . . . I reckon she still does.

30

Yer ma took real sick an' died jest hours after she was borned. Yer pa couldn't take care a her an' my aunt took her. It weren't long after that when yer pa packed ya all up and came out here, leavin' the little one with me an' my aunt. I knowed he couldn't take care of the young one, an' I promised ta take care a her fer him." Carson's voice grew unsteady. "God forgive me! I thought I was doin' right!" The cry was full of deep anguish and heartbreak. "Ty, ya got ta help me make it right!"

"Make what right? Carson, what happened?"

It was only after a few minutes of struggle that Carson could continue the story.

"Fer three years Aunt Kate an' I raised her, my little sunshine. Aunt Kate had given her the name of yer ma, Eleanor, but I jest couldn't bear ta call her Ellen as yer ma was called. It were in the late summer that Aunt Kate took sick. I jest couldn't take care a her an' Sunshine, so I let a family take the little one jest til my aunt were well. I still remember the day I brought yer sister back ta the cabin. Aunt Kate had some flowers on the table an' we was all jest as happy as can be. Then, Ty, I ain't never forgiven myself fer it, but only a little while after that I went out on a huntin' an' trappin' trip. I promised her I wouldn't be gone more'n ten days. I promised her! Ty." Carson's voice sunk, and he looked at his companion.

Ty's heart beat so hard he could scarcely get his breath.

"The troubles I faced on that trip— my horse went lame, I took sick, early snows forced me ta stay with the Indian family that took me in. The passes were covered in snow, the creeks flooded in spring an' it were six long months 'fore I got back. When I did get back, Ty, Aunt Kate had died an' my trust, yer little sister, was no where ta be found. I did learn that the family she'd stayed with had taken her. Some folks said they went further west an' others said it were back east. I've looked fer her every place I been ta an' ain't found one clue yet. I've lost her, Ty, lost her! An' her the trust a the best friend I ever had. Ya got ta help me find her! Ya got ta!"

Ty stared at his friend. Could this be true? Was this one he was to find his "baby sister"? If Carson, who knew about her for so long, hadn't be able to find a trace of her, how was he expected to? Where should he start? Who was the family she was with? So dazed was he with this story that he gave no reply to his older companion's heart wrenching cry for help.

Carson had buried his face in his hands and now sat silent and motionless.

Outside, the sun climbed higher and higher, doing its best to melt much of the snow before it must slip behind the mountains once more. A lone rider was slowly wending his way through the woods on the now slippery trail. Pausing often, he looked about as though to make sure he was still on the trail and had not missed it. His horse's breath made little clouds of steam in the still air.

Inside the cabin, with a sudden shake of his head, Ty squared his shoulders and drew a deep breath. This was no time for endless puzzling. Now was the time to work out a plan, if possible.

"Carson," Ty began. "What was the family's name that took . . . her?" He couldn't quite decide what to call this newly discovered sister of his.

Carson lifted his head; he spoke slowly, "I don't rightly remember. I know it started with West, but I ain't never been able ta recall the rest a it."

It was Ty's turn to frown now. This made things even more difficult. How was one to find a girl after all these years without knowing the last name? He tried again.

"Would there be anyone back near where ya was livin' that might know?"

"There's no tellin' what some folks might remember, an' it's no tellin' if'n any a the same ones is still there. After all, Ty, it's been a dozen years since I was back that way."

"Still, it wouldn't hurt ta check."

"No, I reckon not. Ya ain't aimin' ta go there alone are ya? How'd ya know who ta ask?"

"I don't know rightly. I was thinkin' a going alone if'n you'd stay here with Sally. Ya know I can't stay. If they was ta get wind—"

At that moment a voice sounded behind him. "I told ya once, an' I'm tellin' ya again, you ain't goin' nowheres without me, Ty Elliot. Now ya jest get that inta yer head."

Both men turned. Sally stood there, hands on her hips and chin squared in stubbornness. Her blue eyes flashed with determination.

"Sally, it ain't gonna be for long. I can leave after dawn tomorrow an' I'd jest be checkin' ta see if'n anyone knows 'bout—"

Sally cut him short. "It don't matter ta me how short a time ya aim ta be gone, Ty Elliot, I ain't stayin' behind."

Ty tried to reason with her, but she remained firm in her obstinacy. If he was going anywhere, she was going too. Nothing would change her mind. She stood there before him with arms crossed and a set to her mouth that reminded Carson of long ago.

At last Ty gave in to the inevitable though he did so with great reluctance. No one spoke for several minutes after Sally joined them. It was she who broke the stillness.

"Ty, who is she?"

Briefly, Ty filled his sister in on what was known. Carson sat still, gazing before him at nothing while he listened to the story and wondered again if it were even possible to find a trace of her.

"Carson," Ty questioned when he had finished, "if Sally goes 'long, what do ya plan ta do?"

"Do? Why I reckon I'll go along with ya. Ain't got any other place ta go that's a needin' me, an' I might be a use ta ya. 'Sides that," his voice dropped and his gaze fell, "I ain't gonna feel quite easy in my mind 'till I see my little girl once more."

Sally stood up. "Well, now that it is all settled, when are we goin' ta leave? Ya know ya can't stay here all winter; someone's gonna find out yer here."

"I know, Sally, I know," Ty interrupted.

"We've got ta leave soon, Ty. If they were ta—" She couldn't go on, for Ty had placed his hand over her mouth.

"Hush that kind a talk, Sally," he ordered. "I reckon we could light out at first dawn. What da ya say, Carson?"

Carson made no reply but held up his hand for silence. A dead stillness settled over the cabin; even the fire seemed to feel a need for quiet, for the logs ceased to snap. Sally fairly held her breath, straining her ears for she knew not what. Yet, try as she would, she could hear nothing. She glanced at Ty as he stealthily rose and drew his Colt repeating pistol from its holster. She reached out a hand to grasp him, but he glided past her outstretched fingers. Carson too had risen and held his rifle at the ready.

The sun, now nearing noonday, shone with blinding splendor on the remaining snow banks. The two men stood waiting. To see out either window would have exposed them to whatever or whoever was approaching. Sally could hear it now too. Steps of some sort were nearing. They were not slow and cautious, but advanced in a sure tread. Now they could hear the faint jingle of a harness. The visitor halted in front of the cabin.

Sally cowered back against the far wall pressing her hands over her mouth to keep back the scream that rose in her throat. Ty's face was set. Had it come to this already? How did they know he was back? His eyes narrowed. They would find that they couldn't always have everything their own way.

The stillness was broken by a deep voice from without. "Elliot! Sally!"

CHAPTER SIX

The words died on the air, and all remained still in the cabin. Sally took half a step forward, cocking her head, listening.

"Sally?" The call came again somewhat hesitantly. This time there was no doubt in Sally's mind, for with quick feet she crossed the cabin and reached the door.

"Mr. Harnnard, ya scared us. Do come in, quick."

As the door shut behind the newcomer, Ty and Carson put up their weapons. There was no need for them now. Mr. Harnnard was a short man with grey hair and beard. His face was leathery from spending so much of his life out in the elements. He walked with a slight limp and began talking right away.

"The missus gave me no peace 'till I said I'd ride out an' see how you an' yer pa was gettin' 'long." He paused at sight of the empty bed. Then turning, he noticed for the first time the two other men in the room. "Why if'n it ain't Ty! When did ya get in boy?" Not giving anyone a chance to answer he kept right on. "Ya know ya can't stay here. But I'm mighty glad ta see ya, an' I'll give ya some advice; leave jest as soon's ya can."

Ty interrupted, "An' why should I be goin' so soon? Is word 'round that I'm back?"

Mr. Harnnard shook his head. "No, no, not for a certainty, but I heard some of them talkin' last night at Sam's saloon an' they're plannin' ta come out here tonight jest ta see if yer back."

"What would happen if he weren't here?" Carson asked.

"They plan on watchin' all the trails 'til he does come. I tell ya, Ty," Mr. Harnnard shook his head, "I don't know what it is that has got them all so riled 'bout you, an' I don't want ta know, but if I was you, I'd get out right quick. An' I'd stay away. Least ways 'till we get ourselves a sheriff."

Ty and Carson exchanged glances.

"How much time have we got?"

"Oh, I reckon not more'n four or five hours. They won't come 'till it's dark, for fear they'd be shot if'n ya was here. If'n ya ask me, I'd say it would be good riddance if they was. Ya can leave Sally with me an' the missus till ya can send for her. I don't reckon they'll be a botherin' us."

Sally was about to protest strongly, but the pressure of her brother's hand on her arm restrained her.

"Thank ya for the offer, but Sally goes with me. With Pa gone, I'm all the kinfolk she knows."

Mr. Harnnard shrugged. "Suit yerself. I reckon I ought ta be movin' on. When did yer Pa—?" he hesitated slightly.

Ty answered in a quiet voice, "Two nights ago."

"I'm sorry 'bout that. Now, ya'd best get a move on if ya aim ta be gone." Mr. Harnnard stepped outside, mounted his horse and turned to leave. "Jest be careful what tracks ya leave, fer there's no tellin' but they'll try trackin' ya." With this parting advice the old man rode off through the woods.

Silence fell among the inmates of the little cabin that lasted for several minutes. No one spoke as they looked at one another. At last Ty broke the stillness.

"Well, I reckon we'd best get ta packin'."

All was business then as Sally and Ty worked to pack such things as wouldn't bear leaving behind. With great care and tenderness Sally wrapped the old family Bible in a quilt she had made.

"Ty," she questioned, "where are the locket an' picture?"

"I have 'em safe," he replied softly.

"Where?"

"The locket's on my watchguard an' the picture's here in my pocket." He noticed Sally's face grow grave, and he rightly guessed why, for he added, "When we reach a place ta stay the rest a the winter, I'll carve a locket for ya ta carry the picture in."

Sally didn't reply in words, but her smile was all her brother needed.

For an hour the three worked steadily. At last all was ready. Carson brought the horses around, and he and Ty tied the packs on the extra horse.

"Let's get a move on now," Ty ordered preparing to help his sister mount.

"Jest a minute, Ty," she paused and looked up at him. "I want a gun."

Ty's eyes opened and his jaw dropped though he said not a word.

"Give me Pa's six shooter, Ty. I'm a dead shot with that. I don't aim ta be ridin' round the country with no way ta defend myself. 'Sides that, it would be a might easier if'n I could jest hand ya a gun 'stead of ya havin' ta try ta find it."

Carson's dry chuckle sounded. "Give her the gun, Ty. I reckon she's got jest as much right ta it as either a us. An' if'n she can shoot as straight as yer pa used ta brag she could, it'd be a shame to lose her skill if'n it comes ta a shoot-out."

Sally smiled as she buckled on her father's six-shooter and mounted her horse. She was a good shot, her father having taught her almost as soon as he had taught Ty. She hated killing anything though she had done it many times to provide food or to defend herself. Never once, however, had she even pointed a gun at another human being, and she wondered if she would have the courage to do so if the need arose.

"Let's ride!" Carson and Ty nudged their horses and headed east with the packhorse following. Sally cast one last long look at the cabin where she had spent all the known years of her life; the cabin where she and Ty had grown up together, and the cabin where their father had drawn his last breath. Would she ever see it again?

For nearly five long hours the trio had been riding. Carson and Ty were careful to leave behind a trail that was so confused it would take a skilled tracker and broad daylight to follow it. Ty hoped fresh snow would cover them though before anyone tried. Darkness had closed in around them some hours before, yet they continued to push on with a steady pace.

Sally was cold, stiff and weary. Her eyes were heavy. She didn't know how Ty and Carson could tell where they were. For all she knew they had been merely riding in a circle. The wind began to blow. Carson glanced up at the sky and noticed the clouds moving in.

"Looks like we're goin' ta be gettin' some snow, Ty," he called back softly.

"Good," was all the reply Ty gave.

In silence once again, the three companions rode. Sally shivered as the first snowflakes began falling, and the cold, icy wind stung her cheeks. She bent her head and with stiff fingers pulled her wrap closer about her.

"Ya all right, Sally?" the voice of her brother startled her, for she had not noticed him ride up beside her.

She nodded. She wouldn't let him know just how cold, yes, and frightened, she really was. She knew that sometime they would stop and make camp. They would have to for the horses couldn't go on much farther. But how could they camp in this weather? The wind was driving the snow against them with increasing fury, and no stars were now visible.

Carson's shout startled both Ty and Sally. "I see a light. We're most there."

Urging their horses on, the brother and sister caught up with Carson, and Ty demanded to know where they were.

"It's the cabin a some folks I know. They're right nice people an' they ain't goin' ta mind some visitors."

"Make sure it's safe first, Carson."

Carson nodded and rode on, with Ty and Sally following at a slower pace.

Only a short time later, all three had reined in before a small cabin. The door was open in welcome, and light shone out through the blowing snow. Ty helped Sally dismount, for she was so stiff and cold she could scarcely move.

"Take the horses to the stable over yonder," the deep voice of a man called over the wind to Carson and Ty. "Then come in and thaw yerselves. Ma ken take care a the lady." With that he drew Sally inside and shut the door.

A stout motherly woman with white hair and soft grey eyes bustled about Sally, taking off her wrap and bonnet, pushing her to a chair before a roaring fire, and removing her shoes. "There now, deary, you jest sit there an' warm up a bit. The coffee'll be ready in two shakes. How far have ya come? Hard ridin' in a storm like this, ain't it?" The woman talked on. She could tell Sally was exhausted and didn't feel like talking. In a matter of moments she placed a cup of steaming hot coffee in Sally's icy hands. "Now jest drink this. It'll put new life in ya. There ain't nothin' like a good hot cup of coffee ta warm ya right up."

With hands that trembled from cold and exhaustion, Sally lifted the cup and gulped down a mouthful of the hot liquid. It felt wonderful, and she closed her tired eyes. With a sigh of satisfaction, she began to relax as the fire, the coffee and a blanket she felt being tucked around her shoulders began to banish the numbness.

After several minutes, the door was opened, and in stamped Carson and Ty. They were both covered with snow.

"Now, Pa," the motherly woman directed. "Help them get out of those snowy coats while I pour some more coffee for them. They must be 'bout frozen. Get those boots off so yer feet can thaw. Now," she ordered, "get over here ta the fire, both of ya. Well, at least you can walk. The poor girl was scarce able ta move! Here's yer coffee. An' there's more of it when ya want it. Pa, why don't ya put another log or two on the fire."

As the woman had talked, Ty and Carson had sunk into chairs before the bright blaze and taken the steaming cups offered them. Ty, sitting beside his sister, glanced at her pale face anxiously while inwardly he chided himself for giving in to her pleadings to go along with him. "It'll be too difficult for her. I should have left her with the Harnnards," he thought.

As though she could read his thoughts, Sally gave him a tired smile and said softly, "I'll be jest fine once I get warm, Ty. An' I wouldn't 'ave stayed behind on any account."

Ty reached out his hand and gave hers a gentle squeeze.

A silence descended on the small group. Even the woman grew quiet once the others were situated to her liking with hot drinks and a blazing fire. Her husband had seated himself on a bench at the table and was smoking his pipe. The woman sat down across from him with her knitting.

At last Carson half turned in his chair.

"I reckon I ought ta introduce ya to each other, though I reckon I never were good at that type a thing. These here are my friends, Ty an' his sister, Sally. Ty, Sally, that is Mr. an' Mrs. Shaw."

"Goodness sakes, Bob!" interjected Mrs. Shaw. "Ain't nobody calls us that 'round here. The folks that know us at all call us Uncle Matt an' Aunt Leah an' we don't want no other names."

The older man removed his pipe and drawled, "That's fer sure, so don't ya go an' be forgettin' it, Bob Carson."

Carson grinned and reached out to pour himself some more coffee. "Aunt Leah," he remarked, "ya sure make the best coffee anywheres. An' that's the truth."

CHAPTER SEVEN

Sally struggled to keep her eyes open, but it was hard work. Leaning back in her chair she yawned. Ty smiled, took the empty cup from her hand lest she drop it and glanced around the room. Aunt Leah must have also been watching Sally for she remarked, "It's gettin' rather late an' Sally an' I'll be headin' off ta bed. You three men folk can bed down anywheres yer a mind to in here or up in the loft. Pa's got a heap a skins stacked over yonder. Come on now child." She gently helped Sally stand up and began guiding her out of the room into a small bedroom. "I reckon the men folk can get along all right without us now."

For several minutes after the ladies left the room, the three men sat in silence. It was broken at last by Uncle Matt. "I reckon you'll be wantin' ta turn in soon. We can have all the time we want ta talk in the mornin' for it don't seem's though yer goin' ta be a leavin' soon the way that storm is blowin'."

Carson glanced at his young companion's face and noticed how worn he looked. "I aim ta turn in, now's I'm thawed out. What 'bout you, Ty?"

With a startled look, Ty raised his head, "What's that?"

Carson chuckled, "I was jest suggestin' ya turn in 'fore ya tumble off yer chair."

Ty gave a tired grin and rose to his feet. "Reckon yer right."

It wasn't many minutes later that two distinct snores were heard issuing from the loft as Uncle Matt blew out the lamp and stretched his old limbs on a pile of skins near the fire and closed his eyes.

It was broad daylight, or would have been had it not still been snowing, when Sally awoke from the first real relaxing and restful sleep she had known since her father had been taken sick. The sleep she had back at the cabin had been one of exhaustion, and she hadn't felt much refreshed when she had awakened. Now, however, things were different. There was no need to worry about "them" coming for Ty. There was a woman to talk to, and no one was ill. With great rapidity she dressed, brushed her long dark hair back from her slender face and twisted it into its accustomed knot at the back of her head.

Stepping out of the small room, she paused to glance about her, for she had been so tired the night before that she had scarcely noticed anything. Now she saw a simple room with a table and a few wooden chairs pushed off to one side. A cook stove, over which Aunt Leah was bending, stood over against the wall opposite the outside door. The fire blazed brightly in the fireplace, and curtains hung on the three windows. There was even a gaily colored rug on the floor which Sally noticed with a smile of satisfaction. She wouldn't mind staying here for a spell; she wouldn't mind at all. Just then her attention was drawn to a tall, broad shouldered youth who had entered the door with an armload of wood. There was something about him that made Sally stare. He was clean-shaven, and his eyes looked bright and cheerful. With a few strides he had crossed the room and in no time at all had stacked the wood neatly in the wood box. As he stood up, he glanced over and saw her standing in the doorway regarding him in bewilderment.

"Well, I see ya decided ta get up after all," he chuckled. "I reckon ya'll have someone ta feed those flapjacks to, Aunt Leah."

"Ty?" Sally questioned in astonishment. With a sudden rush she had her arms around his neck while he swung her around the room. She was laughing and finally managed to gasp out, "I didn't know ya until ya spoke. Ya look," she paused for the right word. "Ya look so young, Ty. Not like ya did the night ya came home. Then ya looked nearly as old as Uncle Bob." She used the childhood name she had long called her father's friend and smiled over it tenderly. "I feel much too old to be yer little sister," she remarked, suddenly pulling her hair out of its unbecoming knot and shaking her head to let it fall loosely about her shoulders and face.

Ty laughed and gave her a brotherly kiss. "Now ya look like the little girl I left long ago. Go eat yer breakfast 'fore it gets cold," and he gave her a gentle shove to the table.

Aunt Leah was regarding them with bright eyes. "Land sakes!" she exclaimed "You two younguns sure know how ta stir things up. Ya look a might more chipper this mornin' than ya did last night." She looked at Sally. "Did ya sleep well?"

Sally sighed in contentment. "I don't remember when I've slept that well. But," she added looking around, "where are the others?"

"Out," Ty told her, "takin' care a the stock. I was picked ta bring in the wood. I reckon though that they'll be in 'fore too long."

Almost as though they had been waiting for those words, the door was flung open and two snowy figures came in stamping snow off their boots and shaking it from their hats and coats.

Sally sprang from her chair and ran to fling her arms around Carson as she used to do when a small girl. "I never really greeted ya back at the cabin, Uncle Bob," she said. "I was so worried then, so I reckon I ought ta do it now." She gave him a hearty kiss.

Carson pressed a kiss on one rosy cheek and then the other. Holding her off at arm's length, he studied her. She was a lovely combination of both parents he decided, and a warm smile crossed his face.

The fire blazed up and sent out a shower of sparks as Ty stirred it up before placing another log on top thus causing the snow on it to melt with a hiss. The day was drawing to a close. The evening meal had just been finished, and Sally and Aunt Leah were washing the last of the dishes. The three men sat around the fire in relative silence enjoying its warmth and Uncle Matt, his pipe. It wasn't until the cabin was tidied up for the night that Sally and Aunt Leah sat down too. Aunt Leah settled herself and pulled out her knitting.

The day had been quiet. No disturbances had occurred to break the peace, and there had been no talk of trouble. Ty knew that questions would come sometime, and indeed he felt the need of wise counsel before setting off again in his search. Now, as he sat silently thinking, he wondered how this all would end. Would he find his sister? It seemed so hopeless, and yet he had promised his father. And always, in the back of his mind, there lingered a slight worry about those he had fled from. Would they try to follow him? Would they continue to wait for his return? Surely they knew he had been back and then had left again. Would he always be running and hiding from them?

His thoughts were suddenly interrupted. "Well Ty, ya goin' ta tell 'em or am I?"

Ty turned with a blank expression on his face and regarded Carson with a puzzled air.

Carson chuckled. "Ya do have a way a not hearin' the conversation that's goin' 'round ya. I reckon I need ta say it all over again. They're wantin' ta know what brought us all out this far from Mel's Ridge."

Glancing around at the small circle about the fire, Ty stretched his legs and leaning back began the tale of how his father had been taken sick. How he and Carson had been away and had ridden back as quickly as they could. How his father had died leaving Ty the seemingly impossible task of finding a sister he had never heard about. "An' when I discovered that 'they' were goin' ta be comin' ta the cabin ta search for me, well, we all jest lit out. Sally wouldn't stay anywheres but with me though it were a long ride. An' Carson led us here," Ty finished up.

Uncle Matt nodded but said not a word. Aunt Leah on the other hand was full of sympathy and clicked her tongue over their troubles. "You poor dears! An' ta think ya rode all that way yesterday an' in that storm too." She shook her head. "No wonder you were all plum tuckered out. Well, ya'll can jest stay here 'long's ya want to."

"That's right kind a ya, Aunt Leah," Ty thanked her.

Uncle Matt spoke up. "Ty, there's jest one thin' I reckon I don't rightly understand. Jest who is 'them' that's after ya, and why did ya have ta run?"

For a moment Ty was silent. All eyes were fixed on him. Even Carson looked interested, for he had never heard the story. All he had known two years before, when he had ridden up to visit his friend, was that Ty had to get out, so he had taken him when he left.

"Well," the words came at last though very slowly. "We could jest say I know somethin' that could well land 'em all behind bars, an' I reckon they aim ta keep me quiet. Ya see, we ain't got no sheriff nor nothin' out there, an' well . . ." Ty left his sentence to die away into silence.

"How many of them are there?" Uncle Matt questioned.

"Oh, I can think a nearly half a dozen, an' there ain't a poor shot among 'em. That's why I knew we had ta get out. Carson an' I are good shots an' Sally can hold her own well's the next man, but ya see, I ain't wantin' ta take justice inta my own hands. It would a come to a shoot-out no doubt 'bout it. I ain't never shot a man, an' would like ta get by without shootin' any neither if'n I can."

Once again Uncle Matt nodded. "Can ya tell the law 'bout them fellows if'n you was somewhere else?"

"I reckon I could, though it don't seem's though it'd do much good seein' as how the law would be in one place an' them others some place different."

Sally spoke up. "Ty, couldn't ya make them believe that ya wouldn't say anythin' 'bout what ya know?"

Ty shook his head. "Even if they'd believe it, Sally, which they wouldn't, it wouldn't be right. I have ta tell if'n I get a chance."

"It was that bad?"

Ty nodded at Carson. "If'n it were jest somethin' little, I don't reckon they'd be comin' after me."

All fell silent for some time as each thought on what Ty had just revealed.

"Ty!"

Ty turned and noticed at once the startled, frightened look that had leapt into Sally's eyes and the sudden quiver of her chin.

"Ty, if they are so determined ta make ya quiet, will they . . . I mean ya don't think they will . . . would they try ta follow ya?"

The agony of fearful suspense that sounded in every word Sally uttered called out for a swift denial, for an assurance that all would be quite safe away from the cabin. However, Ty knew he had to be truthful. His very soul agonized over the terror he knew his words would cause in his sister's heart, yet she had to know the danger. She had to know everything was not what one could wish.

Ty laid a hand gently on Sally's clenched ones and looked her straight in the eye. "I don't know, Sally. They could try ta find me, an' I reckon we must always be on our guard."

CHAPTER EIGHT

Sally shivered, but uttered no sound. Her white face and clenched jaw betrayed her agony.

Carson couldn't bear to see the fear written in her eyes nor Ty's helplessness with the truth. "Well," he stretched out his feet before the fire and clasped his hands behind his head, "I reckon we can all sleep well fer many a night ta come since there ain't no way any a them can find us here seein' as how no one even knows we're here." He chuckled. "An' the tracks we done left from the cabin would shore 'nough confuse even the best a trackers."

"Yep," Ty added, thankful to see the terror gradually fading from his sister's face. "An' even if they was ta have started trackin,' that there storm'd jest cover all signs up. Ya don't think I'd be wastin' my time getting all nice an' shavin,' which I ain't done for two months, if'n I were thinkin' they might show up soon, do ya?"

Sally smiled. True, it wasn't a full, lighthearted one such as she had earlier, but it was a start.

Several minutes were spent in silent thought. The wind could be heard softly whistling about the chimney. Hungrily the flames in the fireplace licked at the fresh logs Ty tossed on them and hissed and snapped like vicious beasts.

"How long ya reckon this here storm'll last, Uncle Matt?"

"Oh, I speckt it'll all be over in a day or so. Winter's on its way out an' spring's acomin' though it don't seem that way tonight."

"I reckon that'll give me time ta carve that there locket for ya, Sally. That is," Ty added with a twinkle in his eye. "If'n ya still want it."

"Of course I still want it. Ya can't get out of it that easy, Ty."

And so the evening spent itself to be followed by several pleasant, restful days. Ty and Carson helped Uncle Matt with the chores. Inside, Aunt Leah found a most capable and helpful companion. Sally seemed to revel in the feeling, however short it might be, of peace. After that one evening when Ty shared the story, the troubles had not been brought up. Talk was held about the missing sister and ways to go about searching for her. Uncle Matt had several suggestions, but most evenings were spent with the men folk swapping stories of trapping and hunting. To these the women listened, sometimes in rapt attention but at other times in skepticism. For, had they not heard some of them before? Only this time the animal was larger and the danger more life threatening. At such times, Sally and Aunt Leah would exchange glances of amusement.

It was during these times of story telling that Ty worked on the locket. He was quite skilful with the knife, and before many nights were over, an intricate locket of red maple sanded smooth lay waiting for the picture. The locket was passed from hand to hand and many were the exclamations it received. But Sally was puzzled.

"Ty, how are ya plannin' ta get the picture in here? Ya didn't leave any place ta slide it in, nor does it have a back that opens."

"I were thinkin' that same thing myself," Carson interjected. "But I know how handy ya are with the knife so I reckon ya have some way?" It was more of a question than a statement, and all waited for Ty's reply.

Holding out his hand for the locket, he grinned as his sister gave it to him. With the tip of his knife he pushed a tiny wedge out of the top of the locket thereby leaving a slit just the size of the picture. After gently sliding the picture down the slit, the wedge was carefully pushed firmly back into place. Sally stared as Ty handed the locket back to her. Where was the wedge she had just watched him put in place? She couldn't detect it. The locket was shaken, but the picture remained firmly in its place, looking as though it had grown in the wood. Sally's delight knew no bounds, and Ty was more than rewarded for his efforts. Aunt Leah produced a ribbon from her sewing basket, and the locket was tied about Sally's neck. Not a word of the evening stories did Sally hear that night as she gazed at her mother's picture.

At last the day came for Carson, Ty and Sally to depart. The snow had melted enough for the three to move on in their search. Uncle Matt gave last minute suggestions and advice and told them to stop by if they were ever that way again. Aunt Leah had packed plenty of food for their trip, and after admonishing Ty to look out for his sister and Carson to look after both of them, she told Sally,

"I reckon you can handle the hard things on this here trip, child, but do try to keep those two out of trouble."

Sally laughed, and the tears that had threatened to fall disappeared. She strapped on her father's six shooter and allowed Ty to help her mount. Uncle Matt handed her the reins, and as Carson and Ty swung up on their horses, she turned her own mount's head to follow. Glancing back, she waved her hand to the two standing in the doorway of their hospitable cabin. Starlight tossed her head causing the bridle to jingle with a happy little tune. The sun was shining, and one bird was heard singing merrily in some tree nearby. They were off. Would they find a clue in the town they were headed to? Would they be able to track and find this sister who had disappeared so many years before? No one spoke these thoughts aloud, but each mind echoed them again and again as they rode steadily toward the east following the snowy road.

For several long, weary days Carson, Ty and Sally had been riding. Over rough mountainsides, down steep slopes through wind, clouds and sunshine they had traveled. Spending nights at some hospitable cabin only to set off again at dawn. Sally was tired. Tired? No, when she let herself think about it, she was exhausted. Every muscle ached from the constant horseback riding. To Carson and Ty, already used to days in the saddle, sleeping out in all kinds of weather and eating in the open every day, this little trip was nothing. Thankfully spring was arriving bringing warmer weather with it, or Sally would have faired even worse. As it was she hardly talked anymore, and each move she made off the horse was slow.

On the fifth day after leaving Uncle Matt and Aunt Leah's cabin, Carson, who was riding in front, pulled up his horse at a fork in the road.

"Well, I reckon we got a decision ta make here," he remarked to his companions as they pulled rein beside him. "If we was ta keep goin' straight, we'd go right by my old cabin, if'n it's still there." Then he added in a lower, husky voice, "That were the last place I seen my Sunshine."

Ty and Sally exchanged glances. Neither of them spoke but sat on their horses in silence waiting for Carson to continue.

After clearing his throat Carson jerked his head to the trail on the right. "An' if'n we was ta take that trail, we'd be goin' right past yer old cabin," adding quietly, "if its still standin'."

A shiver ran up and down Sally's spine. They were that close to the cabin where she and Ty, yes, and this unknown sister, were born? Would it still be standing? Mechanically, without even thinking about what she was doing, she turned her horses head towards the latter trail.

Ty also felt a pull to that spot down in the woods before them. What was it, he wondered, that tugged at his heart so forcefully to go back to the place of his beginning? Could it be his mother's grave? Or were memories, which flickered through his brain like some hazy dream, drawing him onward? He didn't know. The only thing that mattered was that he go.

His voice was quiet as he turned to Carson and said, "I reckon we both be aimin' ta go this way."

Carson nodded. Deep in his heart he was relieved. He wasn't sure he could handle going back to the old home knowing that Aunt Kate and Sunshine wouldn't be there to welcome him. With a sigh he too turned his horse onto the old familiar trail and followed his younger companions.

For several minutes the trio rode in silence, each lost in thought and full of mixed emotions.

At last Carson called up, "Jest round this here bend an' to yer right is where the cabin was."

Sally gasped. Would it be there? Instinctively she slowed her horse and allowed Ty to pass her. Everything was quiet save for the steps of the horses and one little bird singing brightly, hidden in the trees above her.

At last the bend was turned and there, before them, stood a cabin. Smoke came from the chimney, and a well worn path led to the door. Ty dismounted and dropped his reins. Carson too swung off his horse and left it ground hitched. Only Sally remained on her horse, too overcome to move until Carson nudged her foot. Then almost in a daze she followed the others and dismounted.

As Ty gazed about him, the door opened and a young, pleasant looking woman with light hair stepped out. "Why, afternoon. You all strangers in these parts?"

Ty pulled off his hat and stepped forward. "No ma'am, the truth is my sister an' me," he looked at Sally, "we was born here, an' our ma were buried nearby. We was hopin' ya'd jest let us look 'round for a spell."

"Why of course!" the woman exclaimed in sympathy. "I can show you right where ta find yer Ma's grave, I reckon. When I first came here, I found it all neglected like, and though I didn't know who it twas that was buried there, well, I just sort of took care of it ever since." As she spoke the woman led the way to a small, well kept area enclosed by a rail fence. One simple cross stood inside marking the last resting place of someone dear.

Carson bowed his head and held his hat in his hand as Ty, with Sally clinging to his arm, knelt beside the cross. The woman, with great kindness, quietly slipped back to the cabin murmuring to herself, "The poor things. All this way to visit the grave of their mother. I wonder where they came from? The man they are with doesn't seem to be their father. I wish I could help them."

"An' so we're lookin' fer a trace a their sister. Come all the way an' aim ta stop in town jest ta make inquiries." Carson wrapped up their tale to their hostess and glanced at Ty. "Reckon we ought ta be gitt'n on 'fore it gets dark, Ty?"

There was no answer. Ever since Ty had come into the cabin an hour ago, he hadn't said more than two words. His eyes had roamed about the cabin taking in every detail, and then, overcome with memories, he just sat and let them take him where they would. He heard nothing going on around him. Even had a band of Indians or outlaws come in with shouts and guns, Ty would have been completely unaware. Had those who were threatening his very life galloped into the yard, he wouldn't have stirred. His mind had taken him far beyond these four wooden walls and his companions. He saw none of it as he gazed vacantly before him.

"Ty?" Sally laid a gentle hand on his arm, but received no response. It was as though Ty was no longer there. His eyes were vacant and his hands limp as they rested on his knees.

The sound of a horse riding up caused the woman of the house to hurry to the door, fling it open and rush out to greet the rider. It was all so like the greetings Ellen used to give Jake that Carson had to brush back the sudden rush of tears and clear his throat several times.

Pausing before his unexpected guests, the rider held out his hand in friendly greeting. "Bob Carson? After all these years!"

Carson grasped the offered hand but looked puzzled.

The man grinned. "You don't remember Tom Jakobus? Only it was Tommy back then."

"Tommy?" Carson stared a moment and then a smile broke across his face. "How could I forget ya when ya was the most troublesome, mischievous youngun I ever laid eyes on!"

The man's hearty laugh filled the cabin. "I hope I've grown out of that."

"He has indeed," the woman added while stirring a pot over the fire. "Else I wouldn't have up an' married him."

After a little more laughing, Carson introduced Sally and tried to rouse Ty, but in vain. "I reckon I'll have ta jest drag him out an' toss him on his horse."

"Why don't the three of you jest bed down here the night?" Tom invited. "The cabin ain't large, but I reckon with the loft, it'll do. 'Sides, I'm wantin' ta hear what brings ya back ta these here parts."

It didn't take much persuasion for Carson and Sally to accept. Sally for the sake of not remounting her horse again that night, and Carson to catch up on things. The two men, talking incessantly, strode out to take care of the horses, leaving Sally to assist Mrs. Jakobus in getting the meal ready.

For a long time the fire burned that night in the little cabin. Carson told their story once again, and Tom listened in silence as his wife had done earlier. For several minutes after Carson had ended, no one spoke.

Then in a voice like one just awakened from a deep sleep, Ty spoke. "If we jest had a clue ta where she is, I'd go anywhere ta find her. If we even knew the family's name that took her it would help."

"I don't think I can help ya much with the name, but--" Tom paused in thought and every eye turned and fastened on him. "I recall hearin' that they all was headin' up ta the Nebraska Territory. I reckon that'll be a right long trip even if'n ya don't take wagons an' such."

Ty nodded. "I'll say it'd be quite the ride."

"Ya aim ta try for it?"

Ty and Carson exchanged glances. Was this really a clue or would it just lead them out of the way? It was just one man's word about something that had happened a dozen years before. Perhaps they could find out some more information from town.

Almost as though he could read their thoughts, Tom said quietly, "If'n I was in yer shoes, like as not I'd ride inta town first thing an' ask 'round. Sure there's got ta be some one who knows somethin'."

Carson nodded in agreement as Ty replied, "We'll do that." Then noting the look on Sally's face he added, "Would ya be agreeable ta us leavin' Sally here while we ask 'round? I reckon she could do with a day outa the saddle."

"Why of course she can stay! I wouldn't think of sendin' her off jest to ask questions. It ain't every day I get company back here and I don't aim to part with it easily." Mrs. Jakobus' warm smile made Sally feel right at home, almost as though they had known each other for years.

It was early the next morning, not long after dawn, when the three men, Carson, Ty and Tom rode out of the yard toward Lowrise Pass. In and out of the woods the trail wound its way eastward. Now the pale blue of the clear sky was above them, now the branches of the trees with tiny green leaves giving an almost moss like look to their dark bark shaded them. Merry little birds sang and warbled madly. There were so many of them that an individual bird was hard to identify from his song.

Carson gave a low whistle as the town suddenly sprang up before them as they crested a rise.

"Quite up an' comin' ain't it?" Tom grinned.

"This ain't a town, this here's a city!"

Ty grunted in agreement as they started down the main street.

It was still early and not many people were astir.

An older, grizzled man walking with a decided limp paused and nodded to the trio. "Howdy, Tom."

"Howdy, Mr. Dunley. You remember Bob Carson?" He nodded toward his companion.

"Bob Carson? Course I do, but that ain't, . . . why I'll be a linxed faced coyote, if that ain't my old friend Bob!"

Carson dismounted and eagerly greeted his old friend. Ty was introduced and the reason for their unexpected return recounted briefly.

"Wal, I don't reckon I ken give ya much help. I always heard it tell they lighted out fer—" he scratched his chin and frowned. "Wal, I'm a thinkin' it might a been Fort Laramie though I ain't sarten."

"That'd be Nebraska Territory," Ty remarked.

Carson nodded, and after a few more minutes of talk, the trio said good-bye and moved on.

The streets were growing more crowded and the noise of a saloon broke rakishly upon the still morning air as the door was opened. A voice sounded.

"I tell ya we'll catch an' string him up. Don't care how long he tries ta hide!"

Ty had his gun in his hand as he gasped out, "Who's that?"

Rebekah A. Morris

CHAPTER NINE

Carson and Tom, who hadn't noticed Ty's sudden reining in of his horse and were somewhat ahead, turned in surprise at his question.

"Who are ya talkin' 'bout, Ty? What's wrong?" Carson questioned riding back to him and noticing his drawn gun.

"That voice," Ty demanded looking toward the saloon, "who is it?"

Dismounting, Tom strode towards the saloon and pushed open the door causing the loud, rough voice of the boaster to be heard in the streets once more.

"I'm a tellin' ya we'll git him. We know he's come this here way an' I say we'll run him down like . . . like . . ." the voice died away as another voice called out,

"Aw, shut yer mouth, Wiley. Yer drunker 'en Ol' Lukus."

The sound of a scuffle sounded as Tom returned to Ty and Carson. Ty had holstered his gun and now gave a wry smile. "Reckon I'm jest a might skittish."

"Only nat'ral if'n ya ain't sure jest where them ones is goin' ta show up."

With a nudge to urge on his horse, Carson spoke up, "I reckon we'll keep our eyes an' ears open, but I don't think they'll be botherin' us none 'cept we get close ta home."

Ty sighed. "Yep, that's so. Ain't no one bothered us none till we were ta be gittin' back."

Through the town now wide awake and bustling with life and vigor, Tom led Carson and Ty on their quest for information. Many an old timer stopped to greet Carson with surprise and pleasure having never expected to see him there again once he left after his aunt's death. Only a few were able to recall the family in question, though none remembered their name for certain nor was a positive answer given about where they went. One was convinced they had returned east, and though a few thought it was to California, most of them thought the Nebraska Territory would be a good place to try. Especially the area around Fort Laramie.

It was nearly dark before the trio set off for the Jakobus cabin. Upon arriving, they found a good hot supper ready for them and while they ate, plans were laid for their trek up north.

Sally listened to it all quietly. Much as she would have liked to travel in the comfort of a wagon, she knew it would be impractical for the quick riding needed. No thought was given to staying behind for she was nearly as anxious as her brother to find their little sister. It was with relief, however, that she heard the discussion to remain there with Mr. and Mrs. Jakobus until the supplies and provisions could be purchased and made ready. All that would take a few days. These Sally intended to enjoy to their fullest.

The dawn was breaking in the eastern sky, a sky rosy and purple with a golden glow outlining the few clouds. The birds were already singing madly out in the woods while squirrels, chipmunks, rabbits and a host of other small animals, who inhabit the wooded and open lands, scampered about busy with their own affairs. Back of the cabin, four deer stood silent and still, prepared for instant flight, yet curious, watching the loading of the horses and listening to the final good-byes as Ty, Sally and Carson prepared to depart the hospitable home which had given them shelter. Ty helped Sally, with her father's gun at her side, mount her horse, and then with the agility of the young he sprang into his saddle without touching the stirrup. Carson was already mounted and waiting. With a final wave, they were off.

For several hours all was silent save for the sound of the horses' hooves and the soft jingle of their bridles. In the open, with the sun shining down upon them, the air was pleasantly warm, yet in the woods where the thick branches effectively shut out the sun's rays, it was cool. Spring had arrived at last. Proof of that lay all about the travelers, from the green grass and daring little flowers at their horses' feet, to the buds and tiny shoots on the trees. Now and then they caught glimpses of birds with twigs or grass in their beaks.

Around noon, the trio stopped for a bite to eat and to give the horses a rest.

"Ty," Sally began when once more they were in the saddle, "what did ya do the two years ya were gone? Pa an' I often talked 'bout ya. Where did ya go?"

Thus started, Ty launched forth into tales of his trip. Side by side the brother and sister rode. To any not acquainted with the Elliots, it would have been easy to guess they were brother and sister. Each had dark hair and eyes. Although Ty was darkened with the rugged look of a man well used to the daily struggle and hardships of outdoor living, there was an air of tenderness and gentleness that bespoke of the right sort of upbringing. His face, once he had disposed of his beard, looked almost as young as his twenty-one years. Sally, three years her brother's junior, was a becoming lass, quiet and with a remarkable ability to turn any place into a home. She had greatly missed her brother, the constant playmate of her childhood and then her confidant and companion in the later years. It was with mixed feelings of regret and relief that she had written that letter which recalled Ty to his home. Relief, because the burden which had fallen on her young, slim shoulders when the father was taken ill could be shared. Regret, for she knew Ty had left for a reason and to call him back might put him in danger. Yet, providentially, everything had turned out all right.

No one knew or dreamed all that would befall them before their journey was complete. Everything now was quiet and peaceful, but how long would it last?

Day followed day, each one warmer than the last as the trio rode steadily on. After all that riding, Sally was growing almost as used to the saddle as Ty and Carson and no longer dreaded mounting each morning as they once again set off.

The nights, still chilly with cool breezes, were spent for the most part in the open with only the trees for shelter, for now they were far from habited areas save here and there where a lonely cabin of a trapper or hermit appeared. To the men, who had spent the last two years out in the wilderness, the nights were common and ordinary. For Sally, to whom all such experiences were new, they were intriguing. Everything was different when the sun sank out of sight in the west with the sounds of the night animals as they began to stir, the biting wind and the warmth of the campfire competing for mastery, the thousands of glittering stars which came out in the darkening sky and the hard ground on which to sleep. All combined to give Sally a feeling she had never felt before. As she lay each night in this, to her, new environment, she often thought of her mother, touching her locket with its picture and wondered what it must have been like for her to leave the city to come out into an untamed land far from those she knew and loved. Her unknown sister also claimed a large portion of her thoughts. What was she like? Would they find her and what had she had to live through? These and various other questions, Sally never could answer, for she always fell fast asleep only moments after lying down.

"I tell ya, Ty," Carson remarked in admiration as Sally's quick and accurate shot brought down a rabbit for their breakfast. "We'll make her inta a trapper yet." The sun was shining brightly and the fire was just right to roast this choice piece of meat.

Ty chuckled and slid his pistol back into its holster. "She might be a good shot, Carson, but I reckon she ain't goin' ta be doin' any skinnin' of it."

"What, ya mean we're eatin' rabbit fur stew this mornin'?"

Sally's cheeks grew pink with blushes from their teasing, yet she smiled. It wasn't very often she could beat Ty on a draw. And she knew Carson would skin the rabbit for her even if he did tease.

"I think yer aim's improved since I was home, Sis. I reckon if'n ya were ta try ta beat me in a contest, I'd walk away in defeat."

A merry laugh rang from Sally's glowing face as she reloaded her gun. Praise was sweet to her ears even if it was far from the truth.

Breakfast was partaken with great relish that morning for fresh meat was rare to these travelers. "It was well worth a delay," Carson grunted stretching out once more as though to catch another forty winks.

Ty gave him a kick. "Well it sure 'nough don't call for more sleep. This here ought ta've been jest right ta keep ya movin'."

Carson snorted and sat up. "Ya mind yer manners, Ty Elliot. An' don't ferget I'm old enough ta be yer pa."

Ty grinned. "Ain't forgettin'."

Still grumbling good-naturedly under his breath, Carson joined in the packing up of camp. Saddling the horses and loading the pack horse with most of their supplies took some time, though now that they were more accustomed to the task, it was shorter than at first. When all was ready, Carson set off with the packhorse following while Ty and Sally brought up the rear.

The trio had ridden for several hours and the sun, in a cloudless sky, was nearing midday. Carson, up ahead with the extra pack horse, called back that they'd have to cross the ravine just up ahead. Ty waved in answer and turned to answer Sally's question. The two of them rode slowly onward. The sun was pleasant, and they didn't want to push their horses up the rather steep slope. Carson soon had disappeared before them.

On reaching the summit of the hill, they paused to look at the ravine before them. A faint trail led down one side. The farther side was covered with trees and rocks. The ravine was wide, and Sally thought she caught a glimpse of Carson's horse near the bottom.

Suddenly, Ty's quick ears caught the sound of a low roar. His head turned and rapidly his eyes darted over the landscape. What was that sound? Where was it coming from?

Not noticing her brother's rapt attention, Sally had started her horse down the trail, carefully watching for loose rocks. She had lost sight of Carson, but believed him to be down at the bottom, therefore, she kept going.

The roar was noticeably louder, and Sally's mount gave a whinny of alarm and began to prance and toss her head against the restraining reins, which Sally held.

"Easy, girl," Sally tried to calm the horse. "Its all right. Ain't nothin' to be afraid of. Easy now!" for the horse was beginning to plunge in a fearful manner.

Just then, Ty, still sitting his horse and listening, knew exactly what it was. When he turned to Sally, he found her already part way down the ravine right in the way of danger! His face paled and his heart seemed to stop. For an instant, only an instant, but to him it felt like years, he couldn't move. He couldn't even cry out! And just as suddenly strength came rushing back.

"Sally!" he shouted. "Get back here!" Flinging himself off his own frightened horse Ty half slid, half scrambled down the steep side of the ravine, not noticing the rocks that cut his hands nor the brambles which tore at his clothes, to where Sally was trying desperately to keep her seat on the plunging, rearing animal.

CHAPTER TEN

The roar had turned into a thunder of sound now as Ty grasped the bridle strap and pulled the struggling animal's head back to the top of the ridge. For a moment the horse seemed to lose its footing, for it stumbled, but the next it was plunging up the rocks with no regard to the trail. Sally clinging in white, terrified silence wondered what was happening.

Then without warning, a veritable wall of foaming, rushing, swirling water came sweeping down the ravine right over the place Sally had been but seconds before! It came so swiftly that had not Ty almost dragged the horse back up the slope, no doubt both horse and rider would have been swept away.

Sally screamed as her horse gave a desperate leap over the last of the rocks to safety thereby knocking Ty nearly off the edge into the roaring river below!

Terrified, both horses reared and tossed their heads. Ty's mount raced away in fright while Sally's would have followed but for the hands on its reins. Sally couldn't move; her face was ashen. She clung fearfully to the reins of the nervous animal. Would it lose its footing and go plunging to its death in the cold river that had so abruptly formed? Or would it too make a dash for some distant place of safety?

And where was Ty? The movements of her horse prevented her from looking for him.

In a moment, Ty was beside her, calming, soothing the frightened beast until it stood still long enough for Sally to slide weakly to the ground. Her knees gave way, and she sank onto a log.

"Sally! Are ya all right?" Ty had both arms about her trembling form. "Are ya all right?" His voice could scarcely be heard for the rushing of the water below them. It was several minutes before Sally could answer.

"Oh, Ty!" and she burst into tears. She was shaking like a leaf and clung to her brother as though she would never let him go. "Ty, Ty!" was all she could get out between her sobs. Never in all her life had she been that frightened.

For several minutes Ty held his sister close and tried to soothe her distress. "Sally, it's all right. Yer safe now. Yer safe."

Gradually her sobs lessened and giving a last convulsive shudder, she looked up. "Ty, what was it?"

"Some ice dam must'a broke farther up the mountains. I reckon this here nice weather's melted lots a snow."

Together they sat in silence eyes focused on the raging, roaring, rushing torrent as it swept by just below their safe retreat.

"Oh!" Sally cried out.

Ty looked at her sharply. "What is it?"

Sally raised eyes so full of anguish and distress that Ty could only wait for her words.

There were only two words and they were spoken low and with trembling lips and quivering chin. "Uncle Bob."

"What about him?"

"Ty, I saw him down on the bottom as I started down. Could he—?" Sally couldn't finish the sentence.

There was no answer. Ty's eyes didn't seem to be seeing anything before him. Presently, as one in a daze, he rose and walked towards the water. For a long time he stood there, staring out over its heaving surface, then slowly, with a hand that trembled visibly, he reached up and took off his hat.

Watching him with tear-dimmed eyes, Sally slipped to her knees and buried her face in her hands. Her mind was in a whirl. It had all happened so fast, so quickly, yet it seemed to her as though years must have passed since that morning when she had shot that rabbit. Uncle Bob, gone! Swept away in that mad, terrifying wall of water. It wasn't right! Everything was hopeless. All seemed black. They couldn't go on without him, could they?

"Sally," Ty's hand was on her shoulder.

She looked up.

His face was haggard and drawn as though in pain. "Come. We must get the horses."

Silently she rose and allowed him to lead her away from that horrible place. Without a word they walked, the roar of the water growing fainter and fainter until it became only a subdued hum.

The two horses, recovered from their fright and grazing contentedly, looked up at Ty and Sally as though to say, "What took you so long? We have been here ready and waiting for some time."

Carefully Ty readjusted the harnesses and saddles and made sure the packs were on securely. He felt as though he must be dreaming. Carson just couldn't be—. He wouldn't let himself even think it. Now, they had to go on, alone. How could he undertake this journey with only his sister? Feeling strongly tempted to turn around and ride back to the friendly home of the Jakobus family and forget the entire thing, he set his jaw and drew his brows together in a frown. His father's dying words rang in his ears. "Ty will do what I couldn't." He would go on! He would leave Sally at the first friendly cabin if he had to, but he would continue! These thoughts along with many others drifted in and out of Ty's mind as he worked.

At last he turned to his sister. "Let's ride a while 'fore we stop for the night." He held out his hand to help her mount.

"Ty!" Sally exclaimed, noticing for the first time, his cut and bleeding hands. "Yer hurt!"

Glancing down, Ty realized why it had been so difficult tightening things. He didn't protest as Sally washed and bandaged them, though he muttered something about not being able to hold the reins.

This delay over, the two mounted and rode quietly away, neither one speaking.

Above, a few wisps of clouds floated lazily along in the blue sky. A gentle breeze fanned their faces and a mountain bird hidden somewhere in the trees sang a bright melody which neither one noticed.

For well over an hour Ty and Sally rode in complete and utter silence. With Carson gone, they both felt a great and heavy loss. Why hadn't Carson noticed the sound? He had heard it enough times, hadn't he?

Ty knew they would have to find some way to get around that river to continue their journey to Fort Larramie. But how? Was it best to try to go around the mountain? Should they try to go west for a while and try to cross it? Would the river go down enough in a day or two to get over it, or would it continue to rage with melting ice and snow from the mountaintops? Wearily he considered all these problems and questions. Normally his mind quickly formed solutions to any problem. He knew the best way was to meet trouble head on, but somehow, today was different. He shook his head. Different yes, all was different now.

"Let's bed down here, Sally," Ty pulled his horse up beside a clump of tall trees whose branches were green with tiny leaves.

Sally dismounted and camp was set up. The packhorse was gone, so all they had was what was in their saddlebags.

In moments, Ty had a fire burning and was pulling out his rifle.

"I'll see if'n I can't get us some meat. Ya wait for me here."

Nodding, Sally finished unsaddling her horse and began to rub it down. When she came to its right foreleg, Starlight moved away.

"What is it, girl?" she asked softly, feeling the leg. "Well, no wonder ya were limpin'. Ya got it cut. Was it tryin' ta get out 'fore the river came?" Her soothing voice and gentle hands calmed the horse. Carefully she washed and bound up the leg. "I reckon perhaps we ought ta jest let ya take it easy for a day or so, till ya get better." Softly she rubbed her horse's nose.

Nickering, the horse nuzzled Sally's shoulder as though to agree.

Sally checked Ty's horse for injury, but found none. With her duties thus completed, she sat before the fire and waited. Every now and then she would get up, put a few more pieces of wood on the flames and then resume her seat.

The sun, which had been sliding down towards the western sky, now cast a last bright gleam around the mountain peaks causing the snow to glitter and glow in a dazzling evening display. In the east, the sky was beginning to change to a dusky blue, and here and there a brave little star peeked its face out as though to see if the king of the day had really gone to bed.

Sally gazed up into the sky as the sun disappeared. No moon was to be seen. Ty had not returned, and Sally began to wonder where he was. A soft whinny from one of the horses made her listen. Soft footsteps were heard. They were limping slightly, Sally could tell, and coming from the other side of the fire.

"Ty?"

No answer.

In silence Sally drew away from the fire's glow into the shadows and quietly pulled out her gun. Who was it? The footsteps halted just beyond the light.

The horses moved a little restlessly but didn't act very frightened. Sally knew it was a human being, but who? And what did he want? She swallowed hard. Her hands were shaking and her heart racing. At last she could stand the silence no longer.

"Come out inta the light, or I'll shoot." She hoped her voice didn't give away the fear she felt.

A soft rustle of leaves and a dark form glided into the light. Sally gasped. It was an Indian, and he had a gun!

For several seconds Sally stared. True, she had seen many an Indian before, but never when she was alone at night on a strange mountainside. Cautiously she too stepped into the light and looked at her visitor.

"Huh," the Indian grunted and sank onto the ground and looked into the fire.

Sally could tell he was old and tired. She grew bolder and stepped closer. "Who are you?" she asked.

"Huh," was the reply.

Another step closer and Sally could see the weariness in his face. "Would ya like some water?" she asked feeling for her canteen with her left hand while her eyes never left the Indian's face, and her right hand still grasped her pistol.

"Huh."

Taking that for assent, Sally handed it over.

The Indian took it and raised it to his lips. After tasting a little at first, he tipped it up and took a long draft. "Much good." And again he drank deeply.

Sally smiled faintly. "Are you hungry?"

A grunt was the answer.

It was difficult to carry on a conversation with someone who only grunted to every question asked, yet Sally kept trying. "My brother went huntin' ta try ta find meat. When he returns, you are welcome ta join us."

"Huh, good," was the reply.

After several long minutes of silence, Sally ventured at last to ask, "Are there more, I mean, are you alone?"

"Alone."

Sally breathed a sigh of relief. If he was alone, surely he was not someone to fear. Now if only Ty would come.

The Indian heard him before Sally did. He arose and held his rifle with both hands.

"It might be Ty," Sally whispered.

Sure enough, Ty's voice called out as he approached. "Sally."

"I'm right here, Ty, an' we got a visitor."

The next moment Ty stepped into the light and saw the Indian who, when he heard Sally's response, had sunk back down and let his rifle rest on his knees.

Ty eyed him a moment and then said, "Welcome."

"Huh."

Ty had brought several rabbits, and soon Ty, with the help of their Indian visitor, had them skinned and roasting over the fire.

CHAPTER ELEVEN

No one talked as the three travelers ate their evening meal. Ty and Sally kept watching their visitor, wondering where he had come from, who he was and what he was doing. Neither could eat much though they at least pretended to, more for the sake of the other than for themselves. The food seemed to stick in their throats, and it was only with effort than they managed to swallow any of it. It was a relief when at last the repast was ended.

The Indian lit his pipe and stared into the darkness. Ty built the fire up to a pleasant blaze. Then settling down beside his sister, he began to talk.

"My name's Ty an' this is Sally. Who're you?"

"Black Eagle."

"What're ya doin' out here?"

"Hunting grounds this. Hurt leg," the Indian grunted while nodding towards his right leg and continued. "See strange fire. White squaw welcome Black Eagle."

For several minutes the Indian smoked in peace before asking, "What white man and squaw do here?"

Briefly Ty recounted their adventures ending with Carson's death in the river. "An' now we aim ta keep headin' north ta Fort Larramie. Can ya tell us how ta git 'round the river?"

The Indian grunted. "When sun come, me show."

Ty expressed his gratitude, but Sally pulled at his sleeve.

"Ty," she spoke low, "I can't ride tomorrow. My horse is injured."

"Bad?"

She shook her head. "No, but she was limpin' 'fore we stopped, an' I found her right foreleg cut."

"She might be better in the mornin'."

No further words were spoken as the darkness deepened about them. The cry of an owl in the woods was heard and in the stillness distant sounds were amplified. The heavens were bright with stars. Gazing up at them, Sally yawned. The day had been long and full of heartache and sorrow.

"Why don't ya get some sleep," Ty asked her, touching her arm gently.

She nodded and in a few minutes was rolled up in her blanket. Clutching her locket with its precious picture, she fell asleep trying hard not to think of Carson.

The night passed quickly for Sally whose overwrought nerves demanded rest, but it dragged by with slow, weary feet for Ty. Their Indian guest, after sitting silent for some time, also rolled himself in a blanket and slept. Into the flickering light of the dying flames Ty gazed, not seeing anything, lost in memories, struggling to accept Carson's death. If this trip was to cost so dearly at the outset, what would the final cost be? Would it be worth everything?

All through that long, lonely night Ty wrestled with himself and with the questions that had no answers. Questions that kept returning to haunt him and which only brought more questions.

As the grey dawn began to steal across the sky, Ty stood to stretch his cramped and weary legs and built up the fire. As he did so, both the Indian and Sally awakened.

"I reckon I'll be goin' huntin'," Ty spoke to no one in particular.

"No," the quiet voice of Black Eagle interrupted any words Sally might have said. "White man sleep now. Black Eagle hunt."

Ty shook his head. "Can't sleep."

"Did ya sleep at all last night, Ty?" Sally questioned somewhat anxiously.

He shook his head.

"Then do try ta sleep now," she begged.

Again Ty shook his head. "Can't," and he turned to the Indian.

But he was not to be seen. No trace that he had been there but moments before were visible.

"Black Eagle?" Ty called, his voice sounding harsh and out of place in the quiet morning air. No answer came back and the brother and sister looked at each other.

"Ya reckon there were an Indian here for real, Sally?"

"I think so," Sally sounded a little uncertain. "We couldn't both be dreamin' the same thing, could we?"

Ty sighed deeply and sank down beside the warm fire. The air was chilly and he felt cold clear through. Right then he wouldn't have cared if a tribe of Indians had been there and then vanished.

"Ty," Sally coaxed, "please lie down an' rest some. I can't be havin' ya get sick like—" The loss of her father was still keenly felt, and she left her sentence unfinished.

Ty reached up and pulled her down beside him. "I ain't goin' ta git sick, Sissy." It was a rare thing for that endearing childhood name to pass Ty's lips and Sally gave a quavering smile. "I reckon I might jest take a bit of a rest if'n ya don't mind the quiet." He smiled wearily.

"Mind the quiet? I've been livin' in quiet for 'round two years with Pa off trappin' or huntin and ya off with . . . oh, Ty!" and the sentence ended in a sob.

Gently Ty put an arm about his sister. "Now, ya jest git some more rest. I reckon ya need it 'fore we travel on."

Sally pulled away from him. Wiping her eyes with her sleeve, she swallowed hard. "I'll rest only if'n ya will too."

"All right," Ty yawned. He knew it was useless to try to argue, and in a few minutes he was sleeping soundly.

For several minutes Sally sat gazing about her in the half-light of early morning. Everything was shrouded in stillness save for the soft chirpings of a few birds. Even the horses tethered nearby seemed to be enjoying their rest. Sally wondered where the Indian had gone and if he would return. Had his presence been a dream? She shook her head. No, he was real. And he had been there. Where he had gone and how were mysteries, which might remain forever unsolved.

A gentle snore issued from the blanket in which Ty had rolled himself. Sally yawned. Then, feeling tired, she lay back down near her brother and was soon, like him, asleep.

It was the smell of a savory, venison stew drifting through the blanket and awakening his appetite that aroused Ty from slumber some time later. For several minutes he remained unmoving, feeling drained of all energy and wishing only to sleep. However, the pangs of hunger would not subside. With a yawn, he threw off the blanket and sat up.

The sun was high, showing that the morning was well nigh past. The vast expanse of sky was a brilliant blue with wisps and puffs of clouds dancing across it. Everywhere in the woods and sky birds were singing, eager to be alive on that glorious day. In the distance, the still snow covered mountain peaks gleamed in the sunlight.

A movement beside him caused Ty to turn. Sally too had been aroused by the smell and sat up.

"Eat." The Indian across the fire nodded towards the pot on the fire.

Needing no urging, Ty and Sally filled their bowls and began. Not for a long time had they tasted such a wonderful stew, and they ate rapidly and in silence.

When at last he could eat no more, Ty drew a deep breath. "I ain't sure jest how it happened, but I feel 'bout ready ta set off again. I ain't sayin' I know jest where ta go or that I ain't goin' ta miss Carson, but I got the courage ta go on again."

Sally nodded. "If my horse is all right, I reckon it might be nice ta get on."

Then Black Eagle spoke. "Horse good walk, no ride. Stew give life. We go. Black Eagle show trail to white man and his squaw."

"We'll be right glad ta go with ya, Black Eagle, but this here," and Ty jerked his head in Sally's direction, "is my sister not my squaw."

"Huh."

Camp was packed up quickly and the trio set off on foot leading the two horses. Each breath of air seemed to infuse new energy and life into every fiber of Ty and Sally's beings. The events of yesterday, tragic and terrible though they were, could not cast a deep gloom today. They would move forward. Hope of success, however distant, seemed to grow brighter with each step they took.

Sally fingered her locket, looking down into the tiny face, and whispered to herself, "We'll find her, Ma. We will."

And Ty, reaching his hand into his pocket pressed the broken locket, muttering with a new tone of determination, "I'll do it, Pa. No matter what it takes! I'll find my other sister."

And so the day moved on. That night they camped and the following morning set off again, still with Black Eagle as their guide. By mid afternoon the old Indian had pointed out a trail, which led north. Farewells were called, and Ty and Sally rode off leaving Black Eagle watching them until they were lost to sight.

The horses kept up a brisk pace, for the feeling of spring was filling all living creatures with its vitality. By evening the two riders had traversed many miles, and on finding a suitable place to camp, halted. There they prepared their supper after taking care of their horses.

Miles away, the slow, plodding steps of horses came through the woods to the keen ears of the watching Indian. Eagerly he listened. The steps came closer. A twig snapped. As the rider came into view, the Indian lowered his rifle and stepped out into the open. At the unexpected appearance, the lead horse snorted and tossed his head. At this the rider looked up.

"Black Eagle!"

"Swift Fox," replied the Indian on foot. "It is many moons since you come here."

The rider nodded. "Yes, many moons."

"Come," Black Eagle beckoned. "We eat. Smoke pipe. Sleep."

"Good."

With his rifle in his hands, Black Eagle led his guest into the woods. Neither talked for both knew talk could wait. Once they had arrived at the Indian's campsite, Swift Fox slid off his horse and stretched his legs stiffly before taking care of his mount and the other horse.

It was only after the simple meal was over and their first pipes smoked, that the two friends begin to talk. Their low voices were dispassionate at first, however, as Black Eagle recounted the last few days experience, the eyes of his companion began to gleam in the firelight.

"One white man and white squaw?" Swift Fox questioned with interest. "Good!"

"Huh."

"Where?"

Black Eagle paused, eyeing the other figure across the fire.

"Where they gone to?"

Grunting, Black Eagle gave a faint nod of his head in the direction Ty and Sally had taken.

Swift Fox quickly looked at the darkening sky, then at the still darker woods about them.

As though reading his thoughts, Black Eagle shook his head. "No find tonight. They ride quick."

"When sun comes again. Black Eagle show Swift Fox the trail. Swift Fox, he find."

"Huh."

Silence fell on the little campsite for several minutes. After knocking the ashes from his pipe, Swift Fox began to talk. In the stillness his voice sounded like the distant thunder of a far off storm. For some time the voice went on with a few solitary comments from Black Eagle. Then all was quiet. Rolling themselves in blankets, they slept.

The sun had scarce risen when Swift Fox set off on the trail of Ty and Sally. He was well mounted, and the horse tethered behind was not one to lag on such a morning. Bidding Black Eagle good-bye, the rider set the horses into a brisk ground eating pace. He scarcely noticed the lush green leaves, which now were to be seen on every tree and bush, nor did he pay the slightest attention to the birds which sang so loudly. He had one fixed idea, to find this white man and his squaw. This he would do. They would not slip from his grasp. He would follow them.

Rebekah A. Morris

CHAPTER TWELVE

The night, which had closed down around Ty and Sally, was dark and still. Other than the glowing embers of the fire, only the sliver of moon and the thousand twinkling stars in the heavens were to be seen. The brother and sister had gone to bed with the sun, having covered many miles that day. All was hushed. No breeze blew to rustle the leaves or grasses and only occasionally would one of the horses stir. The silence was intense.

With a start, Ty suddenly was jerked awake. For a moment he lay staring into the darkness and straining his ears. Softly reaching beside him, his hand grasped his rifle. Whatever it was that had awakened him would find him ready. Lying quietly back down, he pressed his ear to the ground, listening. Hoof beats. Faint though they were, there was no mistaking them.

Moving stealthily over to where Sally lay still wrapped in a deep slumber, Ty placed his hand over her mouth and whispered, "Sally!"

She was awake in an instant, her eyes wide with alarm. Not a sound did she make as Ty drew away his hand.

"Someone's comin'. Get yer gun an' get behind the trees."

Sally nodded and, slipping out of her blanket, drew her father's six-gun from its holster. Then noiselessly she disappeared into the gloom. Ty followed and together they crouched in the blackness, waiting.

It wasn't long before they could both hear distinctly the sound of horses. They weren't moving rapidly, but they came on at a steady pace. In another moment they would be there.

Beside him, Ty heard the soft click of the six-shooter as it was cocked.

"Don't shoot 'till we know who it is an' what they want," he hissed.

"I don't aim ta. Jest ta be prepared."

Ty smiled rather grimly. He was glad Sally was taking things so calmly, yet wished she didn't have to face this at all.

On came the steps of the approaching horses. A welcoming nicker from one of their own mounts greeted the new arrivals as they drew near the camp site. From the shadows Ty could make out the form of one rider who halted and looked around.

"Ty? Sally?"

That voice! It couldn't be, and yet— Ty heard Sally gasp as once again the stranger called,

"Ty? I know I ain't taught ya ta sleep through someone ridin' inta camp. Where in thunder are ya?"

"Uncle Bob!"

"Carson!" The answering cries came at once as both Ty and Sally rushed from the trees, the one to grip Carson's hand while the other threw herself about his neck.

It was indeed Carson. He had returned as it were, from the dead. Questions flew so thick and fast that he had no time to answer any or get a word in edge wise. At last, having disentangled himself from Sally's embrace and pulled his hand out of Ty's viselike grip, he cried out,

"Quiet!"

Instant silence prevailed. "I'll answer yer questions soon's I can, but I'm near famished an' the poor beasts must be plum tuckered out. An' how 'bout a little more light."

Sally built up the fire and pulled out some dried meat while Ty saw to the horses. It wasn't very long before all three were sitting around the blazing fire. All thought of sleep had vanished.

"Uncle Bob," Sally began, "How'd ya manage ta get out a that river?"

"Weren't never in no river, girl."

"But," Sally protested, "I'm sure I saw ya down in the bottom of the valley, right 'fore the water came."

Carson snorted. "Well, it weren't me. Why I was plum up the other side when that there flood come a rushin' down. I was scairt for you an' Ty. Couldn't get them ornery beasts ta get anywhere close ta the edge ta look for ya neither. By the time I did get back, there weren't no sign a neither a ya. I even fired my gun, though it ain't likely ya could a heard it, seein' I couldn't hear it none too well myself. I did light a fire a hopin' ya'd see the smoke."

"I didn't even look for smoke, Carson. Sally had been so sure ya was in the bottom that we both gave ya up for dead."

"Ya ought ta know it'd take more'n a little water ta get rid a me." Carson grinned and stroked his beard with his hand.

"But how'd ya find us?" persisted Ty.

"Why, I met Black Eagle. Used ta hunt an' trap together years back. In fact, yer pa used ta come with us 'fore he went an' got hitched ta yer ma. Ain't seen Black Eagle fer some time an' it were right nice ta see him 'gain. He called me Swift Fox an' yer pa, never one ta talk much, was Silent Hawk."

"Ty, maybe that's why Black Eagle kept lookin' at ya. Ya reminded him a Pa."

Ty didn't answer for several minutes. Then he turned with a question to Carson. "How come Black Eagle didn't say he knew ya?"

Carson shrugged his shoulders. "I reckon we ain't goin' ta ever know. He did come a lookin' ta see if'n I were really dead. An'," Carson couldn't help chuckling, "he found out I weren't. He set me on yer trail an' here I am. But, by thunder, Ty, I well nigh couldn't catch ya fer ya travel powerful fast. An' now," he yawned, "I reckon I could use with some shut eye." With that, he stretched out by the fire, after wrapping himself in a blanket, and was soon snoring.

"Well, would ya look at that," Ty shook his head. "He's gone from dead ta snorin' by our campfire. Huh." Looking across the fire to his sister, he asked, "Ya reckon we ought ta join him?"

Sally giggled. "Jest long's I don't have ta snore like a grizzly bear."

Ty grinned. "I reckon not."

Daylight found the three united travelers stirring, and it wasn't long before they once again set off for Fort Laramie in the bright sunshine. As they traveled along, Ty, with help from his sister, told Carson all that had happened to them since they were parted at the river.

It was a long journey that lay before them, over rough country, in much of which no white man dwelt. Each day brought its own challenges. The spring rains and melting snow caused flooded streams, which had to be forded. Winter avalanches of snow and rock had blocked many trails, and Carson and Ty spent time trying to find the best way around them.

At last their trail led them down into the foothills where spring had arrived with a blaze of color. The riding was easier then, and they made good time. There were also settlers here and there. These welcomed the travelers gladly and shared their store of provisions, meager though they might be, with them. Sally, especially, was thankful to sleep under a roof now and again. And at each place they asked about the younger sister, hoping against hope for just a hint, some clue that would show them they were on the right track, but always it was the same.

"We're right sorry, but we ain't heard nor seen a any sech folk." The man scratched his scraggly beard. "Ya heared a any, Ma?"

Thus questioned, the woman shook her head. "Land sakes, we ain't never had no strangers round these here parts 'cept trappers, here Billy, climb down off that table 'fore I take this spoon ta ya, and traders till ya'll came a ridin' in. And, land sakes, Clara Jane, how many times must I tell ya don't climb in that there cradle with the baby! It's down right nice ta see a lady." Continuing to chatter volubly as she bustled here and there, the woman served up a fine stew and fresh bread.

Days passed into weeks and still Ty, Sally and Carson traveled north. Sally was beginning to grow dark from the sun. No longer did a long day's ride wear her out, for she had grown as accustomed to the saddle as her brother and friend. When they rested for their noon meal, Ty began to teach his sister the fine art of knife throwing. Sally was a quick learner and though she never could match her brother's skill, she was a credit to her teacher. Carson now and then would join in and then Ty had hard work to hold his own, for the older man had many more years of experience with the best of instructors: Indians.

Although Sally couldn't always hit the center of a target with a knife, she was a crack shot with her father's pistol. Even a rifle made little difference in her shooting though she preferred the former firearm. Even if she didn't talk much about him, Sally often thought of her father as she rode along feeling the weight of his gun in the holster by her side.

"Ty," she asked once, late in the afternoon, "Ya reckon, if'n Pa were still alive, he'd a come with us ta find her?"

For a moment Ty was silent, watching the clouds race across the sky as though they were chasing one another. "Hard ta tell, Sally. It ain't likely he'd a even told us 'bout -- her." Pausing, Ty sighed. "I jest can't help wonderin' why he wouldn't never tell us till he was dyin'. It seems, well, sort a un-right somehow."

"Ya got a right ta wonder 'bout that," Carson put in, leaning down over his horse's neck to avoid a low tree branch. "But I reckon it ain't as unnatural as it 'pears. Never have I seen a man so in love, as yer pa was with yer ma. Why he fairly worshiped the ground she walked on. I reckon his love were so deep an' the baby sech a part a her, that when she died, half his heart died too." He squinted over at Ty and Sally from under his hat. "Nope, neither one a ya's got the look a yer ma. Sally has a might a it when she's arguin' with Ty, but it's jest her chin and maybe the tip a her head."

Ty glanced at Sally and began to laugh, for her cheeks had grown quite rosy under Carson's scrutinizing gaze.

Grinning, Carson continued. "Now, Ty, ya ain't a particle like yer ma. Ya ain't headstrong now 'cept when ya've thought it all through, but, by thunder, when ya was a young whipper-snapper—" Carson shook his head, and Sally chuckled. "I recall a time when ya was set an' determined that ya weren't goin' ta wash yer hands fer supper. Yer ma said ya would. Yer pa were out back or I reckon he would a took care a ya right quick."

By now Ty was beginning to grin rather self-consciously.

"Well, yer ma gave ya a lickin' an' ya still weren't goin' ta wash. Seem's like it took 'bout two more lickin's ta get ya ta mind, but ya did. An' right 'fore yer pa come in too. I always wondered if'n ya knew yer pa were comin' an' gave in ta save yer hide."

A hearty burst of laughter came from the three riders as Carson finished his tale, and all dismounted to walk up a hill and stretch their legs. "I don't recall that time, but I ain't never goin' ta forget Pa's lickins. Why he could tan a fella's hide till it felt like fire," and Ty rubbed his seat as though he could still feel the sting.

"But Carson," Sally questioned, "Did our sister look like Ma?"

"Look like her?" Carson repeated, "Why, she was the spittin' image a her! I seen babies that folks say look like their ma or pa an' I couldn't see it, but Sunshine— Well!" Carson drew a long breath before he continued. "Sally, that picture ya got in that there locket is jest like yer sister's goin' ta be lookin' right 'bout now. I'd bet my last bullet on it."

Drawing the locket out of her dress, Sally gazed at the face inside. It was a sweet face that seemed to look back at her, one that wore an expression of gentleness. Kind eyes with just the hint of a smile about them, under a perky little hat with feathers, seemed to match the bright smile of the full lips.

No one spoke as Ty also looked long at their mother's face as it hung around Sally's neck. "Well," Ty spoke at last. "I reckon perhaps we can find her after all."

Two days later, Carson, Ty and Sally found themselves at a crossroads in their journey. They had passed the night in the only hotel of Rock Valley, which stood at the foot of the pass leading to the other side of the mountain range and Fort Laramie. A tall, rough looking, dark bearded man, having heard them mention where they were headed, now offered his services as guide for a shorter, though less traveled, trail.

"I know the trail. It'll take two days off yer travels."

"How traveled is it?" Carson questioned shrewdly, wondering if the guide was being honest.

"Well, not many travel it at all. Fact is, not many know of it."

"And why should we follow it 'stead a the traveled one?"

"It's lots quicker. But," the man put in, glancing over at Sally. "You are planin' on comin' back through here ain't ya?"

Ty spoke up suspiciously, "Why?"

"The trail is a might dangerous, especially fer a lady. It'd be best if'n ya left 'her'," and he nodded in Sally's direction, "here till ya returned."

Ty's eyes narrowed. "Why?" was all he asked, but he was roused. What was this man trying to hide? Did he really know a trail or was it just a trick? And why did he want Sally to stay behind?

Having heard what the man said, Sally moved up beside her brother, her eyes flashing at the very idea of being left behind.

"Well," the man began and then hesitated, evidently a little embarrassed by Sally joining the group. "Like I said, it's rather dangerous. An' well, no offense ma'am, it ain't safe fer one who can't hold his own to defend himself should we be needin' it."

"I'll have ya know, mister, that I can shoot jest as well as you can." Sally fairly bristled with indignation.

"Well, that ain't all exactly, ma'am," he began, somewhat flustered.

The man's evident hesitation was causing both Ty and Carson doubts about the man's honesty and purpose. "Then get on with the rest," ordered Carson. "We're wastin' time."

"Well, like I said, it's dangerous an' ain't well used. But it's quicker. Oh yes, two whole days quicker, but there's a few places that the trail goes right along the cliff an' ain't much more space than a horse with a full load. An' . . ." The man paused and his eyes became hard. "There's a mountain lion roamin' the trail. Larger 'an any ever seen 'fore an' meaner 'an ten she bears. I been tryin' ta kill 'im fer nigh upon three years. An' I aim ta get 'im, if'n it's the last thing I do."

Sally turned slightly pale at the mention of a mountain lion. Gladly would she have pleaded then and there to go the other way even if it took a week longer, had not the man been looking at her with his cold, dark eyes. Was he trying to scare her into remaining in town?

Ty wondered the same thing, for his keen eyes and ears thought they detected a cunningly devised tall tale. There might be some truth to it, however, and Ty made a promise to himself that he would find out. Now he only remarked, "Seems like a mighty rash offer ta lead us over this trail with a wild cat so dangerous 'bout."

"Well, I figured on goin' myself," protested the man indignantly, "but when I knew you were headin' that way, I thinks ta myself, 'Vin, three guns is better'n one an' ya might get 'im that a way.' An' so I jest offered."

"Much obliged," Carson grunted. "Give us time ta sleep on it."

"Oh sure," the man became suddenly very polite. "Ya jest talk it over. I reckon ya'll figure out I was right 'bout leavin' her here till ya return." With that, the man bowed to Sally and strode off down the street with a swagger in his steps.

"Ty, ya ain't goin' ta do it, are ya? I ain't goin' ta stay here! I'd rather—" Sally didn't finish for Ty silenced her."

"Hush! This ain't the place for that. Let's go, Carson. I reckon I know a skunk when I smell him."

Silenced, but still ruffled, Sally followed her brother down the street towards the hotel. She noticed his easy stride and thought of how at home Ty was in the saddle as well as out of it. It was Carson who appeared slightly out of place.

"Never did like these here fancy towns," he grumbled.

Before the trio reached the hotel, Ty paused and crossing the street, entered a saloon. Sally gasped inwardly but then realized that Ty was only trying to find some things out. With a fast beating heart, she waited with Carson on the porch wondering what Ty would discover.

Striding up to the counter, Ty leaned his elbow on it and eyed the bartender.

"What can I get ya?" the bar tender asked looking casually at him.

"Some information," Ty replied coolly without moving.

The man glanced around before leaning down to Ty's level. "What kind of information?" The man had lowered his voice.

"What do ya know about a man who calls himself 'Vin'?"

CHAPTER THIRTEEN

"You a stranger 'round these parts?"

"What if I am?" Ty boldly challenged the barkeeper.

The man behind the counter shrugged. "Figured ya must be not ta know Vin."

"What about him?" Ty was determined to keep the conversation from getting sidetracked.

"He's a slippery sort a snake. Ain't never sure jest what he's up to. I heard the sheriff's been keepin' an eye on him now he's back in town."

"Where's he been?"

"Mountains."

"Ever hear tell of a mountain lion bigger'n ever seen 'fore and meaner 'an ten she bears?"

Suddenly the bartender straightened up. After another quick glance about the room he leaned back down and spoke in a hoarse whisper. "I ain't jest heard about it, I done see it! It's the most awfullest bigg'st fiercest cat anywheres. I never want to see the likes of it again!"

For a moment Ty stared before him, thinking. This man claimed to have seen the mountain lion, but he was a saloon man, how could he have? It wasn't likely that he had gone out into the mountains with this Vin. "Where'd ya see this cat?"

"At a house on the edge a town. It had come down from the mountains, an' the sight was enough to turn yer legs to jelly."

Ty nodded and stood up. "Thanks."

It was all he said, but the way he said it caused the man to wish he hadn't told so much and he muttered, "Vin, ya fool, get out of town an' don't mess with him."

Ty took no more notice of the man than if he had suddenly vanished as he stood for a few seconds glancing about the half empty room, but his quick ears had heard the muttered words, low though they were. With a quick straightening of his broad shoulders, Ty strode out of the saloon to rejoin Carson and Sally.

"What'd ya find out," Carson queried as Ty, having glanced first up and then down the street, turned his steps to a small building not far away.

"Ain't sure. Let's go have us a talk with the sheriff."

Carson nodded while Sally, who had grown warm in the sun, flung back her shawl revealing her holstered six-shooter.

Ty noticed and chuckled. "I don't reckon Vin would 'ave said what he did if'n she'd a shown her gun."

"Then I should have shown it. I ain't a coward." Sally frowned. The man's words still rankled her spirits.

Ty attempted to soothe her. "No, ya ain't. I reckon if'n ya made the attempt ta kill that legend of a mountain lion, ya'd do it 'fore three years was up."

No more talking was done then for they had reached the town jail. The sheriff, along with his deputy, was leaning back against the side of the building watching the trio approach. Both men touched their hats to Sally as they reached them.

"Howdy, folks," the sheriff greeted, in a quiet, pleasant voice. "Can I help you?"

"I reckon so," Ty spoke up. "We're lookin' ta find out about a man who calls himself Vin."

The sheriff and his deputy exchanged glances before the sheriff replied, "I just might be able to help at that. I'm Sheriff Mead and this is my deputy Griffin Thompson."

"Ty Elliot, my sister Sally and friend Bob Carson."

"Won't you three come in where we can talk undisturbed." And Sheriff Mead led the way inside.

Inside was a room, which, by all appearances was the sheriff's office, and back behind that, in another room were the jail cells. No one was in them, however, and Sheriff Mead bade his visitors be seated while he perched himself on the corner of his desk. "Now," he began, "you were askin' about Vin."

Carson and Ty nodded.

Crossing his arms, kicking one heel of his boots against the desk leg, glancing out the window into the street, Sheriff Mead cleared his throat. "I can tell you about him. At least, all I know. Griff can fill in anything I miss. Where Vin came from, no one seems to know. He showed up here, oh, I'd say maybe six years ago. Doesn't hang around the town much. Claims to be a trapper and guide. I locked him up a few times for saloon brawls but, though he seems rather suspicious, we've never been able to pin anything on him. Last year he offered to lead a couple of men to Fort Laramie through the shorter trail. They went with him and we never heard of them again. Vin won't talk about it, which has several of us here in town mighty alert for dirty work."

"So there is another trail?" Ty cut in.

"Oh, yes. Been over it myself a time or two. It is a shorter way, but so downright narrow in places that only stout hearts should venture."

"What about the mountain lion that's bigger'n any ever seen 'fore and meaner'n ten she bears?"

A hearty chuckle from Mead and Thompson confirmed Ty's suspicions.

"There's a mountain cat all right, but each tale I hear grows bigger and meaner."

Carson turned to Griff who had just spoken and asked, "Then why's Vin sayin' he's been after this here cat three years an' ain't got it yet?"

Deputy Thompson shook his head and shifted his position in the doorway. "That's one of the questionable things 'bout him."

"We'd round up a posse to find out if we had something to go on. As it is, we sit here and wonder."

"I'd like ta help ya out, Sheriff, since this man seems so unusual, but I got my sister an' wouldn't want ta put her in no danger."

"I can defend myself if'n I have to, Ty Elliot. Don't forget I can match ya at a draw any day an' shoot jest as straight."

The sheriff nodded at her gun, "If you carry that around, I reckon you know how to use it."

"I could go up with Vin, an' leave you an' Sally ta take the other trail."

Carson's offer was rejected at once by a horrified Sally, and an astonished Ty, who added, "If'n anyone's ta go, I'd do it. Been takin' care a myself with 'them' after me for more'n two years now. I reckon I could take on another."

"No! Ty, I ain't goin' ta let ya do that. I'd go 'long on that trail jest ta keep ya from goin' alone. An' don't think I aim ta be left behind either." Sally's eyes flashed and her hand rested on the handle of her gun.

A hearty laugh filled the room. The sheriff shook his head with a grin. "Well, I don't know what's goin' on except none of you seem content to go by the long trail. You could go with Vin, but I don't know what he's up to."

"Excuse me, Sheriff," Deputy Thompson broke in, "Look's like you might have some company."

Boots clumped on the hard floor as Sheriff Mead vacated his seat on the desk. In three strides he was at the door with his deputy looking down the street. "I wonder what they're so riled up about."

"Hard tellin'."

At the news of company, Ty, Carson and Sally rose and prepared to depart, but the sheriff put up a hand. "Just wait a minute, if you would. Let me check this out first."

"Sheriff!" a loud voice called as four or five tough looking men with pistols and rifles crowded around the porch before the two officers of the law.

"Well?" The quiet reply seemed to calm the men somewhat, for when the voice spoke again it was lower.

"Vin's in town again, an' this time we aim to see what he's up to. He don't know most of these men by sight, so we thought we'd try ta get him to take us over his trail."

The sheriff shrugged. "Then why come to me? Vin's probably at the saloon or stables."

There was a moment of silence broken only by the clink of someone's spurs out in the street. At last one of the men spoke quietly, "We'll visit him next, Sheriff. First though, we wanted to find out what you think of our plan."

Scowling every time he walked past her or glanced in her direction, grumbling about the extra work she would bring, the danger she would be in, the bad luck it would be to have her along, muttering dire predictions under his breath, Vin at last got his followers ready to head up the mountains through the little used and known trail, Sally, her brother and Carson included. He wasn't sure just how it had all come about that his offer to guide two men had multiplied into nearly a dozen and even included that woman. He had eyed them all suspiciously but couldn't well refuse. Now he took his place at the front of the line and they were off.

Ty, Carson and Sally found themselves at the tail end of the caravan. Sally's chin was up and her eyes gave off sparks, though she refrained from speaking. Vin's looks and manners hadn't escaped her notice. Neither had they escaped Ty and Carson's sharp eyes. Both men were on the alert for the slightest double crossing or crooked dealings from the leader. Ty especially stuck near his sister, ready to ward off any unwanted attention she might receive as the only female.

It wasn't the most talkative group and hardly a word was spoken until they halted for the night. Vin directed that watchers would be stationed around the camp that night in case of wild animals.

"Huh!" Carson grunted in low tones to Ty and Sally. "He jest gave himself away. He ain't no trapper nor hunter neither. Ya don't post guard fer animals, ya build a fire."

Ty nodded.

"Perhaps there's other dangers besides animals, an' he ain't wantin' ta tell us," Sally suggested as Carson moved away to converse in low tones to a few of the other men.

"Could be. But what?"

Glancing around before she replied, Sally noticed the preparations for an evening meal. "Robbers."

"What?" Ty looked quizzically at his sister.

"I mean," Sally began again, "What if there ain't no real threat from wild animals, but a group of outlaws live here an' Vin brings their victims to them."

"Then why post guards?"

"With this many people, perhaps it is ta make it look like he was protecting them."

His brows drawing together in deep thought, Ty mused in silence for a while. He was still deep in thought when the call to supper came. Moving over to the fire beside Sally, he sat down and accepted the cup of coffee handed him.

"Augh! Terrible!" Ty choked and spit out the mouthful of coffee. Coughing and nearly gagging on what he had swallowed, he threw the rest of the contents of his cup into the fire and demanded, "Who made this stuff?"

"I'll have ya know that I made that coffee an' I know how ta make the best coffee." It was Vin.

The others were cautiously tasting it themselves and each declared it undrinkable. One by one they poured it out into the fire or tossed it over their shoulders into the woods.

"Isn't there anyone who can make a decent cup?" one of the men questioned. "I know I can't."

"Sally," Ty urged, "Ya make the coffee. Carson an' I can vouch for ya."

"Yep, go to it," Carson added.

Thus urged, Sally went at once to work and in a few minutes had the pot washed out and new coffee made. Handing a steaming cup to Ty she waited until he had tasted it before serving the others.

It only needed Ty's satisfied sigh to bring the cups out all around the fire. Sally was highly praised and made official coffee maker for the trip. Vin only glowered.

That night Ty and Carson took their turn on watch along with the other men. Sally slept fitfully, waking often to listen. All was still in the dark. No animal came near and only the snap of the fire as fresh wood was added disturbed the serene silence of the still night.

As dawn approached, Sally, wide awake, arose and began to make coffee. Ty quietly joined her to build up the fire and start breakfast. Then, one by one, the other men of the party roused themselves or were roused by the tantalizing aroma of Sally's coffee, and the day began. Before long camp was packed up, horses once again loaded and the fire put out. Vin taking his place at the front, set off.

The day was beautiful. As the sun rose higher, the sky grew richer in its robe of deep azure with here and there fleecy puffs of white dancing along on the breeze. Shining brightly, the sun cast its warm rays over the landscape. Everywhere the pine trees, their branches loaded with green needles and cones of varying sizes, showed signs of new growth at the tips of their branches. In places where there were no trees to block the sun, flowers of different colors and shapes lifted bright heads to welcome the king of the day. Miriads of tiny insects buzzed from flower to flower. It was all so lovely that Sally let her horse lag behind.

"Sally, come on," Ty called, noticing her distance from the group.

Urging her horse on a bit, Sally soon joined her brother at the end of the line of riders. "Oh, Ty," she breathed in ecstasy, "ain't it just, well—" She couldn't seem to find the right words to describe it. But her gaze took it all in, from the distant snow covered peaks to the lush valley far down below them, from the blue of the sky above, to the green grass at her horses' feet; all seemed to breathe hope and tranquility. Surely no danger could be lurking in these mountains, no crooked dealing men, no fierce beast of prey. It was too fine a day to even think such thoughts.

Ty nodded. "Yep, it's jest that. But if ya keep laggin' behind, we'll never reach Fort Laramie."

With a lilting little laugh Sally pulled her horse in front of her brother's and followed Carson, calling back over her shoulder to Ty, "Then I reckon ya'd better ride behind me or I may not come at all."

Continuing to travel in relative silence, the riders pushed on over the narrow mountain trail which wound its way northwest towards Fort Laramie. After a quick halt to rest the horses and eat a bite or two, Vin urged them on again. He seemed in a hurry and ordered them all to dismount and lead their mounts when they came to the cliff.

Sally and Ty, still in the rear, were some distance behind Carson when they saw him dismount and set off on foot, his horse and their pack horse following.

"That must be the cliff up yonder, Sis."

Sally nodded, not saying a word. How wide was the path along the precipice? Dismounting slowly, she advanced with bated breath. Then, there it was, a sheer drop of several hundred feet. The trail led right along the side of the cliff wall, turning around a sharp edge and disappearing. The sight of it was too much for Sally, stout hearted though she was. Backing way from the ledge, she grasped a pine branch nearby and held on, her knuckles turning white and her breath coming in gasps.

Also dismounting and moving forward, Ty halted beside his sister. "What's the matter? Sally, ya all right?"

"That . . . that . . ." she couldn't go on. Her eyes were full of terror.

Ty moved out to take a look. "Whew," he whistled softly between his teeth. "Looks like a right nice place ta not miss yer step." Then coming back to Sally, he said, "Well, I've been over wors'n that, so come on."

Sally shook her head. There was no way she would set foot on that tiny lip of a trail. She was starting to tremble and her face to lose its color at the very thought.

"We've got ta go on, Sally," Ty urged gently. "Here, give me yer reins an' I'll lead yer horse 'long with mine."

From a hand that visibly shook, Sally let her brother take the reins, but still she clung to her branch.

For a moment Ty looked at her. How was he to get both horses and Sally across that narrow walkway? The horses shouldn't present a problem, but Sally . . . I'll be right beside ya, now come," he coaxed. It was useless. Sally clung all the tighter to her branch. "Sally, ya can't stay here," Ty went on, laying one hand over hers on the branch. "Didn't ya tell Carson an' me back in the town that ya weren't afraid?"

"I ain't afraid, Ty," Sally whispered. "Jest scared ta death! I ain't goin' on that. I'd rather face any number a bears, mountain lions an' such than put one foot on that—that death walk."

Working gently but persistently, Ty had been unclasping her fingers from their grip on the branch. "Sally," he remarked slowly, "this ain't goin' ta be the only place yer afraid, but ya can't let that stop ya. Ya got ta face yer fears an' move on."

It was only then that Sally noticed what Ty was doing. With a cry she tried to tighten her hold once again, but Ty had her fingers in his firm grasp and was pushing her away from the sheltering arms of the tree.

Just at that moment, with sudden whinnies of alarm, both mounts began to rear and plunge in terror. Ty, unprepared, staggered and fell flat on his back.

Catching a glimpse of a face above them, Sally screamed!

CHAPTER FOURTEEN

"Ty! Look out!"

Sally tried to draw her gun, but she was shaking too much. Ty, lying on the ground, had also seen the face and just as the huge mountain lion, with a snarling scream, sprang down from its high perch above them, drew his Colt revolver and fired.

The shot was true and pierced the lion's heart. Rolling quickly to one side, Ty managed to escape the full impact of the now dead animal though the hind legs with their dangerous claws raked his shoulder and thigh. With a quick move, Ty freed himself, and still clutching his pistol with one hand and the horses' reins with the other, stood up.

"Ty—"

He cut her short. "The horses, Sally. They got ta be calmed now."

He was right. If they broke free, they could rush headlong over the cliff or disappear into the mountains never to be found again. At the very least, they would hurt themselves. Still rearing and pulling on the reins that held them, the horses, in terror at the smell of the mountain lion, struggled to get away.

"Here, Sally, take Starlight's reins!" Ty shoved his pistol back in its holster. "Whoa, Par! Easy now," Ty spoke soothingly to his own horse while separating the leather straps and thrusting those belonging to Starlight into Sally's hands. "Calm her," he ordered.

That was easier said than done. For both horses, nearly maddened by the strong scent of a hated enemy were frantically pulling away. After the first few seconds of the struggle, Ty recalled an old Indian trick. Leaning down, he rubbed one hand over the fur of the dead beast then he spread the scent over Par's nostrils. After a shake or two of his head, the horse, perhaps perplexed by the fact that all he could smell anywhere now was mountain lion, calmed down. Ty patted him gently talking all the while. "That's right, Par. Easy now, Ain't nothin' ta fear now for it's dead."

"Ty!"

Sally's cry brought Ty over to help her at once. Using the same trick he had used on his own horse, Starlight was soon under control.

In the sudden silence that reigned, Ty and Sally looked at each other. For a moment neither of them spoke. At last Ty, with a slight grin, remarked, "Well, I reckon this ain't the place ta stop an' rest. What say we take that there big cat along with us?"

"Will Par let ya?"

For answer, Ty hoisted the large cat, slung it over his horse's back and stepped away. The horse didn't move. "I reckon he'll carry it. Least ways till we catch up with the others." As he spoke he securely tied the animal. "That's that. If'n we don't get on, Carson'll be back ta fetch us. That ain't goin' ta make Vin very happy."

Slowly, with reluctant steps, Sally followed her brother; the horses followed calmly as though no danger had only moments before terrified them. At the beginning of the narrow, cliff hugging trail, Sally paused. There was no way to go back, for the horses were behind her, and yet, how could she walk along that ledge?

Ty, seeing her hesitate, took her hand and drew it through his arm. "Put yer right hand on the wall there an' let's go."

"Ty, I can't, I'm goin' ta be sick. I feel dizzy, an' . . ." her words trailed off as she closed her eyes and leaned against the cliffside.

"Jest look at yer feet, an' keep yer eyes half closed," advised Ty pulling her forward a few steps.

She tried it, but it was only with great effort that she could continue at all.

Ty tried to distract her thoughts from the dangerous path they were treading footstep by footstep. "Ya think that mountain lion's the same one Vin's been after all these years? Sure would be a right nice present ta give him, if'n it were."

When no answer came, Ty fell silent.

It seemed like years to poor Sally, who was fighting to keep from showing the terror she felt. Every time she tried to open her eyes and see how much farther they had to go, a sudden wave of dizziness swept over her, leaving her strangely lightheaded. Her grip on Ty's arm was tense and she moved mechanically forward. How wonderful it was to hear Ty say quietly that they were almost to the end. Then they were off the cliff and onto a trail carpeted with pine needles. Sally drew a deep breath and sank limply down beside the path.

Opening his mouth to say something, Ty stopped with the words on the tip of his tongue. On the trail up ahead, he had caught a glimpse of Carson standing with head cocked as though listening to something and a hand up for quiet. Bending low over his sister, he quietly placed the reins in her hands and nodded in Carson's direction, breathing, "Wait here till I see what's up."

"There seems ta've been an ambush an' all are held up by outlaws," was Carson's low reply to Ty's questioning look. "It seems ta me ta be a set up."

"Vin?"

"Yep."

"How many?"

"Maybe half a dozen."

"Doesn't he know we ain't there?"

"Reckon not."

The wind was blowing the sounds towards them and both strained their ears to hear what was being said. After hearing a few sentences, Ty was slowly reaching for his pistol when a hand was laid on his arm. He turned. Sally, drawing her father's gun from its holster, handed it without a word to her brother. Then, taking the reins of Carson's mount and the pack horse, she nodded, again without a word, towards the sounds of conflict.

Ty noticed that her cheeks had color once more and her eyes again flashed sparks like some one stirred with passion. Here was a danger she could face without flinching.

Carson, taking his rifle from the scabbard, cocked it and whispered, "Let's go."

Ty nodded grimly. Leaving his own gun holstered as back up, he advanced down the trail beside Carson with his father's six-shooter gripped firmly in his right hand.

Pausing before a turn in the trail, both men listened. Rough voices could be heard. After a cautious look through the screen of bushes and pine trees, Ty nodded to Carson and, throwing all caution to the wind, they dashed out into the open.

The sharp crack of Ty's six-shooter as he shot the gun out of one of the outlaws' hands was the first anyone knew of their presence. Consternation was written all over Vin's face as he realized too late that not all of his party had been present. As for the other travelers, no sooner had they caught sight of their comrades than every gun was drawn before the surprised bandits could collect their startled senses enough for flight or resistance.

It was all over in a matter of minutes. When one of the men began tying Vin's hands, he protested.

"Ya can't tie me up. I've got ta lead ya over the rest a the trail."

"We've come as far as we care to on your trail," the man replied grimly. "Vin, you're under arrest."

"I tell ya, ya can't arrest me. Ya ain't the law."

At that, the man pulled off his vest revealing a deputy sheriff's badge. Vin stared wide-eyed and open mouthed. "The sheriff deputized me before we even came to you. An' now, I think he'll be rather pleased with what we have to bring to him."

"But . . . but, that mountain lion. I ain't seen him yet, an' he'll kill ya all!"

Ty, who had been assisting with the tying up of the outlaws, grinned. "How would ya be knowin' one mountain lion from another, Vin? This one got any special mark?"

Nodding, Vin replied, "It's left ear is torn and missing a piece where my bullet went clean through one time."

Beckoning to Sally who had approached with the horses, Ty chuckled. "Hmm, perhaps ya'd like ta identify this here large cat I jest kilt on the other side a the cliff. I were kind a short on time an' didn't get much of a chance ta look 'im over."

Untying the cat, Ty hauled it off his mount and dropped it down before the astonished gaze of the entire party. It was an uncommonly large mountain lion, evidently a grandfather one with huge paws and, sure enough, his left ear was torn and part of it was missing.

Several of the men, leaving their prisoners under the watch of the others, began to examine it more closely, asking how Ty had come to shoot it with such accuracy as to kill it with one shot. Therefore, Ty, to the great pleasure of the rest, related the tale and his shot from the ground.

Suddenly Carson, who had listened with great interest, broke in. "Ty, we'd best get them scratches on ya washed real good."

"Scratches?" The very word brought two of the other men to their feet in a hurry. "Come on, Ty," one of the men ordered. "Wild cat scratches aren't things you want to mess around with."

The other adding, as Carson pulled his younger companion to his feet, "Got a younger brother who got scratched by a bobcat. He was mighty sick for a long time, I'm tellin' you."

Ty merely laughed. Grinning at Sally, who had looked startled when she realized Ty had been hurt, he pulled her gun out, which he had tucked in his belt, and handed it over. "I reckon ya can put it back. An' don't ya worry none 'bout me. I'll go 'long with 'em seein' as I ain't got much choice." The last was called over his shoulder as he was hurried away.

After slipping her gun back into its holster at her side, Sally noticed many of the men staring at her. Coloring slightly, she turned to her horse, realizing that probably no one knew until now that she even had a gun.

"Can you hit anything with that?"

Sally turned around. The question was asked respectfully, yet with a note of skepticism too. The speaker was the quietest and possibly the youngest one of the men who had gone to talk with the sheriff back in town. Sally nodded.

Glances were exchanged between several of the men. Sally didn't volunteer to show her skill, thus unknowingly casting doubt on her ability as a markswoman. However, nothing further was said until Ty returned with Carson and the two others. His shoulder was bandaged and he walked with a slight limp. The washing of his scratches hadn't been the gentlest, and he now felt the pain, which he hadn't noticed before.

"Ty," the young man questioned, "Can your sister really shoot with that six-shooter?"

Ty snorted. "Can she? She can match me at a draw most any day an' can hit any target I can. Ya want ta see?"

"Ty!" Sally protested softly, turning scarlet.

A murmur of assent rippled through the men, prisoners and guards alike.

"Jest pick a target ya can hit an' let her try." Ty was proud of his sister's shooting and wanted to enjoy seeing the faces of those who doubted it when she proved her ability.

Accordingly, the young man pointed to a tree a good distance away that had a knot about half way up.

Sally was given the opportunity to go first, but she shook her head. He had challenged her, so he shot first. Carson and Ty nodded. They had no doubts that Sally could hit it.

The young man was a good shot and hit the outer rim of the knot. Then Sally stepped up. For a moment she remained motionless, gun in its holster, arms down at her side, studying the target.

All at once the gun was drawn, followed almost instantly by its sharp report and then the gun was back in its place, and Sally moved away to her brother's side. For a moment a stunned silence lay over everyone, for Sally had not only hit the knot, but had beat her opponent!

The vanquished youth grinned self-consciously as cheers for his opponent filled the air. When they had somewhat died down, he approached Sally and said, "I beg your pardon, Miss, for doubting. You are a better shot than I am an' I don't mind saying so."

Sally smiled and shook the offered hand.

"Well, let's start back an' hand these men over to the sheriff, now that our little party is over." It was the deputized man who was now the unspoken leader of the group.

During the activity of gathering horses, arranging prisoners and such, Sally grasped Ty's arm and whispered, "I ain't goin' back over that cliff, Ty. I jest can't."

"Now don't go gettin' excited. 'Course we ain't goin' back. We're headin' ta Fort Laramie an' ta Fort Laramie we're goin' ta go. Carson," Ty called to his friend.

When Carson made his way over, he remarked, "I reckon we can make the rest a the trail ourselves, Ty, 'stead a goin' back."

"That's what I was aim'n ta do."

Thus it was that when the posse with their prisoners headed back over the trail they had come, Carson, Ty and Sally waved good-bye and were soon left alone on the mountainside.

Ty, unwilling to leave his mountain lion for the beasts of prey, soon had it skinned, and the three companions set off once more for Fort Laramie.

The trail, though narrow in places and but roughly marked, was relatively easy for such woodsmen as Bob Carson and Ty Elliot to follow, and they made good time. There were no more cliffside walkways to traverse, only rocky paths and icy streams to ford. These didn't require such stout nerves, and Sally made no complaint.

On the following day they spied the fort ahead with the flag of the United States floating over it in the breeze. The very sight quickened the blood in their veins and, urging their horses on to a brisk canter, they headed forward, hearts beating with eagerness for they knew not what. Surely their travels would be rewarded somehow. None dared hope for complete success to their quest at once, for this was the first lead they had followed, yet all felt certain that in some way there would be something to guide them on, to lead them forward, closer to their goal, closer to the long lost sister whom Ty and Sally had never met.

Riding into the fort, their first stop was at the hotel, for though this was a fort, it was also a stopping place on the wagon trail to Oregon and California. After caring for their animals and eating a hearty meal, Carson, Ty and Sally walked about.

For the next few days, the three travelers wandered the fort, asking "about a family named Westlake or Weston, anyway, it began with West." Nearly always the answer was no. Now and then they came across someone who had known a family by some such name, but never did it seem to be the right ones. Each day brought fresh disappointment, and before the week was out, Ty had become so discouraged that he nearly missed out on an important clue.

Carson had gone out early in the day and hadn't yet returned. Not seeming to care any more, Ty remained behind at the hotel with Sally. They were planning on leaving the following morning, yet Sally felt restless.

"Do come out once more, Ty," Sally begged.

Ty stubbornly shook his head. "It ain't any use, Sally."

"Ya could at least come down an' eat," she begged.

"I ain't hungry."

Sally's jaw tightened and she planted her hands on her hips. "Well, even if'n ya ain't hungry, I am."

With a reluctant sigh, Ty got up and followed his sister down to the dining room of the hotel. Once there, Sally continued trying to persuade Ty to search a little longer, but he shook his head.

"I said it ain't any use. It's been 'bout twelve years since anyone heard a 'em, an' it ain't likely we'll find anyone here that knows 'em now."

"But there might be one person we haven't talked to yet," she urged.

"Sally," Ty sighed in exasperation, "we've been checkin' an' there ain't no one left ta ask."

Before Sally could think of another argument, the woman wiping off the nearby table turned suddenly towards them. "You know who you ought to check with—Captain Roland. He's been here, oh I'd say fifteen years, and he doesn't forget a name or a face. He seems to know every person who comes through this fort. Go talk to him if you want to find out about that family."

Ty was on his feet in an instant, suddenly alert. "Where is this Captain Roland?"

The woman pointed out the officer's quarters, and Ty and Sally left in great excitement. Meeting Carson just returning after another fruitless search, they eagerly imparted the news, and with quickening pulse, he joined them.

Captain Roland welcomed them cordially and when all were seated, Ty asked the question.

Frowning thoughtfully, the captain stared at the opposite wall in thought. "No," he began slowly, "no one was here named Westlake. Twelve years ago or so you say? Hmm, there was one family, Westline, no, Westlin—"

"That's it!" Carson nearly shouted. "Westlin! I remember it now. Were they here, did ya say?"

Captain Roland hesitated before replying, "There was a family by that name who came through here, I'd say about eleven years ago." He paused, thinking, remembering. "Let me see now . . . yep, they had four or maybe five little girls. I remember they all looked alike, except one."

CHAPTER FIFTEEN

The friends fairly held their breath. Would this be the right family? Was Sunshine with them? The pause the captain took as he recalled the family seemed to drag on for hours to that eager trio, when it was really only a few seconds.

"Yep, one little girl was different. The others were dark haired and rather large. Oh, not in an unpleasant sense, but they seemed like it next to the other one. She was small and had golden hair. Seemed almost like spun gold when the sun shone on it. She was a lovely little thing. Seemed a might peculiar seeing as how both the parents were dark haired."

"What was her name?" The question from Ty startled the captain it was so hoarse.

Knitting his brows together, Captain Roland frowned and getting to his feet, he paced the room striving to recall the name that had been there only moments before. At last he shook his head. "It's gone. I'm sure it'll come to me, but I can't think of it right now. I'm sorry."

Long sighs of disappointment came from each one present. Ty slumped in his seat. Would he ever know her name? Carson dropped his head and neither one noticed Sally. As she sighed, she instinctively reached for her locket with its precious picture. Inspired with a sudden thought, she drew it from its hiding place and holding it out to

Captain Roland, who appeared nearly as disappointed as his visitors felt, asked, "Did the little girl look anything like—her?"

Turning the picture to the light, the captain studied the sweet face. "Yep, I'd say that sprite of a child is looking just like her right about now."

"You're sure? There's no mistake? You wouldn't be mixin' that picture up with some other girl, now would ya?" Carson had sprung to his feet, his words quick, almost frantic.

"No, there's no doubt in my mind. This must be her mother. You all related too?"

Thus assured, Carson sank back down in a daze murmuring, "Sunshine . . . my little sunshine . . . here," while Ty, with heart full of gratefulness, whispered, "Thank God! News at last!"

Both men were so overcome with emotion that it was Sally who told the story to the kind captain. He listened sympathetically.

After all was told, he handed back the locket and said, "I'll help you all I can, but it has been eleven years and much can happen in that time. Now let's see. I know they were going farther west, but how far I'm not certain. They could have gone all the way to California or even Oregon. I reckon if I were you, I'd take the old trail towards Oregon and check at some of the forts along the way. The trails aren't used much now days, but they'd sure make easy riding if you have good mounts."

Carson and Ty assured him that they were well mounted.

"Well, I wish you all the very best of success. It might be a long, hard and even dangerous journey, but . . ." and Captain Roland paused to look steadily at each one of his visitors. "I have a feeling you will find your sister. And after you do, Ty, the army could use such an experienced and determined man in the scouts."

Ty smiled. "I'm afraid the army'll have ta do without me. I jest ain't the type."

Captain Roland laughed, "Well, it's the army's loss. Good luck to you all."

"Thank you, sir."

Carson, Sally and Ty were already out of the room and several steps away when suddenly the captain jerked open the door behind them and called out, "Eleanor!"

"What's that?" Carson asked.

"Her name. I just now remembered it!"

"Eleanor," gasped Carson, "how did she get given her mother's name?"

No one could answer that.

The sun was coming up in a blaze of glory promising a beautiful day for travel as Ty, Sally and Carson set off from Fort Laramie. They now had five horses with them, having acquired another pack horse with the sale of Ty's mountain lion skin, so as to carry more supplies and to ease the burdens of the other animals. All the party, the riders as well as their mounts, were in fine spirits. Though it was still somewhat chilly, the rising sun would soon warm things up.

Captain Roland had been right; the well-worn trail was easy to follow, and they made good time. "Much faster'n the folks makin' the trail in wagons," Ty said as they cantered along.

And so, day followed day, easy riding, and mile after mile covered. It soon became rather monotonous and they began to long for a challenging hill to climb, a rushing stream to ford or even a wild animal to shoot.

At last they reached South Pass where they halted for a few days. By dint of diligent questioning, they discovered two people who thought they remembered a family named Westlin, and after considerable more thought, they reached the conclusion that they had left the trail and headed south. Where they were going, neither informant knew.

This information was received with a mixture of thankfulness and regret. Regret that no one seemed quite sure of anything and thankfulness that they could leave the well-worn trail they had been on. Neither Carson nor Ty enjoyed such well-worn trails. They both preferred the open, unmarked countryside where one must cut his own trail, where one could ride or wander to his heart's content, where only the print of wild beast or his own horse were to be found. This turning south meant all that to the two men for, aside from a few settlers here and there, a few little towns scattered far and wide, the country to the south was still the untamed plains, mountains and even deserts Ty and Carson loved so dearly. They would go south.

They were thankful also that even if it was slight, they still found news of Eleanor, which meant they hadn't lost the trail.

Sally would have followed her brother and friend into Canada or back east to the big, crowded cities and towns which her mother had known, if they had chosen to so lead her. As it was, the thought of vast expanses, with no human being close by except her companions, held an intriguing thrill as well as dread of the unknown to this girl who had known loneliness and few friends all her life; however, she longed even more to reach the end of this journey and find the sister she never knew she had, to settle once again in a cabin, to sleep with a roof over her head every night, to sweep the floor, eat at a table every day; above all, she wanted a home where Ty felt safe from unwanted visitors. Perhaps this trip would lead them to a new place of safety where they could live in peace. Only, how could she leave their father's grave, away, oh so far away, in the mountains? Would she ever get to return there? Never would she abandon her brother on his search. Unknowingly, her eyes had brimmed with tears over these thoughts and now began to trickle down her cheeks.

"Sally? What's wrong?"

Glancing up at her brother, she felt a tear drop on her hand. "I reckon I were jest thinkin'."

"Home?"

Sally nodded. "I'm jest gettin' tired, Ty. Ain't nothin' happened since we left South Pass last week."

Ty grinned. "Ya jest wantin' ta use that six-gun a Pa's," he teased.

This brought forth a merry retort and Sally's tears were forgotten in lighthearted banter.

South the trio rode day after day. The challenge of cutting their own trails once they left the great basin added some excitement to their travels, which soon turned into weeks. No more news of the Westlin family or of the missing sister.

"We could a passed their cabin days ago an' never know it," Carson sighed one evening as camp was being made.

"Don't think I weren't jest thinkin' that same thing," agreed Ty, carefully adding small sticks to the bit of flame he had just started. No one spoke again until the fire was a bright blaze and Sally was making coffee and preparing their evening meal.

"Carson, I don't know 'bout you, but jest travelin' like this with nothin' but 'south' ta follow, is 'bout ta get ta me. It ain't as though we knew where we were goin'."

"I feel the same way, Ty. Somethin's got ta happen or—" the sentence was left unfinished. Each knew in his heart that they would continue the search until they found either Eleanor or her grave, no matter how difficult it was. Right now all three felt discouraged and low spirited. The constant travel with no fixed destination had begun to wear them down. Perhaps not physically but emotionally all were on edge. Though none would admit it, the sudden and exciting news received at Fort Laramie had kindled a bright flame of hope in each heart; hope for more clues and yes, secretly, hope for a rapid conclusion to their search. Now, however, that hope was dying, bit by bit with each week, each day, and at times, each mile that passed by empty.

One by one the stars came out over the campsite of the weary travelers and the moon cast a pale light, which sifted through the leaves of the trees. The evening chirps of the birds ceased, and all was hushed. The fire died to a glow and no one made a move to replenish it. In silence they sat, motionless, each one lost in his own thoughts while now and then a whisper of air faintly stirred the leaves overhead and the grasses beside them. The air was still warm, for summer was upon them at last. Into the stillness of the night came the far off cry of some nocturnal animal. At last, Sally, who had been falling asleep where she sat, wrapped her blanket around her and, lying down near the fire, drifted into sleep, too tired to think anymore. Carson soon followed her example. Ty, however, remained where he was, his body tired, but his mind giving him no rest.

Was this trip a waste of time? Right then it felt so. It was an impossible task his father had given him. Why not forget it all? Ty knew why. He never could forget this unknown sister. This quest, which had been given to his trust, would find an end. He had given his word to his dying father and he would fulfill it if it took the rest of his life. Once given, Ty never went back on his word. His father never had and he never would. All the same, he wondered what this would cost him. "I'll do anything to find her," he promised himself as he, too, at last, stretched out near the fire.

Had he known what lay in store just ahead, he might not have slept so well. It is better that he didn't know, and he rose the next morning with renewed determination and hope.

It was early in the afternoon when Ty, who was in the lead, reached a wooded area. A quick glance showed a slight trail through the trees and Ty urged Par on. This way and that the trail wound among the woods. Ty kept his eyes and ears alert for signs of man or beast, but none were found.

At last he reached the open ground once more and as Par shook his head, making his bridle jingle, Ty let him have his head. With a snort, Par dashed forward tossing his head.

Suddenly, Ty felt his horse stumble; a rifle cracked, and a searing pain shot through his left shoulder nearly knocking him from the saddle!

CHAPTER SIXTEEN

The sound of the shot startled Carson and Sally, and they looked up in time to see Ty nearly falling from the saddle. Sally screamed. Dashing forward through the remaining trees on Starlight, she reached her brother's side and grasped his arm, crying out as she did so, "Ty! What happened? Who was it? You're hurt! Oh, Ty!"

Carson, having ridden nearly as quickly as Sally, had come up on the other side and, grasping Par's reins, instructed, "Keep him steady, Sally. Ty, don't try ta get off now. We've got ta get away from this clearin' an' out in the open where we can see the shooters 'fore they shoot us." As he spoke, Carson had wrapped the reins around his saddle horn and, keeping one hand on Ty to help steady him, nudged his horse into a faster gait.

Ty, his face grey and dotted with drops of sweat, fought to keep in the saddle. Every move of the horse beneath him was agony, and if it hadn't been for the firm hands on either side of him, he surely would have fallen. The left shoulder of his shirt was crimson with blood, which was rapidly staining more every second.

Carson knew the flow of life-giving blood needed staunched quickly, but he also knew that stopping while still in range from a hidden gunman in the trees could be fatal to all of them. Consequently, it was several minutes before he halted the horses, sprang off and caught the now nearly fainting Ty and laid him on the grass. Ripping open his shirt he found the wound. The bullet was lodged deeply and would take quite some probing to get out. Knowing that the best place for Ty now was a house, not out in the open, Carson thought quickly as he tried to staunch the blood of his friend.

"Sally, we need somethin' ta help stop the bleedin' an' bind this here wound up."

Sally had already slipped off one of her petticoats and was busy tearing it into strips, remarking in a half hysterical attempt at cheerfulness, for Ty's pallor and the sight of the wound frightened her more than she would admit, "I always knew a petticoat would come in handy for somethin' besides gettin' in my way."

At that, Ty opened his eyes and tried to smile reassuringly at her, but at that same instant Carson pressed the wad of petticoat against his shoulder causing the smile to turn into a groan, which he couldn't suppress.

"Oh Ty!" Sally cried. "What are we going to do?" She looked at Carson with tear-filled eyes.

"Here, Sally," he directed, "keep pressure on this till I come back."

"Carson," moaned Ty, struggling to make his voice audible, "don't try ta find 'em."

"Ain't goin' ta." was the short answer as he strode away leaving the brother and sister alone.

For several minutes Sally knelt in silence, one hand stopping the flow of crimson and the other gently wiping the sweat from Ty's brow. All was quiet. The five horses with reins dropped stood calmly nearby eating a mouthful of grass now and then, looking with seeming curiosity at Sally and the motionless Ty. There was no sound from the woods they had so rapidly left. Ty lay still on the grass, the only movement from him was the rise and fall of his chest with each breath he took. Even this was somewhat painful, and Ty lay with clenched hands and tightly compressed lips.

How long this silence and inaction lasted neither Ty nor Sally ever could tell. It might have been hours or days even before Carson came back. "I can make out some smoke jest a couple miles away. Where there's smoke, there's most likely a fire, an' a fire this time a day speaks of a house. Can ya ride a bit, Ty?"

In answer Ty opened his eyes and tried to sit up. Carson, using the rest of Sally's petticoat, bound up the shoulder as best he could. Then together with Sally, he helped Ty to his feet, and after a bit of difficulty, into the saddle. There Carson steadied him until Sally was mounted and could hold on to Ty.

And so, with Carson and Sally on either side of their wounded companion, the trio set off slowly towards the wisp of smoke Carson had observed in the distance. It was the longest trip any of them had ever taken before. Each step of the horses sent jarring pain through Ty's wounded shoulder. The bleeding, never fully stopped, continued to slowly seep through the rough bandages.

It was with great anxiety that Sally watched her brother. She fought back the tears, which filled her eyes, and breathed a prayer as they rode. Carson, too, was alarmed at this sudden turn of events in their journey. Eagerly he watched the smoke that seemed never to be any closer. Would they ever reach that fire? Would it not be better to leave Ty and Sally and ride there himself? But what if something happened while he was gone? They had to stay together.

At last, as evening was rapidly approaching, he observed a trail heading towards the smoke. Here it was easier going, for no longer did they have to travel up and down hills. Then, just when it seemed as though they would never reach it, the lights of a small, but in their eyes, wonderful house shone in the gathering darkness.

"Hello!" called out Carson.

The door flew open and someone stepped out calling, "Who is it and what's wanted?"

"We've got a wounded man here an' need help."

Instantly several more persons stepped out as the tired trio rode into the yard. The horses' bridles were grasped and Ty was lifted off his horse. Sally, too, was helped down, and in a daze, she followed the two fellows as they carried their living burden between them into the light of the house.

Sally didn't notice anything as she followed them into a room where Ty, now unconscious, was laid tenderly on a bed. One of the young men bent over him listening to his breathing and then began removing the bandages with skillful fingers. Sally didn't notice the other fellow place a chair next to the bed until she was pushed gently into it, someone saying softly to her, "Just sit here by him; Ma'll bring you some coffee."

"I need some hot water, Joe," the fellow examining Ty ordered quietly.

"It's coming. Ma's got the kettle on," replied the other.

In a daze Sally watched the young man as he worked over her brother, washing the wound and then skillfully, expertly, extracting the bullet from the shoulder. Someone put a cup of hot coffee in her cold, shaking hands, but she didn't realize it. She just sat, shivering, her eyes never leaving Ty's face, pleading silently that his life be spared, oblivious to anything or anyone else around her.

Meanwhile, Carson, after seeing his young companions in the hospitable house, led his own horse, along with their two pack horses, to the barn where two men had taken Par and Starlight. While the three men unsaddled, brushed and bedded down the five tired horses, Carson introduced himself.

"I'm Bob Carson an' my two friends are Ty Elliot an' his sister Sally. We've been traveling since spring's come an' ain't sure jest when our travels'll be over."

One of the men, evidently the father, shook hands with Carson. "I'm glad to meet you, Carson, I'm Jim Fields. This is my youngest son, Jed. Our home is always open to those in need whether they be friends or strangers."

The young man, Jed, after closing the stall door behind him, held out his hand. He was a tall, well built youth with the broad shoulders that come from hard work. His hand, as it gripped that of Carson, was rough, yet his face was pleasant. "Glad to meet you. What happened to your companion?"

As they all walked back to the house, Carson told of the shot from the trees. "If'n Ty weren't hurt so bad, I'd a gone ta see who did it."

"We could ride out there tomorrow and check it out, don't you think, Pa?"

Jim Fields nodded. "I'll go with you and we'll take a couple of the hands. That ought to be enough to deal with whoever is out there. And don't worry about your friend," he added turning to Carson, "Jack just got back from medical training back east. The good Lord led you to just the right place."

"Yep," Jed put in, his hand on the door latch "There isn't another doctor for over a hundred miles. Jack sure comes in handy in this wilderness."

Sally didn't notice Carson come softly into the room nor feel his hand on her shoulder, nor did she hear his low voice urging her to come eat. All she saw was Ty and all she heard was the slow, uneasy breathing of her brother and the moans that now and then came from his grey lips. The coffee turned cold in her hand and was replaced with more, yet she neither moved nor responded to anyone. So absorbed was she in her brother that she didn't know she was being talked about by the group in the doorway.

"I ain't never seen her like this 'fore," Carson shook his head. "Even when her pa were dyin' she knew what was goin' on 'round her. Now she jest sits an' looks at him."

Jack nodded. "Sometimes that happens when someone receives a shock like this must have been. And it doesn't help any that she was probably already tired and worn out by the long travels."

"Think Ma can do anything, Jack?"

The young man turned and, glancing first at his brother and then across the room to his mother, shrugged. "It's worth a try. She isn't going to do him any good if she takes sick as well." The others knew he was referring to Sally and not his mother.

A few moments later, Mrs. Fields took one of Sally's hands in her own kind, worn ones and began talking softly. At first there was no response from the girl sitting so motionless in the chair, then, as the voice continued, something in the tone seemed to reach her brain, for slowly her eyes moved from Ty's still form to the kind motherly face before her. It took several more minutes for her tired, exhausted mind to understand what was being said.

"Come, Dear, you need to eat if you are going to keep up your strength for him. The others will stay with him. Come on. You are worn out and need rest and food, then you can watch again. You really must eat."

Sally looked back at Ty and slowly nodded, too weary to argue. She was helped to her feet and gently led out of the room while Jack moved to take his place beside the bed of the wounded man.

Anxiously Carson watched Sally listlessly begin to eat. If anything happened to Ty, what would she do? Would the search be even possible to continue without him? He began to think the trip was too much for her. They should never have let her come along.

No one in the room seemed inclined to speak for several long minutes. At last, Jim picked up a book off the mantle, remarking quietly as he did so, "Let's have a bit of reading from the Good Book. The Lord will give much comfort and help through His Word." Without waiting for a response, if one had been expected, the book was opened, and in a voice that seemed to feel the truth of the words, he read: "In the Lord put I my trust: how say ye to my soul, Flee as a bird to your mountain?"

CHAPTER SEVENTEEN

"For, lo, the wicked bend their bow, they make ready their arrow upon the string, that they may privily shoot at the upright in heart . . . The Lord is in his holy temple, the Lord's throne is in heaven: his eyes behold, his eyelids try, the children of men . . ." Then the good man bowed his head and prayed.

Carson, never having been much of a praying man himself, having gotten out of the habit when off trapping on his own, now listened with great respect. This man knew who he was talking to and seemed to expect an answer. He swallowed hard, suddenly recalling his Aunt Kate as she used to pray with Sunshine in their old cabin. From there his mind drifted back a few more years, and again he seemed to hear his friend Jake as he prayed one day with his beloved Ellen by his side. Another voice came to echo in his mind, a voice from long past, a voice from his childhood. Even the tones were distinctly heard, and the weight of his own father's hand on his shoulder seemed to be felt once again. His father was speaking to him, repeating words from the Bible. It was all so clear, so real. "'The steps of a good man are ordered by the Lord, and He delighteth in his way.' Remember, Bobby, the only good men are those who place their trust and life in the hands of the Lord Jesus Christ and let Him direct their paths. Wherever you may go, never forget that you have given yourself to Him."

Carson's head dropped into his hands and he sat bowed with the remembrances, which that one heartfelt prayer had roused. "God help me, I did forget," his heart cried out. He knew it was no use to pretend differently, for the gentle drawing of the Shepherd was strong in this wandering sheep. Never had Carson intended to forget the only One who had been his comfort when his mother and father were taken from him. Nor the One who, when Aunt Kate and Sunshine were taken from him, had guided him still. Somehow, however, he had forgotten. Not completely, for the knowledge of that Someone had kept him safe in many a temptation, yet he let days go by without a thought for the One he had sworn allegiance to. It was all too much. Rising abruptly, he left the house. He had to settle this thing alone with only himself and his God.

In the house, Sally continued to sit in the daze she had been in since their arrival. Only when Mrs. Fields talked to her, did she seem to rouse.

"Come, Sally," that good woman ordered gently, laying a hand on Sally's arm. "You must get some rest now. There is a bed in the room right next to your brother's. Things will look better in the morning." And so, with Joe's assistance, Sally was helped to her feet and led from the room.

How long she slept was uncertain. All was still and quiet when she opened her eyes. Again she seemed to see Ty slumping in the saddle, saw the blood staining his shirt and the petticoat beneath her hands, saw the well loved face so white and still. With trembling limbs, she rose. Was Ty still alive? Had he died while she slept? She should never have left him!

"Ty," she moaned, "I can't lose ya too!"

Choking back the sobs that nearly strangled her, Sally crept from her room into the large and equally dark one beyond. Pausing a moment to listen at the door where her brother lay, she placed one hand over her wildly beating heart trying to quiet it. She felt her locket. Clutching it tightly, she drew a long, deep breath. Not a sound could she hear. All about her was quietness. Slowly she pushed open the door and stepped into the dimly lit room.

As the door opened, Joe, who had been keeping watch for the last hour, turned. The sight of Sally standing in the doorway with her long, dark hair hanging loosely about her pale, anxious face and over her shoulders, one hand clenched over her heart and her eyes filled with unshed tears, was a sight the young man never forgot. Silently he stood, but before he could take a step towards her, Sally had staggered across the room and dropped on her knees beside the bed. One hand was laid on the motionless hand of Ty while her face was buried in the bedclothes. The silent shaking of her shoulders gave the only indication of the anguish within her.

Tenderhearted and full of sympathy, Joe watched the girl without stirring, until a muffled sob reached his ears. Then he quietly moved to her side and, kneeling beside her, placed one hand on her arm, whispering, "It will be all right. Jack isn't giving up and everyone is praying."

The only answer was a fresh burst of tears.

Compassionately, Joe stayed by Sally, alternately watching Ty's face and whispering comforting words to the distressed girl beside him. The gentle, calm voice gradually soothed Sally and her sobs grew less intense. After a little while, the hand, which had clutched her locket, loosened and stole over to timidly touch the hand still on her arm.

"Do you want to come sit and wait until Jack comes?" were the softly whispered words Sally heard as she drew a long, shuddering breath and grew still. When she nodded faintly, she felt herself being lifted up and half carried to the chair. Swallowing hard and blinking away the tears, Sally looked at the face of her brother as it lay still upon the pillow in the dim room, watched, and waited, and prayed.

Stationing himself nearly behind her chair, Joe stood also watching, waiting and praying as the minutes slowly ticked by.

When Jack entered the room some time later, moving on soft feet to the bedside of his patient, Sally fairly held her breath. Ty hadn't stirred at all since she had come, was he—? She blinked her eyes rapidly and then, as the tears refused to leave, drew her sleeve quickly across her face clearing her vision for a few minutes at least.

Jack straightened up. "No change," he whispered to the watchers. "I'll take a turn now, Joe." He nodded to his brother. "And Miss Sally," he continued, "go back to bed and get some sleep. You'll need your strength for tomorrow if you are going to do any watching then." Jack added the last when he saw her beginning to shake her head at the mention of leaving.

"Come on," Joe put in a little coaxing. "Jack will wake you if there is the slightest change. If you don't sleep now, how are you going to keep up?"

Feeling torn by conflicting emotions, Sally looked first at one face and then another, lingering finally on Ty's pale one on the pillow. "If there is any change, please promise—" she pleaded, her dark eyes on Jack's face above her.

"I promise."

With a little sigh, Sally allowed Joe to help her to her feet and guide her to her own door where he left her with a gentle pressure of the hand.

Meanwhile Carson was having his own struggle out under the stars. Wrestling with his thoughts and his fully awakened conscience, he tramped for hours over the fields in the silence and quietude of that moonlit night. At last fully exhausted, he flung himself on his knees behind the barn and prayed as he had not done for nearly a dozen years. Pouring his whole soul out before his Lord, Carson wept and pleaded for forgiveness, for strength to continue on, for life for Ty, and, with tears coursing down his rough cheeks, he pleaded to find his Sunshine once more before he died. As he knelt thus, unmindful of the time, a gentle feeling of peace began to steal over him until at last he sank down and lay quiet and still in the grass. The stars above looked like tiny candle flames flickering faintly in a far off window. The moon cast its silvery shimmer across nature. Carson gazed about with a new wonder until he felt his eyelids begin to close. With great effort, he roused himself.

Back at the house, he made his way in and, finding a blanket left on a chair for him, he rolled himself up and slept a deep, dreamless sleep.

The sun was shining brightly in the eastern sky and all living things were still basking in its warm ray. Across the plains half a dozen horsemen could be seen cantering along. Jim Fields, his son Jed and three of their cowhands were following Bob Carson back over the trail from yesterday. As they neared the bottom of the hill where Carson had spied the smoke from the Fields' chimney, he halted; dismounting and dropping the reins, he cautiously made his way up the hill, rifle in readiness for anything. For several minutes after he reached the summit, he remained nearly motionless scarcely turning his head as his quick, sharp eyes examined the woods stretching out before him. There was no sign of danger. No voices were heard, no movement observed. Slowly he stood to his full height. Nothing changed. All remained as it had been.

Beckoning the others, Carson waited until they rode up and Jed handed over his mount's reins. "I reckon if we were ta split up, we could circle 'round in both directions. It'd keep us all from walkin' inta an ambush too."

Heads nodded as all eyes took in the lay of the land.

Gesturing with his hand, Carson continued, "Right down yonder, 'bout where them pines are gowin' is where I reckon the shot come from. I aim ta look there first."

"I'll go with you," Jed volunteered immediately.

"Just where was Ty when he got shot?" queried Mr. Fields.

"See how them trees makes a U shape 'round that bit a grasslands?" When heads nodded he added, "Well, I reckon he might a been 'bout in the middle a that there U. Sally an' I were still in the trees behind him. Now I reckon we ought ta get movin'. Ya ready, Jed?"

"Ready."

Carson and Jed rode off towards the left, circling to get back in behind the trees somewhat before making their way through them. Jim Fields, with one of his men, headed his horse for the U in the middle while the other two cowhands moved to the right. No one spoke. Each was listening and watching, alert for any possible danger. All guns were held ready.

Suddenly Jed pointed ahead into the trees. There seemed to be something there. Swiftly Carson dismounted, handing the reins this time to Jed instead of dropping them as he usually did.

"Wait here," he whispered, moving forward with catlike tread. Soon he beckoned and Jed rode forward and dismounted at the edge of the trees. Leading the horses, the two advanced into the woods. All was still. Jed watched in amazement as Carson, with no noise and scarcely seeming to move any branches or grass, slipped along before him.

Before long they came to a small clearing with the charred remains of a fire to one side and on the other a small path. Dropping down to examine the ground, Carson touched the ashes. They were cold. But on probing a little deeper he discovered warmth still existed. "Fire ain't out all the way. I reckon they left in a hurry."

"They?"

Carson nodded. "I see two, maybe three sets a tracks 'round here." He frowned in silent thought.

Jed, who had also been looking around gave a low exclamation, "Would you look at this! I think it explains everything."

CHAPTER EIGHTEEN

Carson looked up. "What'd ya find?"

"A branding iron."

Carson raised his eyebrows.

"You don't brand cattle in the woods unless you are trying to hide it," Jed said. "The way I figure it is a few cattle rustlers were using this as a re-branding place. They could easily get a few cattle from a herd about anywhere, bring them here and brand over the brand already on them. They were here yesterday when Ty rode out of the trees. Of course, being thieves with guilty consciences, they either thought he knew about them or was about to find them. So, one of them shot Ty and then they all left in a hurry, not bothering to make sure he was alone or dead, or to hide their evidence."

The experienced trapper listened to this explanation in silence, now and then nodding slightly. "I reckon ya might be on ta somethin'. Let's see if'n we can't find where the shooter was waitin'. An' then I reckon we ought ta check out that there path."

Jed nodded, yet wondered how Carson could find where the one had been standing when he shot Ty. He didn't have to wait long, for already Carson was examining the ground in some nearby brush.

"Right here," he remarked, pointing. "Ya can see his footprints. Jest the same as one near the fire. I reckon they heard the horse comin' 'fore they saw him. An' look there, that leaf was clean shot in two. A shot from here'd hit right where yer pa is."

"It looks like he found something!" Jed declared, watching his father spring from his saddle and look intently at the ground. "Should we go find out?"

Thinking a moment, Carson agreed, saying they could check the path later.

It wasn't long before the entire search party was gathered around Mr. Fields. "Look," he was saying as Carson and Jed rode up. "See this hole? From the looks of it, I'd say Ty's horse stumbled in it and that is why Ty got hit in the shoulder instead of being killed outright."

For several minutes Carson examined the ground around the hole, gazed into the woods where the shot came from, and with his eye, traced yesterday's path back into the trees. At last he nodded. "Seems reasonable. I remember Par were limpin' slightly by the end a the day."

"It seems like an act of Providence," Jed remarked quietly, "that Par should stumble then."

"I agree, Son. But who did it?"

"Rustlers."

Jim Fields glanced at his son quickly. "Sure?"

Jed nodded. "There is even a brand in the woods."

"Mr. Fields, I'm beginnin' to see how we've been losin' cattle," one of the hired hands put in.

"Yes, and we need to put a stop to it." His face was grim. "You boys ready?"

"Just say the word, Boss."

"Carson, I don't like to put you in danger, and you can go on back to the house if you want; though I'll admit having one more gun as well as your ability to read sign would—"

He got no farther for Carson interrupted him. "I aim ta spend the day lookin' for 'em myself, an' I reckon yer company would be downright nice. Even jest knowin' it were rustlers an' not 'them', gives me a better feelin'."

"Them who?" questioned Jed, puzzled.

"Long story. I'll tell ya tonight," Carson promised, mounting Flint and heading for the trees.

Sally, though clearly exhausted, couldn't sleep long, for her mind replayed her brother's accident over and over even in her sleep. The sun had barely risen when Sally again slipped into Ty's room. No one was there except Ty.

"Oh, Ty," she moaned, bending over him and gently brushing back his dark hair. "Ya have ta get better, ya jest have ta. I can't lose ya an' Pa. Besides, we have to find our sister, Ty. Ya have ta help me." Still talking softly, pleadingly, Sally perched on the edge of the bed.

There was no response from the still form of her dearly loved brother, the companion of so many childhood hours, the one who understood her better than had her own father. Would he ever open those dark, searching eyes of his again? Would those grey lips ever smile? Would she ever again hear that voice tease her as before?

"Ty!" she cried, tears spilling down her cheeks and dropping onto the bed clothes, "Ya can't die!"

A hand was placed on her shoulder. She looked up. Jack stood there looking down at her. "Go and eat some breakfast."

Sally shook her head. "I can't."

"Try."

Again Sally shook her head. "Ain't no use, I'm stayin' by Ty."

"Ty's just the same as he was last night. He is weak from loss of blood, and it might be a while before he is rested enough to wake up. Go and eat. You can come back as soon as you're done."

If Jack had known Sally, he would have seen by the sudden determined tilt of her chin and a look in her eyes that she was not going to change her mind. She continued to sit beside her brother, her fingers softly playing with those stronger ones of his. When Jack again touched her shoulder, she didn't even look at him, but shook her head. "Until Ty wakes up, I ain't leavin' him."

Frowning, Jack withdrew from the room.

In a few minutes, Joe appeared beside Sally and asked softly, "How is he?"

She looked up, "Jest the same."

He beckoned her over to the side of the room.

Reluctantly, after some hesitation, she followed.

"You need to—" Joe began but never got to finish his sentence, for at that moment, a groan came from the bed, and Ty muttered something.

In an instant Sally was back beside the bed while Joe hurried to the door and in a low but insistent voice, called Jack.

"Got ta get Par saddled," Ty muttered feebly, trying to push back the bed clothes. "We'll never make it at this rate, Carson."

"Easy, Ty," Jack was beside the bed with one hand on the sick man's pulse. "Par is just fine right now. You need to rest." As he spoke, Jack had laid his cool hand on Ty's flushed and feverish face.

"Carson? Dan!" Ty's words were growing excited. "Dan, where's Carson? Ya saw him last! Where is he?"

"Carson is out riding, Ty, there is no need for alarm. He'll be back."

Momentarily calmed by Jack's soothing words, Ty's eyes closed and his tense shoulders relaxed. Jack began bathing his face with the cool water, which Mrs. Fields had brought. Sally sat in stunned silence. Ty had awakened but he hadn't said one word to her. And who was Dan? Why did Ty talk of him instead of her?

As though in answer to her thoughts, Jack told her softly, "He's delirious, Sally. He doesn't know where he is or what is going on."

"What can I do? I have to do something!" her voice was frantic and full of suppressed emotion.

Jack glanced at Joe who stood near the distressed girl, nodded at her and then jerked his head in the direction of the door.

Understanding his brother's unspoken order, Joe gently pulled Sally to her feet. "Come on," he whispered sympathetically, "we can talk out here."

Before Sally really had time to comprehend where she was being taken or to resist, Joe had her out of the sick room and seated in a rocking chair near the table. She shook her head when offered something to drink and attempted to rise, but Joe pushed her gently back down.

"Sally," he said softly, looking into her tired face, "you have to eat. You must," he added when she shook her head, "if you want to help nurse Ty. Jack won't let you back in the room unless you eat."

"He has to, he's my brother," Sally swallowed hard and her chin quivered.

Resolutely Joe shook his head. "Ty is also Jack's patient. If there is a sick person, Jack is in charge and what he says is law. You have to eat something if you want to go back in there."

For a moment Sally looked like she was going to continue to resist, but just then Mrs. Fields pulled a fresh loaf of bread from the oven. The tantalizing aroma was too much for Sally and after one more longing look at the closed door, she nodded slightly, sure, however, that she couldn't swallow a mouthful.

"Good girl," Joe sighed, getting to his feet. He wasn't sure what he would have done if she had insisted on not eating.

Having managed to eat two slices of the fresh, hot bread, Sally begged to go back to her brother, and Joe nodded assent. Ty was sleeping when they entered the room. Quietly she sank down in the chair beside him. "What can I do?" Though still fighting back tears and fright, Sally managed to speak calmly. The food and glass of fresh milk had seemingly given her new courage. Jack let her bathe Ty's face and hands while he and Joe stepped to the far side of the room.

So intent on her brother was Sally that she didn't hear their low-toned conversation.

"How is he?"

Jack shook his head. "I don't like the look of his shoulder. I expected a fever, but I'm afraid it is going to go much higher than it is now. He is already weakened by lack of blood not to mention a long journey, and if the fever lasts too long, well . . ." his voice trailed off significantly.

"We'll keep praying."

"That's all you can do right now. That and try to keep his sister from completely wearing herself out. We don't want her sick too. If you can keep her resting and eating, I'll do all I can for her brother."

"I told her you wouldn't let her back in the room if she didn't eat," Joe smiled slightly.

"Glad you thought of that." And Jack looked over at the dark haired girl beside the bed. "Maybe it will help her to keep up."

Ty began to mumble and move restlessly, and Jack left his brother to hurry to the bedside of his patient.

All that day Sally remained by her brother's side. Leaving only for a few minutes at a time when Joe, with persistence and skill, made her eat a little. Thankfully she didn't see Jack's face when, as the afternoon turned into evening, Ty's fever continued to rise making his delirium worse. He muttered and talked, called for Carson and kept trying to get up. Never once did he call for his sister or seem to notice her. When he saw Jack, he called him Dan and ordered Joe away from his horse, which he fancied was in the room with him.

During one of his cries for Carson, Sally, with sudden terror grasped Joe's arm and whispered hoarsely, "Carson!

Where is he?" She had just at that moment realized that he hadn't been around all day.

"Come out here, and I'll tell you."

Seeing that Jack and Mrs. Fields were both with Ty, she followed with pale cheeks. Once they where out of the sick room, Joe told her of the search to find those who had shot her brother.

Sally turned even more pale and clutched at her locket. She began to shake and her breath came in gasps while she looked at Joe in wild-eyed terror.

"No!" she gasped out. "No! Not Uncle Bob too!" A wild burst of sobbing broke from her and had not Joe caught her, she would have dropped. With great sobs shaking her, she buried her face in her hands unmindful of the encircling arms while she continued to cry, "Not Uncle Bob! No, not him too!"

CHAPTER NINETEEN

Joe didn't know what to say, for he wasn't about to admit that he had begun to grow slightly worried himself at the long absence of his father, brother and their companions. True, he didn't know what they had discovered or where they had gone, but surely, surely they would be back soon. Now he could only try to comfort the girl in his arms, but she was so upset, how could he? His heart went out to Sally in her anguish and distress. Instinctively, almost without realizing it, his arms tightened as though to protect her from the terror and fright that beset her while in low tones he began to pray. One sure Refuge he knew could help and comfort Sally and to this Refuge he turned.

It was several minutes before Sally's heartrending cries subsided into pitiable moans. She continued to tremble as she drew each shuddering breath. Joe waited in silence for her to recover her composure. His own emotions had been deeply stirred by seeing Sally so overcome.

A clatter of hooves in the yard outside had the effect of bringing Sally's face, streaked with tears though it was, out of her hands. Joe released her and stepped to the window. "They're back, Sally," he told her quietly.

Flying to the door, Sally threw it open and, on seeing Carson dismount, rushed to fling her arms about him and begin to cry once more.

"Hey, what's this? Sally, Ty ain't—" and Carson looked at Joe quickly.

"No," Joe answered the unspoken question. "He's sick, but still alive."

"Thank God!" Carson breathed earnestly. "Ya had me worried there, Sally. What ya all upset 'bout?"

"I thought they would get ya like they promised ta do ta Ty," she whispered, shuddering again at the thought.

Carson hugged her close. "It weren't 'them', Sally. Jest some cattle thieves. We rounded 'em up an' Jim and his men are takin' 'em ta the sheriff right now. Jed an' me thought we'd come back ta see how Ty was."

"Why don't I take care of your horse for you, Carson," Jed offered, holding out his hand for the reins.

"I'm much obliged, Jed." Carson patted Flint's neck. "An' would ya check on Par?" he called.

"Sure."

Carson was quiet as he followed Sally into the sick room and saw Ty moaning and muttering on the bed. Jack was putting a new bandage on his shoulder, but looked up as Carson approached.

"I'm glad you're here," he remarked softly. "Perhaps you can keep him calm."

Even as he spoke, Ty opened his eyes and began calling once again for Carson, his tones hoarse and urgent. "Carson! Where are ya?"

"I'm here, Ty. Right beside ya," Gripping his friend's restless hand he added, "What ya so worried fer? I ain't goin' ta leave ya."

"The letter, Carson," gasped Ty, eyes fixed on the face above him. "Did ya read it?"

"Sure, sure. Ain't nothin' ta get excited 'bout."

"But it's from her!"

At that, Carson turned quickly and looked at Sally. What was Ty talking about? What letter? Who was the "her" that had written it? Just as he was about to ask, Ty spoke again.

"Dan! I ain't stayin' here." His glazed eyes were fixed on Jack's face and his breathing was coming in gasps. "Give me the letter!" he demanded.

"Hey, Ty, jest ease up, I got the letter. Dan ain't goin' ta touch it. He ain't got the brains ta get it from me. Now why don't ya jest have a drink," as Jack hurriedly placed a cup in his hands and nodded at Ty. "That's it," for Ty accepted from Carson's hand the drink he had been refusing from Jack for the last hour. "Now ya jest get some shut eye an' I'll take care a some other things 'round here. Agree?"

"Agree," Ty murmured, worn out by his struggle.

Neither Carson nor Jack stirred from their posts until Ty's deep, steady breathing told them he was asleep at last. Then Jack drew a long breath and let it out slowly. Standing up, he beckoned Carson to follow him while Mrs. Fields slipped past them to take up her post.

Once all were out of the room, Jack turned to Carson. "Thank God you came when you did. Another fifteen minutes of that raving could have had dire results. He's been calling for you most of the day."

"An' I weren't here," the regret in his voice was evident as he paced the room. "Well, I ain't goin' ta leave him now. Not if'n I have ta stay all summer!"

The door opened and Jed came in. Curiously he glanced at the gathering, noticing Carson's disturbed face, Jack's grim look and the worried and sympathetic expressions Sally and Joe wore. "What's going on? Is Ty worse?"

Jack shook his head. "Worse than he was this morning, but not worse than when you got here. Where are Pa and the men?"

In a few words Jed explained, adding in answer to Carson's look, that Par would be all right after a few days rest and that he had bandaged his leg to give him more support.

"Uncle Bob," Sally began hesitantly, "why didn't Ty ask for me?"

The reply came slowly. "I reckon his mind's gone back ta the time him an' me were off trappin'. Ya heard him talkin' 'bout that letter didn't ya?"

Sally nodded.

"Well, I kind a think that were the letter ya wrote when ya told him 'bout yer pa's sickness."

"How do ya know?"

"'Cause a his talk 'bout Dan." Here he looked over at Jack with a slight grin, "Hope ya won't take it personal 'bout what I said back there."

"About the not having brains?" Jack returned the smile, though his was rather tired. "I long ago learned not to pay attention to what a sick man says or those who are trying to calm him."

"But Uncle Bob, who is Dan?"

"Dan? Well, Dan were a kind a hanger on in our camp. He weren't smart, jest seemed ta have enough brains ta get him in trouble. Dan did try once ta take somethin' a Ty's, but--" and Carson shrugged as though to express how ridiculous the very thought was.

Sally sighed almost unconsciously with relief. Without realizing it, she had begun to be afraid of Dan, whoever he might be. Her shoulders, which had been so rigid and tight, dropped.

Jack noticed and at once ordered her to eat and then go to bed.

Supper was made interesting as Carson and Jed told of their adventures. Sally ate without really realizing what she was doing and made a good meal. When the tale ended with Carson and Jed's return, Jack glanced around the room. All was quiet.

"Carson, do you mind sleeping near the door to Ty's room? I'd like you on hand if he calls you again. You seem to be what he needs to calm him."

Carson nodded.

Jack continued. "Joe, you can get some rest until later. Jed, are you up for a little watching? Good. I'd like you to relieve Ma. I'll check on Ty in a few minutes and then get some rest too. If there is any change, call me at once. Understood?"

"Got it," Jed answered in a steady voice before his brother went on.

"Joe, I'll let you take the second watch, but before you do, I'll look in on him once more. And the same instructions go for you: any change, I'm called. Miss Sally, you are to go to bed and not worry. If there is any change that you should know about, I'll tell you. You need rest for tomorrow."

Opening her mouth to argue that she wouldn't be able to sleep and that she would stay with her brother as she had done with her father, Sally found that Jack had already turned to Carson again, seemingly as though he expected her to do just as he had ordered.

"Carson, I don't know how much sleep you'll get tonight. I hope you don't mind."

"It weren't never a problem with me. I can sleep anywhere or not at all if'n I have ta."

"Jack!"

Instantly Jack was on his feet and heading for the sick room with Carson right behind him. Sally started to follow but Joe held her back.

"I'm goin' ta Ty," Sally declared trying to pull away.

"Listen," Joe soothed, "Ty is asking for Carson. He doesn't want or need you right now. But he may later, and you have to be rested. Now Jack ordered both of us to bed. How about we follow those instructions?" Joe spoke quietly, hoping Sally would give in.

She, however, tired though she was, just wouldn't let herself give in. How could she sleep with her only brother lying so ill in the next room? "I won't sleep!" she declared actually stamping her foot in vexation. "I can't." The tears were beginning to trickle down her cheeks. "Ty needs me. I'm his sister. I tell you I won't sleep while he's sick!"

Mrs. Fields, coming out of the sick room, saw and guessed what was going on. "Jed," her voice was gentle, "Jack is ready for you." Then she turned to Sally. "Let me make you some tea before you sleep."

But Sally shook her head, blinking back the tears. She wanted nothing but to stay by her brother's bedside and cry and wait until he spoke to her. Nothing would tempt her to leave. She had slept last night, but now Ty was worse. There was no telling when he might call for her. Didn't anyone understand? She could leave the sick room for a little while, but sleep? That was simply out of the question.

Joe's quiet voice interrupted her thoughts. "If you won't sleep, at least sit down. There is no use wasting your energy by standing."

Fighting back the strong desire to rush to Ty's beside, Sally reluctantly sat back down and a few minutes later Mrs. Fields was placing a steaming cup before her. She gave an involuntary shiver as the hot liquid went down her throat. For several minutes no one spoke. The only sounds to be heard in the stillness of the evening were the low voices in the sick room.

Suddenly, realizing that she was beginning to fall asleep where she sat and that Joe and Mrs. Fields were watching her, Sally shook her head and straightened up in her chair.

"Why don't you go lie down for a little while, Sally?" Mrs. Fields asked softly.

"No, I'm staying up," persisted Sally, trying desperately to keep her eyes open.

"Come on, Sally," Joe had moved to her side and was bending over her, "Don't be an idiot. You have to rest." His voice was a mixture of sympathy and firmness. When she didn't move, he pulled her chair out and ordered, "Go to bed."

If he had coaxed her or showed any signs of giving in, Sally would have refused to go though she was so tired and sleepy that she swayed on her feet. As it was, when that order was given, she gave in, too tired to argue any longer.

She was glad for the steady arm of Joe to lean on as she walked, or staggered rather, to her room. Once alone she sank onto the bed and was asleep before her head even touched the pillow.

It was a long night in the sick room. Carson didn't get much sleep, for Ty called for him so often that finally he gave up trying and just sat by his young friend's side through the wee hours of the morning. The watchers changed as Jed and Joe took turns, while Jack came in every little bit to check on his patient.

It was just as dawn was breaking that Ty started up in terror from a restless slumber.

Rebekah A. Morris

CHAPTER TWENTY

"Sally! Where is she?" he demanded of Joe, his breath fast and uneven.

"She's sleeping in the next room—"

"I said, where is she!" Ty was growing frantic and struggled under Carson's restraining hands to get up. "My gun," he panted, eyes darting around the darkened room. "Carson, let me have it. Where is she?"

Jack rushed into the room. "Joe, get Sally. Hold him still if you can, Carson. I don't want that shoulder to start bleeding again. Easy, Ty. Joe is getting Sally."

For a brief moment, Ty relaxed under the soothing words, then he began to struggle anew until Sally pushed past Carson and grasped her brother's hand.

"I'm here, Ty, an' I ain't leavin' again." She glanced at Jack as though defying him to order her away, but Jack was intent on his patient and didn't appear to notice. "Now ya just rest, that's right," as he lay back struggling to catch his breath.

"They ain't hurt ya none?" Ty mumbled.

Sally smiled. "I ain't hurt a bit. Why Ty, everything is goin' ta be fine once ya get well." She laid her face against her brother's hand. "Ya have ta get well, Ty," she begged. "Please."

And thus the long days wore slowly away. Ty tossed with fever, calling frantically for Carson and Sally, talking of 'them,' asking about the sister he was looking for and muttering words that no one could make any sense out of. Jack used every ounce of skill he had and prayed. The whole Fields family was praying for this unexpected guest.

Carson also prayed, often going out alone when it was dark and Ty was sleeping. He found great rest and peace in those times alone and would come in ready to take up the watching with renewed strength. At other times, when he could be spared from Ty's bedside, he ate and slept, knowing how important it was to keep up his strength.

With Sally, however, it was different. She had no place of real rest. Vaguely she knew of the Father who would help her, but though she prayed, she often felt as though her prayers never went higher than the ceiling. It was with great difficulty that she was persuaded to eat or sleep. Her one desire was to be with Ty. Even when he was sleeping she would often refuse to leave his side. Only Joe seemed to be able to get her to follow orders somewhat. Whether it was his tender, sympathetic spirit that found a response in the girl's nature, or whether it was the fact that he had been with her through that long, trying first day when Carson and Jed were off, no one knew. Perhaps it was a combination of it all. Whatever the reason, Joe, by coaxing or ordering, could get Sally to do almost anything.

It was several nights later; Jack came out of Ty's room, and there was a look on his face that caused everyone to pause. What was it? Surely Ty wasn't—dead? Jack walked over to the window and looked out at the setting sun a moment. Then turning, he looked at those gathered in the room and spoke quietly. "Tonight is the crisis. There is to be no noise if it can possibly be helped. Carson and Jed, I am going to let you two watch, each for a two hour shift before changing."

He gave other orders, but Sally scarcely heard them. For the first time since the accident she realized that Ty might not live. Could she go on without him? Knowing that she was going to cry, and realizing that even her tears could be harmful to her dearly loved brother, she pressed her hands over her mouth and fled from the house.

Carson watched her go with troubled eyes. Why did life have to be so hard for this young friend? No mother's love and care, her father taken from her by sickness, her only sister unknown and only God knew where, and now, her only brother lying at death's doorstep. If only she would go to her father and mother's Friend, yes, and his Friend too.

Almost as though reading his thoughts, Jack asked quietly, "Carson, do you want to go to her?"

Carson shook his head sadly, "She won't listen ta me. I've tried. I jest don't know what ta say."

"The poor, weary girl," Mrs. Fields sighed. "She isn't used to a woman's help or I would go to her, but she doesn't open up to me."

"Send Joe."

All eyes turned to Mr. Fields. He nodded as though he knew what he was talking about. "I don't know what Ty is really like, but for some reason his sister will take from Joe what she won't from anyone else. Send him if he can be spared from the sick room."

As a result of that talk, Joe, relieved of his post, was soon moving quietly towards Sally. He prayed as he walked. He doubted that he was the best person to send, yet his heart, stirred deeply by all that had happened, beat rapidly as he drew near, whether from pity and a longing to help or from some other cause, he didn't know.

Sally had thrown herself on the grassy slope of a hill and was sobbing bitterly, crying out as she sobbed, "Ty! Ya can't die! Ya can't, ya can't!" Her whole soul cried out with each passionate word revealing something of the terrible agony she was going through. Never had she felt so forsaken and alone. Even when her father was so ill and Ty and

Carson were so far away, she had the comfort of prayer. Now, however, even that refuge seemed to have forsaken her and she cried out, "Ya can't leave me, Ty! I'm all alone!"

A hand touched her shoulder and Joe's steady, tenderhearted voice broke into her sobs. "You aren't alone, Sally. There is a Refuge! Jesus Christ will never leave you if you come to Him."

"I can't!"

"Why not?" that gentle voice persisted. "He has promised that all who come to Him, He will in no wise cast out."

"I can't pray." The misery and distress in Sally's voice was more pathetic than even the heartrending cry for her brother had been.

"Why not?" Joe repeated.

For several seconds, Sally could only cry, then, in a voice muffled by her hands, she answered, "My prayers n— never seem to go h—higher than the ceiling a—and I know God doesn't hear them." The last words ended in a sob.

"Oh, you poor child," murmured Joe, his face, had she seen it, betrayed his compassion. "Sally," he began gently, "if you and I were in the same room, and you asked me something, do you think I would hear you?"

"Y—yes," Sally stammered, sniffing.

"You wouldn't say I couldn't hear you, even if I was standing behind you and you couldn't see me?"

"No." This time Sally ventured a timid look at the face of her companion, wondering what he meant. Of course he would hear her if he was in the same room even if he was behind her.

"Then have you never read the words of the Lord Jesus when he said, 'Lo, I am with you always, even unto the end of the world,' and again 'I will never leave thee nor forsake thee'? If He is with us always, then why must our prayers reach beyond the ceiling? He is with us wherever we are."

For a moment she looked at him, her eyes full of this new thought, then suddenly she buried her face once more in her hands and sobbed forth, "Then why doesn't he heal Ty?"

"Sally," very gently, "do you trust me?"

The question, so unexpected, caught Sally off guard. Did she trust Joe? She knew instinctively that she did, but why? What was it about him and the rest of his family that made her feel that she could trust them? They were perfect strangers to her only a few days before.

"Do you?" the question was repeated softly.

Wordlessly, Sally nodded, her face still buried in shaking hands.

"Then, if you were to ask me for something and I was to tell you to wait and trust me, would you say I hadn't answered you?"

In the fast, waning light of day, the shake of Sally's head was almost undetected, but Joe was watching. "Sometimes the Lord Jesus tells us to wait and trust Him. Can't you do that, Sally?"

It was a full minute before Sally spoke and then in tones so low that had not the evening hush already closed over the world, even Joe, who was sitting beside her and listening, wouldn't have heard them. "I want to trust. Help me."

And there, out in the peaceful evening, as the stars came out one by one, Joe and Sally prayed. And in heaven, the angels were rejoicing over the new lamb brought home to the fold.

At last Sally gave a long, weary sigh and looked up. Her face, still streaked with tears and showing signs of her struggle, wore a look of peace which Joe had never seen before. She shivered and he, pulling off his jacket, wrapped it around her, for the air was growing cooler. Neither one spoke. Sally was gathering strength to face the night with its unknown results and trying to hush the tiny voices of worry, which still persisted in tormenting her. Joe sat and waited.

At last, when Sally still didn't move, he spoke, "Are you ready to go inside?"

She looked up at him, nodded, and allowed him to help her to her feet. "Thank you," she whispered as they started toward the house.

A smile and a gentle pressure of the hand was his only response.

Pausing on the doorstep, Joe turned to the girl at his side and asked in low tones, "Will you not go and try to get some sleep now? Jack doesn't think there will be any change before midnight."

Only an hour before Sally would have rebelled against such a thought and have insisted on sitting up even if she couldn't be in the sick room. Now, however, her heart was at rest and, feeling exhausted, she nodded assent but added, "Promise you'll waken me if there's a change? I want ta know."

Joe promised, and Sally, without a word to anyone, slipped into her little room and shut the door. There, before she lay down, she dropped on her knees and prayed. What did it matter if her prayers only reached the ceiling? Wasn't there Someone there in the room with her? With that comforting thought, she closed her eyes and slept.

A hand gently shook her shoulder and Joe's soft voice called her name. Starting up quickly, her heart pounding wildly, Sally waited for the news.

"The fever has broken, and Ty's sleeping."

In that moment of relief and excitement, Sally did what she would never have done otherwise; she flung her arms around Joe's neck and kissed him. "Oh!" she gasped, letting go, her cheeks flushing scarlet at the realization of what she had just done. "I'm so sorry, I don't know what I'm doin' an' ya've been just like a brother ta me, an'—" she broke off in confusion.

"It's all right," Joe said, and Sally could tell he was smiling. "I know I'm a stand in for Ty right now. Jed is with him, and Carson is sleeping. I'd suggest that you get some more sleep or Jack will give me what for for waking you."

"I'm glad you did. Thank you." And her words were full of feeling.

"You're welcome. Now sleep," Joe whispered back from the doorway as he slipped out.

After a prayer of gratitude to her loving Friend, Sally slept again and it was quite late when she again opened her eyes.

CHAPTER TWENTY-ONE

"Sally," Ty's voice was low and feeble. He looked over at her as she sat beside his bed.

Gently she placed a finger over his lips. "Hush, Ty. You know Jack said you were to sleep an' not talk now. Rest." She spoke softly but there was a hint of stubbornness in her tone which Ty knew.

He gave a slight smile and his eyes closed once more.

As a shadow fell across the bed, Sally looked up. Jack stood on the other side of the bed. His expression was a pleased one and after placing soft fingers on Ty's wrist, he turned towards the door, motioning Sally to follow.

She did so with a light heart. Ty was getting better. The fever and loss of blood from his shoulder wound had left him weak, but each day he seemed to gain more strength. The wound was healing nicely and Jack said only yesterday that his arm would be as good as ever in a few weeks.

Out of the sick room, Jack turned to Sally and instructed, "Go out and get some fresh air. Ty should sleep for a while and I'll be here if he needs anything."

Sally nodded. Only a week or so ago, she would have stubbornly insisted on staying by Ty, but now all was right. "Where is everyone?" she asked, pausing before the door.

"Well, I think Carson and Jed are out with Pa looking for some stray cattle. Ma is out in the garden and Joe is around somewhere. More than likely, he's out with the horses."

The warm summer sun shone brightly out from a deep blue sky dotted here and there with cotton ball clouds. Loosening her hair, Sally let the breeze blow it about her face while she drew in deep breaths of the fresh air. Slowly she meandered across the yard towards the barn and garden, stopping now and then to look at and admire a flower blooming in the grass. A bright butterfly flitted by and Sally paused to watch it; the delicate little insect flying from flower to flower, enjoying the sunshine, fluttering its colorful wings and mounting up, up into the vast expanse of sky above, it disappeared at last from view. Sally, who had watched until it vanished, lost in her own thoughts, was brought back to earth by a voice.

"Don't trip, Sally," it warned.

Sally looked down and smiling, walked around the pile of stones. Mrs. Fields was watching her from the garden.

"Did you come out to get some sunshine?" she asked pleasantly.

"Yes," Sally replied simply, adding, "Oh, let me help. I ain't had—" she broke off quickly, blushing and then started again. "I never had a garden. Not a real one. Pa, Ty an' I lived in the woods an' there jest weren't no— I mean there wasn't any place for one." In the weeks since Carson, Ty and Sally had dropped in on the Fields so unexpectedly Sally had noticed how differently she talked from the others. Never before had she had the daily influence of a woman like Mrs. Jim Fields. Slowly, with persistence and much encouragement, Sally was beginning to learn those fine arts which only a true woman can teach. So subtly were the changes coming to her that she scarcely noticed them except in her speech, which she was quite conscious of.

In the weeks that followed Ty's start on the road to recovery, while Sally was learning from Mrs. Fields, Carson was learning about cattle ranching. Always one to try his hand at something new, Mr. Fields soon found him a valuable assistant especially in tracking down missing cattle. In this Carson was an expert. Having trapped nearly all his life, learning to read sign from the Indians and with a keen eye and quick memory for the tiniest details, he found tracking cattle to be much like tracking anything else. Jed Fields, fascinated by Carson's skill, went with him everywhere and learned much from the older man.

These two, Carson and Sally, each busy in their own way, were content to stay on where they were for months if need be. Sally had the companionship she had unknowingly craved, and Carson was out in the great world, his world of nature, always occupied. It was Ty who was growing restless. The idleness, which his illness had forced upon him, was to him, a great affliction. Never had Ty remembered being so weak. He fretted at staying in bed. He wanted to be up, to ride out with Carson, to stroll across the fields with Sally and have one of their long talks such as they used to have when they were growing up. Now he found that he couldn't stay awake and talk without growing tired. Sometimes he felt as though he wasn't improving and would lie moody and silent, becoming gruff and even impatient with his sister or with anyone who happened to be with him at the time.

Even if Ty could see no improvement, Jack could and was encouraged by his patient's rapid improvement, for Ty's strong constitution stood him in good stead now as he struggled to regain his former strength. As he grew stronger, Jack first allowed him to sit up, then, with help from Joe, Carson or Jed and carefully watched by Sally and Mrs. Fields, he was helped to a chair in the large room beyond or on warm sunny days, he was even allowed outside. Those days were of great pleasure to Ty, but often were followed by days of restless fretfulness.

After one such day, when Ty was lying moody in bed, Jack came and sat down beside him.

"Ty," Jack began quietly, "you are not helping yourself in the least by this fretfulness. It wastes your energy and you wear yourself out. If you want to regain your health quickly, stop fighting against what you can't change. You are improving, but these moods of yours are setting you back."

Ty was silent. Staring up at the ceiling a moment, he sighed. "I reckon I ought ta follow yer orders an' if'n ya say I've got ta quit frettin', well," and he sighed again, "I reckon I'll have ta." He looked at Jack and gave a slight grin.

Standing up, Jack returned the grin and said, clapping him gently on the shoulder, "Get some rest now, and I just might let you sit outside for a while this evening."

"Anything ta get outside again, Doc." And Ty yawned and closed his eyes.

In two more weeks, Ty, still looking pale, having lost much of his dark tan during his illness, was up and about. His only thought now was to get back in the saddle and continue the search. Jack was somewhat hesitant about it, but since Ty's shoulder wound was healed and other than not having regained his former strength and stamina, he was fit if he went easy, he didn't protest. Carson and Sally, much as they had enjoyed their stay, were likewise ready to be on the move once more. And so, preparations began for their departure. Not much time was needed, however, for the threesome traveled lightly with only two packhorses.

"Now, Sally," Mrs. Fields admonished the following morning after preparations were complete and Jed and Joe were helping Carson saddle the horses and load supplies on the pack animals, "do write to us each town you come to if you can so that we can hear how things are going."

"I will," Sally blinked back tears. She was going to miss this motherly person more than she thought it was possible. "Thank you for everything," she murmured, looking so like a child, that Mrs. Fields instinctively kissed her cheek.

"Don't mention it, Dear. Just let us be hearing from you often."

Nodding, Sally, accompanied by Mrs. Fields, went out of the house to where the men were gathered.

"All ready, Sally?" Ty asked, eager to be off.

"Yes."

"Carson?"

"Any time, Ty. I reckon we ought ta get on if'n we aim ta reach any place by dark."

"We'll reach it," Ty grinned. "Any place out under the stars'll work. I got a hankerin' for some campfires an' sunsets. I ain't complainin' 'bout stayin' here, mind ya."

"Sure you aren't," Joe chuckled. "Maybe it was just the bed you're tired of."

"You should have let him sleep on the floor, Jack," Jed put in, and everyone laughed.

Carson handed Sally her father's six-shooter and she buckled it on, remarking to Ty as she did so, "I don't know which of us is the better shot now."

Ty couldn't help grinning. "I reckon we'll find out 'fore long."

"You all take care of yourselves," Mr. Fields directed as Ty, Sally and Carson mounted their horses, and, turning their heads towards the south, waved a final farewell to those gathered in the barnyard behind them.

"I'll write," called back Sally with a bright smile, and then they were off.

Not wanting to break the silence of the late morning, enjoying the sunshine, feeling the fresh breezes sweeping down from distant mountain peaks, each lost in his own thoughts, the trio rode in silence for several miles. It was good to be on the back of a horse again. Ty sighed in satisfaction. How he had missed this vast expanse of nothing but nature. Looking back, he could no longer make out the faint wisp of smoke, which marked the hospitable home of the Fields. At last they were once again traveling on towards their goal of finding Eleanor Elliot, his missing, youngest sister. How long would it take before the search was ended? Weeks? Months? Years? Ty didn't know. But this he did know, nothing but death would stop him from fulfilling his father's dying request, unexpected though it was.

It was Carson who at last broke the silence. "How far ya feel like ridin' today, Ty?" he asked.

Ty hated to admit it, but, it had been so long since he had been in the saddle or had done anything except sit or lie around, already he was feeling rather faint and weary.

After a quick glance at her brother, Sally saved him the trouble of admitting his weakness. "I haven't been riding much, so if it's all right with both of you, I'd like to take a rest. Those trees look pleasant and shady.

"That'd be right fine by me," Carson agreed. "Ty?"

Ty nodded but didn't speak.

No sooner had they dismounted than Ty, stretching himself out with a deep sigh of satisfaction, fell asleep, more worn out than he thought was possible after such a short ride.

Sally built a fire while Carson set off to see if he could shoot a rabbit or squirrel for their noon meal.

It was several hours before they set off again, this time halting as the sun was beginning to sink behind the mountains in the west. Sitting around their campfire, Ty watched the flickering flames, listened to the last good-night chirps of the birds and enjoyed the taste of his sister's cooking. "I missed this," he said simply, quietly, to no one in particular.

"I didn't know how much I missed it as well until tonight," Sally whispered.

"It jest ain't the same livin' under a roof with other folks. Don't matter how nice they are," added Carson. "An' I aim ta enjoy them stars above fer a while 'fore I sleep." So saying, he lay back on his blanket with his arms folded under his head.

Following his example, Ty also lay down, but before many minutes had passed, his star gazing was over, and Sally, watching him, saw his eyelids close and his whole body relax and knew he was asleep.

"It worked, Uncle Bob," she breathed. "He's asleep. I don't think he knew how tired he really was."

Carson rolled over, propping his chin up in his hands. "I reckon we can all take things easy fer a spell."

"Uncle Bob," whispered Sally, pausing as she was about to lie down, "Do you think Ty really is strong enough for traveling? Joe told me that Jack didn't give Ty his full approval before leaving."

Yawning, Carson gazed into the fire before answering. "I reckon it wouldn't a hurt Ty none ta've jest stayed a few more days or weeks ta kind a build his strength back. He ain't been in the saddle none since he was shot. That's a mighty long time. But, I reckon if'n we take it easy, Ty'll get his strength an' ain't goin' ta be none the worse. Sure Jack didn't want him leavin' but he could tell Ty'd jest be frettin' 'bout goin' an' that weren't goin' ta do 'im no good." A soft sigh in the darkness told Carson that his words had relieved Sally's fears. Now he added a few last ones. "Jest be sure ya tell 'em how Ty's doin' when ya write them there letters yer supposed ta. I reckon that'll set all their minds ta rest. The other thing we can do, Sally," Carson spoke slowly, as one not sure how to say it.

"What, Uncle Bob?"

"We can pray fer him."

"I do."

"Then I reckon the good Lord'll take care a him."

A deep, peaceful silence fell over the little group of travelers resting beside the glowing embers of their campfire under the thousands of bright, twinkling stars in the heavens above while a soft breeze caressed their cheeks and gently stirred their hair. All was hushed. Sleep, with gentle persistence, claimed Carson and Sally before further words were exchanged.

For several days following that first one back on the trail, Carson and Sally set an easy pace. Ty noticed it but didn't say anything, for, until he regained much of his earlier strength and stamina, he knew he wouldn't make it to the next town if they pushed on as they had done before he was wounded.

Often as they traveled they were silent, but now and then one of the trio would make a remark and a lively, serious or reminiscing conversation would ensue. It was Sally who began it this time.

"Ty, when you were sick you didn't seem to like Joe. You would order him away from your horse or tell him to leave your things alone."

"Hmm, could be I thought he were the kind ta take what ain't his."

"Joe would never do that," protested Sally warmly.

"Huh, well I ain't too sure 'bout that. I reckon it were a right smart thing we left 'fore he had more chance." And he turned to look at Carson. "Ain't that right, Carson?"

"I reckon so."

Sally was indignant. "Ty Elliot, Joe would never take what weren't—wasn't his, especially not from someone else."

Ty grinned slyly at Carson before replying, "Ya think so, huh? Well, I ain't none too sure. I reckon the only reason somethin' weren't taken was 'cause he decided ta wait till I had another one."

"Another what, Ty?" Sally questioned innocently.

Ty only looked at her with such a teasing grin on his face that Sally felt the blood rush to her cheeks, and she looked away, slowing her horse until she was the last of the line. Not another word did she say for several miles.

As the days passed and still the companions rode south, Ty's strength was rapidly returning. The sun and wind were darkening his face and arms once more and when Ty was able to beat Sally on a draw, he knew they could travel at a faster pace. He was eager to reach someplace where news might be obtained.

It was while they were picking their way down a rocky hill that Starlight stumbled. Sally was jolted in the saddle but managed to stay on. Patting her horse's neck, she murmured, "Easy, Starlight. Did you step on a loose rock? Take it easy now, we're almost to the bottom."

With those gentle words to reassure her, Starlight recovered herself and continued down the hillside. At the bottom Sally slid off and ran her hands down her horse's legs. None of them appeared hurt, so, remounting, Sally nudged Starlight forward to catch up with the others.

Carson and Ty, noticing Sally wasn't with them anymore, pulled their horses to a halt and looked back. She was just remounting and as she came up it became obvious that Starlight was limping.

"Sally," Ty called out, "Yer horse is limpin'."

"I know." Sally rode up and dismounted once again. "She stumbled coming down that hill. I checked her legs, but they all seemed fine."

Ty and Carson had both dismounted and now Carson said, "Could be a shoe's loose. Let's take a look see."

It only took a few minutes to discover that the shoe on her right fore foot was missing and the foot was cut in a few places.

"No wonder you were limping," Sally crooned, stroking the chestnut's neck and rubbing her face. "You don't like walking on rocks without your shoes on. And I made you hurry. I'm sorry, Girl."

"Well, what do we do now?" Ty looked at Carson. "She can't be ridden, least ways not till we've got another shoe on her."

"I'll walk," answered Sally simply.

"Ya can't walk for days," Ty protested. "Ya can ride Par an' I'll walk."

"I reckon Sally'd rather ride Flint 'n Par," Carson put in. "Besides, ya ain't strong enough ta walk that far."

"If'n I ain't, then she ain't either," retorted Ty.

Shaking her head, Sally started forward leading Starlight. "If you two want to stand there and argue, go ahead. You can catch up with us when you have finished. For now I'm going to walk. It feels good to stretch my legs."

For a few brief seconds, the two men could only stare after her. Then, with slightly sheepish grins, they both mounted and soon caught up with the pair before them.

CHAPTER TWENTY-TWO

Agreeing to take turns walking, Ty, Sally and Carson continued on their way. It was slow traveling now for Starlight wasn't used to walking without shoes and now that she only had three, she walked with a limp, favoring her shoeless foot especially over rocky ground. For three days they traveled thus and on the fourth day, as Sally was walking beside her horse, she noticed Starlight was limping more than usual.

"Ty, if we don't find a town soon and get another shoe for Starlight, she'll be a dead horse before long. Or at least an injured one. The poor thing can hardly walk as it is!"

Ty dismounted. "Yer right 'bout that, Sally. An' if'n we do find us a town today, I reckon she'll have ta rest for several days 'fore she can be shod. Carson," he asked, turning to the older man, "What ya think if'n one a us rides lookin' for a town?"

"I think it'd be right smart. We ain't got the money for a new horse 'sides the fact that Sally's used ta Starlight. I'll jest ride . . . Why, wouldn't ya know!" Carson exclaimed looking off at a distant hill. "There's someone comin' our way."

Ty and Sally looked also. A lone rider was coming rapidly down the hill and across the valley towards them. It

167

only took him a few minutes to reach them and at Carson's wave, he drew rein and halted.

"Howdy," the stranger greeted them, touching his hat to Sally.

"Howdy," Carson returned his greeting.

"In trouble?"

"We're jest need'n a town with a blacksmith," Ty explained. "Horse's thrown a shoe."

The stranger grunted and jerked a thumb back over his shoulder. "'Bout five miles. Dead Horse. Ask fer Herr Rohbar or whatever his name is. Furriner, but the best blacksmith I ever seen."

"Thanks."

"Yep. So long!" And the stranger rode off in a cloud of dust.

"'Bout five miles. That ain't too far. Let's make tracks," and Ty gently urged Starlight forward.

"Dead Horse, ugh," Sally made a face. "It doesn't sound like a very nice town even if they do have the best blacksmith. I just hope poor Starlight doesn't give them a reason to change the name of their town to Dead Horses."

The five miles were at last ended and a small town was to be seen. It wasn't exactly small but neither was it what one might call large. The main street was lined with the usual buildings: hotels, saloons, a post office, general store and jail. Boardwalks lined either side of the dusty street.

Ty asked the first person they saw where the blacksmith was.

"Jest down there 'bout four houses."

After thanking the man, Ty led the others down the street indicated and soon stopped before the blacksmith's shop.

A short, broad shouldered man stepped out wiping his hands on his leather apron. His dark hair and beard gave him a sturdy look while his dark eyes twinkled in friendliness.

"Can I help you?" he asked, his thick accent showing plainly that he was indeed a foreigner.

"Are you the blacksmith?" Carson asked.

"Ja, I am Herr Rohbar. You in need of vork done, nein?"

Ty nodded. "This horse threw her shoe couple a day's back. I reckon she'll have ta rest a bit 'fore she gets a new one."

The blacksmith with gentle but sure hands lifted Starlight's leg. "Ah, ze poor horse. You are right. Zis horse should rest for a few days. You have place to stay?"

Carson shook his head. "I reckon we'll jest find us a hotel."

"Nein! Zat vill not do. And the Frau, your vife?"

"Sister," corrected Ty.

"Ah, the fraulein, she ish tired. Mine good Frau Senora Juanita vill get all you a cool drink, nein?"

Before Carson, Ty or Sally could say anything, the good blacksmith called out, "Juanita, ve have company."

The door of the little hut behind the blacksmith flew open and a lovely Mexican woman came out with a small child in one arm and two more about her skirts.

"You called, my husband?"

"Ja, my Nita, ve have guests. Zis Fraulein ish veary of her journey an for zees mine herrs, a glass of vater you bring, bitte."

The dark eyed Juanita beckoned for Sally to follow and led the way into the small hut, the little children following.

In a voice soft and sweet, Herr Rohbar's Frau Senora Juanita spoke, "If the senorita will sit, soon I shall have cool water for her to drink, si?"

Sally sat as she was bidden and watched the small woman move swiftly about the tiny hut. She was clothed in a brightly colored skirt and blouse and her dark hair was in a knot at the back of her neck. With a mixture of Spanish and English she directed the children. The oldest a boy and girl of about six and four looked more like their mother with her darker skin, black hair and dark eyes while the smallest child looked so like his father that Sally half expected him to say something in a deep German voice.

Soon a mug of cold water was handed to Sally and the Senora took some out for Carson and Ty, leaving the three children to stand staring wide-eyed at Sally. She offered a smile and said, "Hello."

"Hello," the boy replied giving a small smile in return.

The younger two remained soberly silent standing beside their big brother until Frau Rohbar returned.

Out in the yard, Herr Rohbar was assuring his visitors that they did not want to stay in the hotels in this town. "Nein!" he exclaimed emphatically, "Zees hotels, zay are full of bugs an ze streets are no place to be after dark. Nein, zay are not ze place for ze fraulein. I vould offer mine house, but it ish shmall. Ah, vait! I know ze very place. Nita!"

His wife appeared instantly, followed by Sally.

Then the blacksmith poured forth such a torrent of mixed German, Spanish and English that the three travelers could only stand in utter bewilderment. Not one of them understood. But the lovely Spanish wife evidently did, for she replied with approval, "Si, si, I will take the senorita in the wagon. The ninos will also go. The senors will follow, si?"

"Ja, zay vill follow as soon ve take care of zis poor horse." Then, turning to his guests he explained, "Ve have house on ze other side of town. It ish large house, but ve have nicht moved in yet, nein? Ve must first move zees shtuff," and he waved his hands towards his furnace, bellows, anvil and tools. "Ze house, she shtand empty. Now you shtay dere vile your horse she goes well an' I make new shoe, nein? Zis very goot. Mine Frau vill drive ze vagon vith your schwester." At Ty's blank look, Herr Rohbar smiled. "Ze fraulein, how you say, sister. Ze go shtart fire, get supper ready, nein?"

"Ya willin' ta go with her, Sally?" Ty questioned his sister softly while Juanita was hitching up the light wagon.

Nodding, Sally half touched her six-shooter at her side. "I think they are trustworthy, Ty. And I like them. Just take good care of Starlight."

"Don't worry. We'll be 'long an' join ya jest as soon's we can."

The Frau Senora Juanita gave a command in Spanish and the three children tumbled into the back of the wagon. Ty helped Sally up beside the blacksmith's wife and watched them drive down the street. He felt rather bewildered at how quickly things were moving along since their arrival in Dead Horse. For several minutes he stood watching the wagon until it turned down the main street and disappeared. He had no fear for Sally for she could take care of herself with that six-shooter of Pa's, besides the fact that Herr Rohbar had an honest look about him.

While Ty stood in thought, Carson and the friendly blacksmith were unsaddling Starlight and leading her over to the nearby livery. The other four horses would be taken to the house and stabled there. The blacksmith loved to talk and Carson wasn't adverse to it himself since both Ty and Sally could be as quiet and closed mouthed as their father used to be. Thus it was that the wagon with the ladies and children had been gone for over an hour before Ty decided it was time they left.

"Carson," he called to his friend, "I reckon Sally's been gone long enough ta cook an' eat the supper. We got a couple a days ta jaw if'n ya feel the need. I aim ta head on ta the house. Ya comin' or not?"

Herr Rohbar broke forth, "Ja, ja, you should go vith your young friend. No doubt ze Fraulien ish vonderin' vere you are. Mine Frau vill be back soon with the kindders. Ve can talk another time, nein?"

"Yep, that sounds mighty fine ta me. Till then." Carson swung up on Flint and nudged him on after Ty and Par.

At the house, Sally was examining everything with delight. There was even a pump in the kitchen so she wouldn't have to go out of the house to get water. "Oh, this is lovely," she exclaimed to her hostess. "It was so kind of you to let us stay here for a few days. It will only be until Starlight can have a new shoe put on."

"Si, this place, she need someone to live in her. Senor Rohbar will bring much tools, heavy things over soon. Then we come. Now you stay, make building feel home, si?"

Sally smiled and nodded. "Home," she echoed. "Oh, if only we could go home sometime. But 'they' are there waiting for Ty," she mused. "They would kill him if they could."

"Banditos?"

"Bad men."

Senora Rohbar shook her head in sympathy.

"But," Sally said brightening, "they are far away. I don't have to worry about them here."

"Si. Now I leave. The senorita will not mind staying alone?"

"No, I won't mind. I'm sure Ty and Carson will be along soon." And Sally looked again in amazement at the pump in the kitchen finally tearing herself away long enough to wave farewell to the three children in the back of the wagon. "Now to make supper." Humming to herself, Sally set about her task with pleasure.

Ty and Carson rode slowly towards the main street of town, their horses, seemingly unwilling to go far from Starlight and the food they smelled in the nearby livery. Turning west down the main street, Ty noticed the sign for the hotel. It was hanging crooked and the whole building presented a sorry looking sight as a place of shelter and rest.

"I reckon that Rohbar were right 'bout that there hotel. I wouldn't want ta keep my horses in that!"

"Yep. It's a purty sad lookin' thing fer a hotel," Carson agreed in disgust. "An' the rest a the town ain't that nice neither."

They rode in silence past the hotel and then, as a clean cut, well dressed man stepped up to them with the badge of a sheriff on his vest and a direct, honest look to his face, they halted. "Howdy," the sheriff greeted them. "New here?"

"Yep."

"If'n you have any trouble just let me know. I'm Sheriff Owen. This town hasn't had a sheriff for over a year an' we're still trying to get it cleaned up. An' welcome to Dead Horse."

"Thank ya, Sheriff. I don't reckon we'll be needin' yer help, but it's right nice ta know the Law's 'round." Ty shook the sheriff's hand before they moved on.

As the rode past the third saloon, neither one of the travelers noticed the men gathered by a window, nor saw that one of them moved out to the porch and watched until they turned into the yard of the new house.

CHAPTER TWENTY-THREE

After dismounting and taking their horses to the stables, Carson and Ty unsaddled and brushed their mounts and then removed the loads the other horses were carrying and took care of them. After feeding the animals, the two men made their way into the house where Sally was waiting for them.

"Ty!" she exclaimed the moment her brother was fairly inside. "Look! A pump in the kitchen. Have you ever seen anything like it? And see how the table looks! And so many windows! Why you can see in every direction if you go in the different rooms. There are five rooms in this house, Ty, five! Three downstairs and two more upstairs. You should go see them."

Ty chuckled. "If'n ya ain't goin' ta feed us any dinner till we take a look see, I reckon we ought ta move mighty quick 'cause I'm hungry."

Back at the saloon, the group of men waited in silence until their companion came back inside.

"Well, was it Elliot? An' who was with 'im? Where'd they go?" This was demanded by the roughest looking of the men, one who was evidently their unspoken leader.

Nodding his head, the young man who had just returned, sat down and reached for a glass of liquor on the table. "Yep, that were Elliot an' the old man 'pears ta be the one who took 'im away."

"That was nearly three years ago. An' ta think we'd find him here," chuckled Shorty.

The fourth man leaned across the table towards the youngest one and half snarled, "Ya never told us where they went, Duffer."

Duffer looked indignant. "I can't tell everything at once, Poker. Don't worry, they ain't gettin' away. They stopped at that new house at the edge a town."

"Anyone else there, Duff?"

"Naw, it's an empty house, an' it were jest the two a them."

Poker and Mason, the leader, looked at each other and then began conversing in low tones. If it was just those two, it shouldn't be too hard to put an end to that meddlesome Ty Elliot once and for all, and they might as well get rid of the old man at the same time for who knows what he might know. Should they get more guns? Poker didn't think so, not after all his bragging about being the fastest draw west of the Mississippi. What most people didn't know was that his fast draws were at the game table not with his gun. Mason sat thinking for several minutes before agreeing that they needn't call for more guns.

"What about Bartram?" asked Shorty referring to their leader.

"He's way off in Californy an' if'n we let Elliot go now, there's no tellin' where he'll show up an' what he might do. No, I think it's best ta jest take 'im now."

"Right now," gulped Duffer setting his mug down with a thud. "While it's still light?"

"Why not? Scared?" Poker taunted.

"I jest don't like that sheriff."

Shorty nodded his head in agreement.

"Well, Mason, what do we do?"

"Shut up a minute an' lemme think." Mason poured himself another glass and drained it before replying. "I reckon we'd best jest get 'im 'fore any others join 'um. They ain't suspectin' us so we've got the upper hand. We'll jest walk in an' take 'em."

"What'll we do after we get 'em?" Shorty wanted to know.

"Take 'em out a town, string 'em up an' then come get us another drink."

"Yeah!" This met the approval of everyone, and Mason, Poker, Shorty and Duffer raised their glasses for one last drink before rising and striding out of the saloon.

"We should each go a different way to the house then no one'll suspect us," Mason ordered in low tones. "Meet behind the stables."

The late summer day was quickly drawing to a close. The sun was nearly hidden behind the mountains and the sky was purple with cherry pink clouds, which were swiftly turning grey in the fading light. Already the moon was to be seen and the first brave star poked her face out to look about. In the town honest folks were inside eating their suppers and preparing for rest. But out in the streets the saloons were just getting ready for their night of drinking, gambling and carousing. Sheriff Owen sighed to himself as he sat down in his office in front of the jail. "I need a deputy. If those strangers are staying, I think the younger man would make a good one. As it is . . ." He left his sentence unfinished as he dozed off.

At the house, Ty and Carson, having inspected the upstairs to Sally's satisfaction, descended the stairs and moved to the front room. "Well, I hope Sally hurries up with that supper," Ty remarked. "I'm getting mighty hungry!"

Carson nodded.

Neither of them, usually so quick to hear signs of danger, heard the stealthy footsteps approaching the house nor did they hear the whispered words.

"Shorty, ya go watch the front door. We don't want 'em gettin' out that way. An' Duffer, ya stand guard at this door. We'll call ya if'n we need ya, but I reckon Poker an' I can handle 'em."

Low murmurs of assent followed these orders and then, with guns drawn, Mason and Poker softly opened the door.

No one was in the dark room, but a light shone from the room beyond. Creeping softly to the door, Mason cautiously peered out. There, near the window stood the man he and the others had been so anxious to shoot or hang: Ty Elliot. Beside him stood that old man.

Mason nudged Poker and suddenly they both sprang into the room while Mason ordered, "Put up yer hands both a you! Don't even think a reaching fer yer gun, Ty Elliot. I ain't the only one here."

"That's right, Elliot. An' don't forget I'm the fastest draw this side the Mississippi," Poker added with a growl.

Taken wholly by surprise, Ty and Carson had no choice but to raise their hands before their captors. Slowly, Mason and Poker, keeping their prisoners covered by their guns, moved into the middle of the room.

"Ya thought you could hide from us, didn't ya?" Mason taunted, leering at Ty.

Ty forced back the urge to take a swing at Mason though his hand above his head clenched.

"Yeah," Poker put in, "he thought he had gotten away. No one gets away from us forever."

"Won't Bartram be pleased when he hears what we caught," Mason asked his companion adding to Ty, "An' don't think a tryin' ta get away, the others are jest waitin' for ya."

"You'll swing yet, Mason," Ty declared between clenched teeth.

Sally had heard strange voices and, moving to the door of the kitchen, beheld the sight that had been her worst nightmare. Ty and Carson were standing with their hands raised while 'they' stood with drawn guns before them! For a moment she stood frozen with horror. Where had they come from? How had they gotten in without anyone knowing it? Could she go for help? All these thoughts flashed through her mind in less time than it takes to write it. Neither Ty nor Carson had seen her for both were watching for the slightest relaxing of the guns pointed at them.

Mason laughed. "It'll be you that's doin' the swingin'. You an' yer friend there. Too bad ya won't be here ta—" He got no farther.

"Drop your guns and reach for the ceiling!" The crisp order startled the two men. "I'm a dead shot if you care to find out. Drop them I say!"

Poker, so astonished and even somewhat frightened by this totally unexpected turn of events, dropped his gun. Mason half turned to see the speaker, letting his gun move away from Ty. That was all Ty needed, for his clenched fist connected with Mason's jaw while his other hand grasped the gun and with a mighty twist, wrenched it from his grasp.

Meanwhile Carson hadn't been idle. When Poker dropped his gun, Carson sprang forward like a panther and the next minute, Poker lay on the floor senseless.

It was all over in a matter of seconds and both the would-be killers were disarmed and unconscious on the floor at their feet.

"That's jest two a them," Ty muttered, swiftly binding Mason's hands behind him. "From the way they talked, I reckon Bartram ain't here, but that still leaves two others at least. I wonder where they are?"

"At the doors?" Carson guessed.

"Why't they come in at the noise?"

Carson shrugged. "Orders, maybe."

"Let's find out," answered Ty, grimly drawing his gun and softly moving to the door. "Put out the light, Carson. Sally, shut the door an' stay in the kitchen."

"But—" Sally began tremulously.

"In the kitchen. An' stay there 'less I call ya." Ty's voice was sterner than he meant it to be and Sally obeyed, shaking and still clenching her father's six-shooter.

With the kitchen door shut and the light put out, the room was left in semi-darkness while outside, things still had a late evening glow about them. Pulling open the door with one quick motion, Ty discovered Shorty standing before him. A look of complete bewilderment swept over his face as he stared at Ty. He had expected to find Mason or Poker, but instead here was the very man they had set out to hang! When Ty ordered him to unbuckle and drop his gun, Shorty just stood there stupefied.

"I said, drop yer gun, Shorty!" Ty barked.

With shaking hands, Shorty finally managed to do as he was told. Ordering him inside, Ty kept him covered while Carson tied his hands and retrieved his gun from the doorway.

"Who else is with ya?" Ty snapped the order out so suddenly that Shorty jumped as though he had been shot.

"D—Duffer," he gasped.

"Where is he?"

"B—by the b—back door."

"Is he armed?"

Shorty could only nod. This turn of events had completely unnerved him and now he sat shaking like a leaf.

Leaving Carson to stand guard over the prisoners, Ty slipped out of the front door and made his way around the house where he found Duffer pressing his ear against the door with his back to him.

"Unbuckle yer holster an' drop it on the ground."

Slowly Duffer stood up and half turned around.

"Drop it now or I will shoot!"

This order was no joke Duffer realized. Perhaps it was the sheriff thinking he was up to no good. If it was, he was sure he could talk his way out of it. Without turning, he said, "Sheriff, I weren't doin' no harm. I jest thought I heard a fight in there an' jest wanted ta make sure it weren't bad, ya know—"

Ty broke in, "I ain't the sheriff, Duffer, I'm Ty Elliot. Now drop yer gun!"

Evidently Duffer didn't believe him, for instead of unbuckling and dropping his gun, he suddenly whirled around and tried to draw. Instantly Ty fired and Duffer staggered back moaning and grabbing his right wrist.

Ty, keeping his own gun ever ready, strode over and jerked the young man's gun out of its holster and opening the door ordered him inside. Prodding him with his pistol, Ty followed him inside and into the room where the three other prisoners were.

Mason and Poker were returning to consciousness and now glared wrathfully at their captors.

"Elliot," Mason growled, "You'll pay fer this. We ain't done with ya yet."

"Maybe ya ain't, but I'm 'bout done with the lot a you. Here, Carson," Ty said, "Bind up Duffer's wrist an' then tie his hands behind him, will ya? I'll keep 'em all covered while ya do."

After doing as he was asked, Carson, with a pistol in each hand, stood watching the four disgruntled and wrathful men while Ty went into the kitchen.

CHAPTER TWENTY-FOUR

After shutting the door quietly behind him, Ty glanced about the room to find Sally standing with white face by the table, clutching the back of a chair with one hand and clasping her locket with the other. Her gun was in its holster upon the table.

"Sally, it's over. We got 'em." He sprang forward, for Sally swayed on her feet.

"Oh, Ty!" was all she could gasp out as she felt her brother's arms go around her. The room whirled, and she hung onto his shirt.

"We'll take 'em ta the sheriff an' let him lock 'em up till mornin'."

Sally looked up. "You got them all, alive?"

"All that were here. Don't know where Bartram is, but he ain't here."

"But, I thought I heard a shot."

"Duffer tried ta pull his gun on me. I shot his wrist. He ain't gonna die. Carson wrapped it up an' now he's tied up like the rest a 'em."

Reaction suddenly set in now that the danger was over and Sally started shaking. Her breath came quickly and her chin trembled.

Ty stared down at her in surprise. He had expected her to be glad and relieved. Hooking his foot on the rung of a chair, he pulled it out and set his sister in it for she seemed hardly able to stand. Swiftly, Ty brought her a glass of water from that wonderful pump and tried to get her to drink it, but she just stared into space, trembling, her hands twisting themselves in her skirt.

"Sally," Ty coaxed, "jest take a drink. Ya'll feel better I reckon."

"Ty, they had guns."

Sighing, Ty placed the glass on the table. "She'll feel better if'n she talks it out," he mumbled to himself pulling out a chair, straddling it and folding his arms over the back as he replied. "Yep, they had guns."

"They were pointing at you an' Uncle Bob!"

"Yep."

"I couldn't do anything. I couldn't even move."

"But ya did. Ya drew Pa's gun an' distracted 'em. That's what we needed an' ya did jest fine."

"I pointed a gun at a person!" Her eyes were wide with horror.

"So did I an' I had ta shoot," he countered softly.

"They were going to kill you."

"But they didn't."

"And then you wouldn't let me come. I was left here not knowing if I would see you alive again!" And Sally burst into tears burying her face in her arms and sobbing.

Standing up, Ty stepped beside her and gently stroked her hair. He knew the tears would help. "I didn't want ya gettin' hurt. An' ya know somethin', Pa would be right proud a ya for what ya done."

The tears were checked and muffled voice came from the bent head. "He would?"

"Sure 'nough. Ya done saved my life an' Carson's too. An' ya did it all without shootin' a shot. Though I'd kind 'ave enjoyed seein' Mason's face an' Poker's too if'n ya had shot a gun out a their hand.

"Ty Elliot!" Sally sat upright and looked reproachfully at him. "I might have shot you or Uncle Bob instead."

Ty only laughed. "Ya don't miss what yer aim'n for, Sis."

"Well, I wasn't aiming! It was all I could do to keep it from shaking. And I was praying I wouldn't have to shoot because I'd have missed by a mile."

Grinning, Ty pulled her to her feet and hugged her. "Well, are ya goin' ta come with us ta the sheriff or stay an' wait for us."

"I'm not letting you two go without me!"

"Then here," Ty picked up the holster.

Sally shuddered at the sight of it.

"If anyone deserves ta wear this, it's you, Sally." And Ty buckled it around her waist. "Come on, I reckon Carson's getting plenty restless an' I reckon they are too."

"'Bout time ya showed up, these here birds are tryin' my patience." Carson holstered one of the pistols and shoved the other in his belt. Grabbing his rifle from where it was leaning in the corner, he looked at Ty and Sally.

Sally had wiped away the tears and, though her face was still pale, she looked resolute. Ty handed her the gun belt he had taken from Shorty and, picking up the two other six-shooters from Mason and Poker where they had been kicked in the scuffle, held one in either hand.

"All right on yer feet an' let's get goin'," Ty ordered.

"Where ya takin' us?" asked Shorty.

"That don't matter, does it?" Ty replied as he helped him with no gentle hand to his feet and prodded him into line with a gun.

Mason was the only one who showed signs of resisting and Ty, relinquishing another gun to Sally, grasped him by the collar. "Don't try any tricks, Mason, 'cause my trigger finger jest might be a trifle twitchy an' I wouldn't want ta shoot ya 'fore the others. It might scare 'em." Ty's tone dripped with scorn, and Mason knew he'd show no mercy if he tried to escape.

Out in the street, with Carson on one side, Sally on the other and Ty right behind the four prisoners, they marched down to the jail past one saloon, then a second. Passed a rundown house to the jail. Here they halted.

"Sheriff!" Ty called out.

A light flickered on inside the building and in another moment Sheriff Owen appeared in the doorway. "What in blue blazes!" he exclaimed when he saw the group before him. "Get inside all of you. I don't want to start a ruckus in the streets."

The seven moved inside while the sheriff turned up the gas. On turning around he noticed for the first time who had brought the prisoners in. "Well I'll be. I thought you didn't need me."

"I weren't countin' on these here low-down, scum-suckin' yellow-livered rat-snakes bein' in town," Ty replied.

"What do you want done with them?"

"Lock 'em up for the night an' we'll be back ta see ya in the mornin'."

Sheriff Owen had taken up a bunch of keys and now unlocked the door behind his office leading to the jail. "And just what am I holding them for?" he asked as he unlocked the first cell.

"Attempted murder ta start with an' I'll fill the rest in later if'n that's all right with you. My supper's callin' me, an' I ain't hankerin' ta miss it." Ty, while he was talking, had untied Mason's hands and pushed him in to the cell followed by Poker.

The sheriff locked it and before long, Duffer and Shorty were locked in the adjoining cell. "I'll hold them for you until morning, but then you'll have to come in and give me the lowdown on them," the sheriff told Ty as they left the jail and returned to the office.

"I'll be here." Ty assured him, turning to go.

"Ty," Sally stopped him, "I don't think I really need two extra guns. One is enough for me."

"That's right; here ya are, Sheriff, the guns them snakes was usin' or tryin' ta use. They never did get 'round ta pulling the trigger, but—" and Ty left the sentence unfinished as he placed the six-shooter he was holding on the sheriff's desk beside the ones Sally and Carson had laid down.

"Fine guns. I'll keep them."

Returning to the house, Ty, Carson and Sally ate their supper and then turned in for the night. Sally didn't know it, but Carson and Ty took turns standing on watch throughout the night just in the event that Bartram or some other unwanted visitor should decide to pay them a visit.

Even when he wasn't on watch, Ty couldn't sleep. Every time he closed his eyes he could see the faces of Mason and Poker behind the muzzles of their six-shooters. Why were they here? How did they know he was here? Was Bartram around? If he wasn't here now, would he be likely to show up soon? Was Dead Horse a rendezvous for 'them'? Ty didn't know the answer to any of these questions, and he tossed and turned through the long night hours. He had thought he was safe this far from home. Must he always be on the watch?

The first faint streaks of day found Ty still awake and he arose with a new thought. He had to tell the whole story to the sheriff this morning. Everything. After three years of keeping it locked up inside of him, what would it be like to share it now? Drawing a deep breath, he let it out in a long sigh and turned from the window where he had been watching the sun paint the clouds a rosy pink and edge them with gold.

Carson too had spent a restless night. He chided himself for not being more attentive and letting them enter the house, and not only that, but to actually pull guns on him and Ty! "I reckon I'm jest gettin' too soft livin' in houses like this. There were a day ain't too long 'go neither, when they couldn't a come within three paces a the house without me knowin' it." And so he fretted for some time, until, as he was pacing the rooms downstairs, he began to realize what would have happened if he and Ty had heard 'them'. "We'd a had guns drawn an' it probably would a come ta a shoot-out, an' I reckon more'n one would a been shot. Perhaps it was providential that they come on us so sudden an' Sally caught 'em off guard. Maybe the good Lord didn't want no killin'." These thoughts made him a little easier in his mind, though he continued to strain his eyes and ears for the rest of his watch.

"Ty," Sally began as the three of them were enjoying a hearty breakfast, "I want to go see Starlight this morning. How long are you going to be seeing the sheriff?"

Ty looked up. "I ain't sure jest how long it'll take, but I reckon I can see ya ta the liv'ry else Carson can." He glanced at his friend. "There really ain't no need for more'n me ta go see Sheriff Owen."

Shaking his head Carson replied, "Ya ain't goin' ta the sheriff alone, Ty. I reckon we can see Sally ta the liv'ry an' the blacksmith, him with the funny name'll see she ain't bothered."

"I ain't goin' ta need ya, Carson," Ty began, "so if'n ya want ta—"

But Carson cut in. "Maybe ya ain't needin' me, but I reckon I'm goin' 'long jest the same. An' it ain't no use fer ya ta think different."

"But—"

Sally interrupted. "I'd really feel better if you were with him, Uncle Bob," she said sweetly. "I don't like 'them' even if they are behind bars. I can take care of myself as far from the jail as the livery. And," she added as she saw Ty frown, "Herr Rohbar and his pretty Juanita will take care of me." She smiled.

Seeing it was useless to argue, Ty agreed reluctantly but added, "Yer wearin' yer gun, Sally."

It was still fairly early when the trio left the house and started down the street. The sun was up and trying its best to shine through the cloudy sky. A cool breeze blew causing Sally to pull her shawl about her shoulders.

"It feels like rain," Carson remarked.

"Looks like it too," Ty agreed. "Sally, maybe we should a left ya at the house."

Shaking her head, Sally kept on walking. "I don't want to stay there alone."

"Come on, Ty, she'll be dry at the liv'ry or at—at—" and Carson floundered for the name of the blacksmith.

"Herr Rohbar," put in Sally.

They had reached the jail where the two men paused while Sally continued on. Suddenly she stopped, turned and, throwing her arms around her brother, whispered, "Be careful, Ty!"

CHAPTER TWENTY-FIVE

Ty and Carson waited until Sally had disappeared around the corner before turning and entering the jail.

Sheriff Owen was seated behind his desk with a steaming cup of coffee in his hands. "Morning," he greeted them.

Ty only nodded while Carson returned the greeting and asked about the prisoners.

"Oh, they're still there. A pretty silent lot, though I think there's one of them that might crack if we pressured him some."

"That'd be Shorty," Ty put in, glancing about the office casually.

"Well, you two gentlemen go ahead and take seats. You might as well get comfortable. You see, I'm eager to hear why those four yahoos attempted to murder you, how you got them and who that pretty gal was with you last night. Who's talking?" And the sheriff looked at his visitors.

"I reckon," Carson began seating himself on a chair and crossing his arms, "that Ty ought ta tell, seein' as they've been after him fer years now. An' that gal, that were Ty's sister." He looked at his companion, who had remained standing and now had his back to them. "Ty," he called, "get yerself a seat an' let's get ta the story."

There was no answer from Ty.

"What's he lookin' at?"

The sheriff leaned over. "Just the wanted list. Maybe he knows one of them. I checked it last night but none of those rowdies were listed."

"That's cause he ain't with 'em." Ty's voice was low but distinct.

"What's that?" the sheriff started up and with a stride was beside his young visitor. "You know one of them? Who?"

Ty pointed. "Bartram. They," and he jerked his head in the direction of the cells in the back room, "work for him."

"You don't say," whistled Sheriff Owen in surprise. "Bartram has a three hundred dollar price on his head. You think he's around here?"

Ty shrugged and turned away. "Hard ta tell. I reckon not. They want me, an' want me bad, so I kind'a figure if'n Bartram were here, he'd a been there last night too."

The sheriff nodded. "What did they want you for?"

For several minutes Ty sat in silence. At last he spoke. "I reckon I still ain't sure on some things. But now I know Bartram's an outlaw, things seem ta be fittin' better. Ya know if'n Bartram's wanted in any place else?"

"Sure. It seems like he's wanted every place west of the Mississippi and south of the Missouri. The U.S. Marshall mentioned him last time he was through here."

"The U.S. Marshall!" exclaimed Ty, and he looked a little startled.

"Yep."

Sitting down, one hand on his holstered gun, eyes gazing vacantly at the floor, Ty thought. Slowly the pieces of the puzzle, which had caused him many sleepless nights, were beginning to fit together. He still didn't have all the pieces, but perhaps the sheriff could help. And there was always Shorty. He'd talk if they got him away from Mason and Poker.

The sheriff waited patiently. He could tell Ty was trying to make sense of something. All was quiet in the room as the two men waited for Ty to speak. At last, with a shake of his head, he looked up.

"I still ain't sure how it all fits together, but I'll tell ya all I know. It were 'bout three years ago an' I were out trappin' back in the mountains where we live. Bein' used ta the woods an' the ways and sounds a the animals there, when I heard a sort a other sound, I reckoned I ought ta go see what it were. Well, I come to a rocky side a the mountain an' see them snakes and Bartram pilin' rocks up 'fore what used ta be a cave as though they was hidin' somethin'. Well, I jest stood an' watched 'em an' then I heard Bartram say, 'When things die down we'll come an get—' An' then he stopped. I knew they weren't up ta no good. Never did trust Bartram. Wasn't sure if'n he saw me or jest stopped. The others promised ta guard whatever it were an' then I must a shifted my foot or somethin'. Anyhow a rock moved an' every one jumped 'bout a mile an' all looked right scared fer jest a second. Then they saw it were me. I reckon they'd a shot me then an' there, only I had my hand already on my six-shooter an' I've beat 'em all at the draw 'fore . . ."

"Well," Sheriff Owen pressed as Ty left his sentence to die in the air. "I know you got away, but how?"

Even the rumble of thunder and the first spattering of rain on the roof wasn't noticed by Ty who sat as one lost, remembering a time past, unaware of his surroundings. It wasn't until Carson shook his arm that Ty was brought back to the present. "Finish the story, Ty," Carson ordered him.

"Ain't much left. I drew my gun, an' backed inta the woods. I knew I couldn't take on five a them at once 'less I had ta. Once under cover I jest disappeared. They all tried ta shoot me, but since they didn't know where I were, they jest wasted ammunition. An' some a them sure were jack asses. I could'a shot Shorty, Duffer an' Poker when they were chasin' me." Ty looked disgusted. "Bartram an' Mason though, they ain't so reckless. But I heard Bartram tell Mason that they had ta silence me. Weren't sure how much I saw. An', I reckon they didn't want no trouble. I went back ta the cabin an' found Carson there. Jest told Pa an' Sally I had ta leave for a while since some were set out ta shoot me or string me up. Carson an' I set out that night for the Colorado Territory. Weren't till earlier this year that we got back."

"So that's why ya rode in an' said ya had ta leave," Carson interjected. "Ya sure was closed mouthed 'bout it all."

"Jest didn't want Pa or Sally ta know nothin'. They'd a worried. Least ways Sally would a." Ty paused a moment before going on. "Pa was dyin' an' Sally had wrote ta me tellin' 'bout his bein' sick. We weren't there more'n a couple days but someone got wind a me bein' back or comin' back an' we had ta light out again."

"Don't you have a sheriff out your way?"

"Nope." Ty shook his head.

"Well!" Sheriff Owen looked astonished. "How long was Bartram around your parts?"

"'Bout two, three years 'fore I left, I reckon," replied Ty after thinking a moment.

"Two or three years," the sheriff mused. "But you left about three years ago . . . yes . . . that might fit . . . I wonder if it's still there?"

"What they hid?" Carson asked.

"Yeah. What do you think, Ty?"

Ty shrugged. "Could be. If'n they're still wantin' ta silence me, I wouldn't be surprised if'n it were there. But then 'gain . . ."

"It might not be," finished the sheriff. "I know."

"Do ya know what they might a been hidin' Sheriff?" asked Carson, quite curious.

The sheriff stroked his chin, stared at the opposite wall and frowned before saying slowly, "It could be money from a stage coach robbery that happened three and a half years ago. They never did find the gold. At least not that I know of."

The three men sat in silence as the rain poured down outside, turning the dust of the streets into mud. The lightning flashed in dazzling display of electric beauty while the thunder rumbled echoing and re-echoing from mountain to mountain, rolling across the sky like a cannon barrage.

Inside, all was quiet and dry. No one seemed inclined to talk, each was mulling over in his mind what he had heard. At last the sheriff stood up. "Anyone want some coffee?" he asked going over to pour himself another cup.

Both Carson and Ty declined.

"I'm going to wire the U.S. Marshall about those thieving foxes, and I'll let him know about Bartram too. I have a feeling he'll be quite interested in it all. You all are sticking around for a while, aren't you? Thinking of moving here, maybe?" Sheriff Owen tipped his chair back on two legs and leaned against the wall and looked hopeful.

Carson answered after glancing at Ty. "Don't reckon we'll be here long lest we have ta. One a our horses threw a shoe an' we got ta wait fer her ta get well 'fore we get another one on."

"Hmm." The sheriff sighed. "Ty?"

Ty turned from the window. "Yep?"

"You wouldn't want to consider sticking around here for a while would you?"

Ty eyed the sheriff. What did he have in mind? He had brought in some varmints, why did he want him around longer?

Almost as though he could read his thoughts, Sheriff Owen continued. "You see, this town is pretty rough. I'm the only law around and I'm looking for a deputy. I think you'd make a real good one, and I sure could use you."

"Me, deputy?" Ty looked incredulous.

"I don't see why not. You managed to bring those four yahoos in with only one shot fired didn't you?"

"Carson did most of it."

"Yep, Sheriff," Carson grinned, "I stood with a drawn gun while he jest rounded up Shorty an' Duffer. Disarmin'

195

Duffer an' scarin' Shorty so's his teeth were knockin' together. I sure did most."

Carson and Sheriff Owen laughed while Ty turned back to the window. After their laugh had subsided, the sheriff stood up and strode to Ty's side. Placing a hand on his shoulder he said, "I mean every word I said, Ty. I really could use you. This whole town could use you. What do you say?"

Ty turned around. His face wore a look of firm determination. "I can't stick 'round longer'n I have ta, Sheriff. It's right nice ta know I'm wanted, but I promised my Pa on his deathbed that I'd find my missin' youngest sister." He paused, drew a deep breath and then continued. "I ain't had much ta go off a, but it ain't been a year an' I aim ta keep goin' till I find her. I will keep my word, even if it takes me all my life." He added the last sentence in tones low and full of feeling.

The rain continued to fall outside and the only sounds heard as Ty finished talking were their drops on the roof and windows. "May it never be said that I kept a man from fulfilling his word." Sheriff Owen held out his hand and Ty shook it heartily. "So, how long is your horse going to be laid up?" He asked returning to his desk.

"I'd say maybe a couple a days, maybe a week," Carson answered.

"An' I reckon we ought ta be goin' ta check on her an' find out where Sally is," Ty put in.

Carson rose. "Reckon we ought."

"Well," said the sheriff as his two morning visitors stepped out onto the porch. "If you find out you'll be here for a week, come and see me. If I had you for a deputy for even a week I'm thinking we could clean up half the town."

Ty grinned. "Ya'd have ta build yerself a bigger jail first," he shot back. He couldn't think of himself as a deputy sheriff. "Let us know if'n ya hear from the U.S. Marshall," he added, stepping out into the muddy street while Sheriff Owen chuckled.

"I'll do that," the sheriff called after them. "Keep your guns dry."

Neither Ty nor Carson talked as they set off down the street towards the livery and blacksmith's.'

Rebekah A. Morris

CHAPTER TWENTY-SIX

It was still raining when the two companions reached the livery. Tramping through the mud had been no easy matter and they were both wet and their boots were filthy. There was no Sally to be seen in the stall with Starlight and, after checking on the horse, Ty and Carson started for the blacksmith's shop. Here they were greeted from the doorway by Herr Rohbar.

"Velcome, mine herrs! Ze fraulein she ish keeping mine Frau Senora company an playing vith the kindders, nein? But mine Herrs! Your clothes zay are vet! Come in by mine fire, zay shall soon be dry. I call mine Nita. She bring you hot drink, nein?" Before either man could protest, if he had wanted to, Herr Rohbar had pulled open the door leading from the smithy to the little house where his family lived and called, "Nita, bring hot drinks for our fraulein's bruder an' friend!"

"Si, my esposo. I bring drinks and food," was the soft reply heard from the other side of the door.

"She come," Herr Rohbar informed his visitors as though they couldn't hear his wife's answer.

Carson and Ty simply nodded. Both were standing near the blazing fire warming up. The rain had been cold, giving them a taste of the coming fall as it penetrated their clothing.

"Glad we ain't out on the trail, Ty," remarked Carson, rubbing his hands together.

"Mr. Rohbar," Ty turned to the blacksmith.

"Ja?"

"Our horse, how soon ya think she can get her shoe on?"

Herr Rohbar thought. "Ze horse, she ish not much hurt. Rest today an' tomorrow. I maybe think I can give her new shoe Monday. You vant much to be gone from Dead Horse?"

"Jest wantin' ta get back on the road 'fore long."

Before more talking could be done, the door opened and Frau Senora Juanita entered with a tray of steaming mugs and a plate of cakes. Behind her came Sally carrying the baby and wearing a look of relief as she caught sight of her brother and Carson.

Ty took the offered mug with a smile and murmured thanks. He was watching his sister.

"Oh, Ty!" she sighed softly, "you are back. I was worried. It was taking so long. They won't get out will they?"

"Not them," snorted Ty in low tones, glancing about the shop. Carson and Herr Rohbar had already begun a conversation, and Mrs. Rohbar was ushering the older two children back into the house. No one was paying any attention to the brother and sister.

Sally shifted the child from one arm to the other. "Isn't he sweet, Ty?" she asked as the young one nestled his head against her neck and offered a timid smile to Ty.

Returning the smile, Ty agreed.

"What is the sheriff going to do with 'them'?"

Trying to smother a yawn, Ty replied, "He's wirin' the U.S. Marshall 'bout 'em cause Bartram is their leader an' he's a wanted man."

Sally looked concerned. "Does that mean we have to stay here until he comes?"

Ty shook his head. "Nope. I want ta leave soon's we can. The blacksmith said he thinks he can get a shoe on Starlight day after tomorra."

"Ty, that reminds me. Tomorrow is Sunday and the Rohbar's invited us to go to church with them. I accepted for all of us. I didn't think you would mind." She looked anxiously up at him. Would he mind going to church? He had gone when he was at home, but that had been years ago. "Please."

"Ya really want ta go?"

She nodded.

"We ain't got any goin' ta meetin' clothes, Sis."

"That's all right. I can wash and mend a few things this afternoon and if you and Uncle Bob, no," she paused as she glanced across the room. "Uncle Bob doesn't shave, but you can. You'll look real handsome after you shave and have some nicer clothes on."

"As handsome as Joe Fields?" Ty couldn't resist asking.

"More handsome," Sally stoutly insisted, though her cheeks flushed.

"All right. I'll go. Ya got ta convince Carson ta go though, if'n ya want him."

"I will," Sally smiled. Her heart was light with the prospect before her, and she began to plan what they would wear.

Soon the call for dinner was heard and Herr Rohbar urged his guests inside to partake. No one hesitated, for the tantalizing smells had been teasing their stomachs for some time and a hot meal on such a rainy day was not to be turned away. Very pleasant it was to sit in a warm, dry house listening to the rain outside and partaking of the marvelous Mexican food, with a few German dishes added, which Frau Senora Juanita Rohbar had carefully prepared.

There was not much talking during the meal and when it was over, Ty rose, thanking the Rohbar's for their hospitality and preparing to depart. Carson and Sally also arose with expressions of thanks. Sally was anxious to hear all about the interview with the sheriff and she knew Ty well enough to know that he wouldn't talk about it before others.

The rain had mostly stopped except for an occasional drizzle, but the streets were a mass of solid mud.

"Ah, mine Herrs," Herr Rohbar protested, rising and stopping before the door in dismay. "You vould not think of taking ze young fraulein out in zat mud! Ja, ze rain, she ish shtopped, but ze road it ish notting but mud. Nein! Her shoes, zay vill be ruined! An' her clothes! Nein, you vait for a leetle vile."

"I'm wearing boots," Sally said, smiling and lifting up the edge of her skirts.

"But your skirt!" The blacksmith was quite upset. "Nein! Nein! Dass ist nicht gut!" In his distress he lapsed into his native tongue. "Vait!" he exclaimed suddenly. "I vill hitch up ze vagon an zen you can ride home vith comfort."

"Si!" His pretty wife agreed.

But Carson protested, "Rohbar, that mud's so deep ya'd sink up ta the hubs a the wheels 'fore ya'd a gotten ta the main street. I reckon Sally can walk on the boardwalks 'long the street an' it ain't goin' ta hurt her any. If'n she's afraid a the mud, she ain't the daughter a my best friend."

After a speech like that, Sally couldn't have been paid to ride in a wagon. "It was very kind of you to offer, Mr. Rohbar, but I don't mind walking. And," she added with a smile for the missus, "a little mud never hurt any of my clothes. Good-bye!"

The trip back to the house took longer than any of them expected, for the mud was so thick and heavy that it pulled on their boots making walking in the street almost impossible. At last, however, the trip was ended, as all trips eventually do, and the trio were sheltered once again in the dry, cozy house near the edge of town.

Ty brought in wood and Carson started a blazing fire while Sally prepared to wash and mend the best of their clothes in preparation for the morrow. Without any trouble she had secured Carson's approval to attend church in the morning with the Rohbars.

The afternoon and evening passed quickly by. As she was mending, Sally questioned her brother and Carson about what had happened during their visit to the sheriff. Though she was relieved that Mason, Poker, Shorty and Duffer were now in jail, she was horrified to find out why Ty had had to leave home so quickly. "Ty, when we get back home, we need to get a sheriff."

"Reckon yer right."

Sally sewed a few minutes in silence. "Ty," she began again, "I can't think of anyone who would make a good sheriff. They're either too old or too busy or something. You could be the sheriff."

Ty snorted and looked disgusted while Carson grinned.

"What?" Sally asked, puzzled.

Seeing that Ty didn't intend to answer her, Carson did. "It's jest that Ty's been asked by the sheriff here ta stay an' be his deputy."

"You would make a real good one, Ty," Sally said slowly.

"I ain't gonna be no deputy," he retorted. "I've got other things ta do an' I ain't stayin' 'round this here town."

"Of course we aren't staying," soothed Sally. "We aren't going to really stay anywhere until we find . . . her." It always felt a bit awkward talking about the missing Eleanor Elliot.

Hardly any more talk was had that evening, and in silence, the trio prepared for the next day.

The sun was shining and the mud on the streets was not as impassible as it had been, when Carson, Ty and Sally set off for the little church. Several birds were singing brightly up in the clear sky on that quiet morning. Sighing a contented sigh, Sally tucked her hand through her brother's arm, and, when he glanced down at her, she smiled up at him, though there were tears in her eyes as she whispered, "It's been so long."

It was a very quiet afternoon which the trio spent back at their temporary home following the church service. Sally wrote a letter to the Fields. It was only the third letter she had written in her life and it took her most of the afternoon as well as part of the evening.

After supper, Carson and Ty sat before the fire, Carson checking over the bridles for their horses and Ty busy with knife and wood, whittling while Sally labored over her letter at the table.

"Ty," Carson began, "if'n we leave tomorrow, where ya thinkin' a headin'?"

"Ain't sure. Jest on."

"Ya know winter's comin'. It ain't here now, but I reckon that cold rain yesterday wouldn't a been so nice out in the open. What ya think a goin' from town ta town, least ways till we get us a clue a some kind. Lest a course ya was wantin' ta change yer mind 'bout that deputy notion the sheriff's got." He grinned as Ty glowered and snorted.

Silence descended for a time with only the soft crackling of the fire, the scratching of Sally's pencil across the paper, a soft brushing sound from Ty's knife and a gentle jingle now and then from the bridles. Outside the shouts and music from the saloons disturbed the Sunday evening hush which was seeking to settle over the town, lulling the townsfolk into slumber, preparing them for the week of work ahead.

Sally laid down her pen at last. "I wrote a letter; I don't know if it is the proper way to write one or not. But Ty, I did want to tell them where we are heading next," she added the last wistfully.

"What about headin' fer Thorn Holler? Rohbar said it's 'bout a five day trek if'n we're goin' slow."

Ty paused in his whittling. "What direction's it in?"

"Southwest."

"Well, I reckon jest 'bout any place'd do, seein' we ain't got anythin' ta go on. I sometimes think we were closer ta findin' her back at Fort Laramie."

"We will find her, Ty," Sally protested. "It hasn't even been a year. We can't give up now."

"I ain't givin' up, Sally. I'll find her even if I have ta go over this here United States on foot!"

Leaning back in his chair, Carson crossed his feet and drawled, "Well, I'm a hopin' we ain't goin' ta have ta do much walkin' I ain't use ta it."

Sally couldn't keep from smiling at Carson's attempt to cheer Ty, and then with great care wrote:

"Ty and Carson said we are going to Thorn Hollow next. It is a five day trip if we go slow. I will try to write from there. Sally."

After fastening the locks Carson had discovered on the doors, the trio turned in for the night.

CHAPTER TWENTY-SEVEN

"Shall we go ta the liv'ry an' check on Starlight?" Ty asked as the three were eating their breakfast the next morning.

No objections were raised and before long Ty, Carson and Sally were in the street heading for the livery. As they reached the jail, Sheriff Owen hailed them.

"What's up?" Carson asked. "Don't tell me ya let them birds fly the coop."

"Ha," the sheriff scoffed. "They're not getting out of this jail in a hurry. At least not on their own. I just have some news." He beckoned them all in.

"What kind a news?" Ty asked questioningly, leaning against the wall and crossing his arms.

"Well," began the sheriff, offering a chair to Sally and then perching himself on the corner of his desk, "I got a wire from the U.S. Marshall. It turns out he's only on the other side of Rockslide Pass and should get here by the middle of the week. He doesn't think it'll be hard to get the evidence we need to hang them all, but he was wanting you," and he looked at Ty, "to tell me exactly where the cave is you mentioned. That is, if you can remember."

"I reckon I can recall it, but what good's it goin' ta do with the Marshall here an' that stuff back there?"

"I don't know for sure, but I think he'll either go there himself or contact the closest law to those parts to look for it. Now, can you tell me where it is?"

"Yep, long's I ain't got ta write it."

The sheriff smiled. "I'll write and you talk."

Ty nodded and for several minutes thought while the sheriff gathered paper and pen and seated himself at the desk.

At last Ty began, "Jest ask any a the town folk a Mel's Ridge how ta get ta Pine Draw. I reckon it's 'bout four miles inta it 'fore ya reach a rock 'bout the size a that saloon 'cross the street."

Rapidly the sheriff's pen scratched across the page. Having had a good education, he was well used to writing and as the pause from Ty grew in length, he looked up. "Then where do you go?"

"Ya got that writ already?" Ty looked astonished.

"Yep."

"Well, I'll be! I ain't never seen no one who could write that fast. Now, lemme think, ya got ta turn north jest after that rock an' folla the trail. It ain't a large one, but the local trappers can find it for ya. Once ta the top a the draw, ya'll come ta woods. Jest take a straight north course an' when ya reach the other side ya'll find the side a the mountain. It's mostly jest rock, but 'bout the middle of the cliff there is, or least there use ta be, a snarly old pine an' jest behind it and up, oh I reckon, 'bout three feet'll be the cave. Course if'n they ain't uncovered it, it'll still be piled with rocks."

"It sure sounds like you know what you're talking about, Ty," remarked Sheriff Owen after he had read the directions aloud and Ty had confirmed them. "Were you ever lost in those mountains?"

"Only once when I weren't more'n eight years old."

Standing up, the sheriff held out his hand to Ty. "Thank you for helping clear our town of four undesirable residents. You sure you don't want to stay for a few weeks and help clean up the rest of the town?"

"Sure," Ty replied, shaking the sheriff's hand. "We're goin' ta check on the horse now an' I'm wantin' ta be gettin' on today."

"Where are you heading?" questioned the sheriff, as he followed the three companions out of the door.

Carson answered, "Thorn Holler."

"Well, if I don't see you again before you leave, good luck and God speed."

"Thanks."

"Ah, mine Herrs and Fraulein, you have come to see about your horse, nein?" Herr Rohbar came out of his shop wiping his hands on his large apron. "Vell, I have good news. Ze horse, she ish ready to have ze new shoe put on. Zees days of rest ver vat she needed. Now she get ze new shoe."

"What about the other shoes?" Carson asked.

"On zis horse?"

Carson nodded.

"I shecked them. I vill put in a new nail in vone of them, but ze others, zey are fine."

Ty turned to Carson, "I reckon it wouldn't hurt none ta have 'im check the other horses. I ain't want'n ta lose another shoe."

"Sounds like a mighty fine plan ta me. Gonna take Sally with us?"

Ty glanced around, but Sally was not to be seen.

A chuckle came from the blacksmith. "You are looking for ze fraulein, nein? Mine kindders, zay come to ze door to see who their papa talk to. Ven zay see their freund, yer schwester, zay fraulein, zey shmile an' she go to zem. Ah, ze kindders, zay vill be sad to see ze fraulein go, an' my Frau Senora Juanita vill too. It ish not many freunds she have here." The good blacksmith ended his talk with a sigh.

Carson and Ty exchanged glances. Then Ty spoke. "Mr. Rohbar, if'n we brought our other horses, would ya mind checkin' their shoes?"

"Nein! Nein! Bring yer horses an' I vill check zem."

It was shortly after noonday that the travelers, Sally, Ty and Carson rode at last out of Dead Horse, heading for Thorn Hollow. All the horses were in fine spirits after their unexpected rest and pranced and tossed their heads in the warm sunshine. Ty had mixed feelings. Though most of the weight had been lifted from his shoulders when he turned Mason, Poker, Shorty and Duffer over to the sheriff, he still wondered about Bartram. Would he, too, show up at an unexpected time? Must he always wonder and watch? Would he never be able to truly put that experience behind him?

Also, the fact that no positive clue of any kind had been discovered about his sister since they left Fort Laramie was causing serious doubts of ever finding her to torment him. The clue they had gotten at South Pass might or might not have been true. Perhaps they should have continued on to California or Oregon. Would they have to backtrack as a tracker does when he has lost the trail? Unknowingly, Ty's brows had drawn together, and he neither replied to Carson's question nor noticed his horse was lagging behind.

"Cheer up, Ty," Carson called, having reined in his horse to wait until Ty rode up and then slapping him on the back.

Ty looked up startled, his hand instinctively reaching for his holstered gun.

Carson laughed and knocked Ty's hand away. "I jest said, cheer up. Ain't nothin' ta shoot. Why Son, yer as grim as an old billy goat who's beard jest got pulled. Ya said ya wanted ta make tracks, well by thunder, let's make 'em! These here horses are jest longin' fer a good gallop since the road is right dandy. Why, even them pack horses seem ta think their pullin' a stagecoach an' are in an awful hurry. Now, are ya goin' ta join us or are Sally an I goin' ta leave ya in the dust?"

Ty looked a little sheepish. "I reckon I'll join ya. Let's go!" And with a loud whoop and a wave of his hat, Ty let

Par have his head, which he had been trying to get for the past mile and away they all went.

Racing down the road in that fashion with manes and tails streaming behind and the wind in his face, brought back memories to Carson of the days when he and Jake Elliot were boys together and used to race their horses on the level stretches of road between their two homes. The race didn't last long and when Ty, who was in the lead, pulled his horse to a walk, there was no trace of the grim expression he had previously worn.

Sally came up with streaming hair, rosy cheeks and laughing eyes. "That was fun," she gasped shaking back her hair from her face. "Starlight didn't want to stop, did you Girl?" and Sally patted her horse's neck. As though in answer, Starlight tossed her head with a whicker causing all three riders to laugh.

"That made me feel like a lad again when yer pa an' I use ta race."

"Who won, Uncle Bob?"

"It were different each time. Ain't sure who won most, it were mostly jest fer fun."

"Well, I reckon we ain't likely ta do much a that kind a ridin'," Ty remarked. "But that were jest dandy. Didn't know Par had it in 'im." Ty gave his mount a gentle slap on the neck.

The trip to Thorn Hollow was made in four days since the trio were used to long days of riding and had good mounts. It was the afternoon of the fourth day when the town came into sight. This town was more up and coming than Dead Horse had been and they found the hotel to be quite satisfactory. On the day after their arrival, Ty, Sally and Carson began their usual questioning of the townsfolk. "Has anyone heard of a family named Westlin? They had many daughters and might have come through about eleven years ago." Always it was the same, "Never heard of them. Sorry."

After three days of fruitless searching, the companions set off for the next town.

There the same story was repeated. No one had heard of the family searched for, but perhaps in the next town they would have news. At each town Sally wrote to the Fields always telling them where they were heading next, always hopeful that the next letter might have better news.

And so the days passed. Towns were one by one reached, the townsfolk questioned and the trio moved on. Hope and faith grew dim and almost dwindled into nothing as town after town only brought fresh disappointments. Could they go on like this much longer? No longer did they race their horses between towns, but plodded along seemingly unmindful of the coolness in the air or the brisk north winds which blew, bringing autumn and winter snows.

Ty especially seemed disheartend and scarcely spoke. Lost in thoughts of the past and full of bleak thoughts for the future, he rode day after day and sat by their evening fires scarcely eating.

Sally began to grow concerned and looked anxiously at Carson when, one evening, Ty wondered away from camp to stand on a bluff overlooking a river. "I just can't stand to see him like this, Uncle Bob," she confessed watching her brother. "Why don't we find out anything?"

"Could be we ain't on the right trail any more. I'm thinking maybe it'd be best if'n we stayed the winter at the next town an' then start up the search 'gain in spring," Carson replied slowly.

"Do you think Ty will agree to settle down?" Sally asked.

Shrugging his shoulders, Carson also watched his young friend. He strongly doubted that Ty would consent to halt the search, at least not until the snows of winter forced him to. What were they to do?

For several minutes Sally watched Ty. She had been praying every day that some clue would turn up. Even if it meant they had to go hundreds of miles, anything would seem good news at this point. At last she stood and, after shaking the leaves off her skirt, slowly made her way over to Ty's side.

Carson watched until she reached him, then, turning away, he wandered away into the woods where in a quiet, sheltered spot, he knelt in prayer for the two young lives so dear to his heart. He prayed also for his missing Sunshine wherever she was at that moment.

CHAPTER TWENTY-EIGHT

Standing a few feet from the edge of the bluff with folded arms, Ty remained still as Sally approached.

"Ty," she ventured softly seeing that he didn't turn to look at her, "you can't give up now. We will find her."

Ty didn't move or even seem to be listening.

Uncertain of what to do or say next, Sally, too, remained silent and looked out across the river. Only the rushing of the waters below, the restful chirps of a lone bird and the rustle of wind through the colored leaves disturbed the stillness of the evening. As Sally glanced down into the waters far below, the sudden remembrance of that dreaded cliff over which they had passed on their way to Fort Laramie swept over her and she caught her breath, grasping Ty's arm fiercely and backing away from the edge.

Startled by her actions, Ty looked down at her. "Sally!" he exclaimed. "What's happened?"

She shuddered, still hanging on to his arm. "That cliff. It reminded me of—" A shiver ran over her before she could finish.

Ty finished the sentence for her. "Of the cliff where that there mountain lion were?"

She nodded.

"Well, we ain't going ta have ta walk 'long this side a the cliff. Ya jest can't be thinkin' 'bout that other place," Ty added pulling his sister back towards the cliffs where he had been standing, but she hung back. "Come on," he coaxed, "ya didn't use ta be scared a cliffs."

"Can I sit down?" she ventured, timidly moving forward once again.

For answer, Ty led her to a large rock which made a pleasant seat. There the two remained in silence, watching the river for several minutes.

At last, Sally, glancing at her brother and noticing the grim look begin to steal across his face, asked softly, "You aren't giving up, Ty, are you?"

"Givin' up?" Ty repeated almost fiercely. "No! It's jest that I ain't sure what ta do now. I can't stop till I got the trail 'gain. An' that," he sighed, "seems utterly hopeless."

"We can pray about it,"

Ty grunted. "It ain't helped."

"But it can," Sally persisted. "Ty," she began again after a moment, "when you were so sick at the Fields, I didn't know what to do. I tried to pray, but it didn't seem to work because I wanted God to make you better right away and He didn't. Then one night, it was the night you began to grow better, I had gone outside and Joe came and talked to me. He explained everything to me and then I knew."

"Knew what?" Ty asked gently, for Sally's face wore a look of such love and peace that Ty was awed.

"Knew that sometimes God says yes right away and sometimes He says no because he has a better plan, and other times he says just to wait and trust Him." Sally had been watching the reflection of the setting sun on the river and now turned her eyes to her brother's face. "Ty, I don't think God has said no to finding our sister, I think he has just said wait."

"Humph," Ty frowned, "then why did we come this way anyway?"

"Why Ty!" exclaimed Sally. "If we hadn't come then 'they' would still be free to try to kill you instead of behind bars where they can do no harm. And if Starlight hadn't thrown that shoe, we wouldn't have stayed in Dead Horse anyway and—"

"Okay," Ty cut her short. "So this here trip weren't a complete waste a time. I jest don't see what we're ta do next!"

"You could try praying. Pa always did, and it helps me. It helps Carson too. He said so." Ty didn't reply and so, after a few more minutes of quiet, Sally rose softly and slowly made her way back to the fire where Carson was waiting.

Alone on the cliff, Ty sat in thought. Was Sally right? Did praying help? From a child his father had taught him from the Bible. He knew in his mind what was promised in it, but never had he tested and proved it. Why not? Honestly he didn't know. He just never had gotten around to it he supposed. Didn't he have time? Plenty of time, but never before did he feel the need of some help outside of his own strength and ability. "I can't find her on my own, Pa," he muttered to himself. "I need help." But still Ty waited, his thoughts in turmoil. Was he wanting to come to God just because he had a problem he couldn't solve? If that were so, would he, once help had been received, not turn his back on the One who had helped him? Such a sudden great longing for a talk with his father came over Ty that he sank down on the rock where Sally had sat and buried his face in his hands while great, silent sobs shook his strong frame. In all his life, never had he remembered feeling so alone and helpless. His father was gone! Never could he go to him in trouble, never would he tramp the woods with him, never hear his voice!

"Oh, God of my father! God of my mother, do not forsake me!" In the darkness of the night no one saw Ty slip to his knees beside that rock, no one but the loving Father who had been tenderly seeking His lost sheep over mountains and plains, leading, drawing and now bringing him home safely on His shoulders. The wrestling was over and Ty knelt, feeling a closeness to God that he had never experienced before. The moon rose, but still Ty remained on his knees unmindful of the fog that rose up around him. At last a great longing, which he had once thought was the desire to find his sister, was gone. He felt satisfied. He knew he would someday fulfill his vow to his father, but he was no longer discouraged.

All night Ty remained on the cliff. As the first grey of dawn appeared, Ty looked up and whispered, "Pa, I ain't givin' up. I'll find her." He stood with bared head, and a look of firm conviction on his face. "God helpin' me, I'll do it!"

When Sally awoke, she found Ty sitting beside the fire while their breakfast was cooking. For a moment she just lay there and watched him. There was a new look on his face. In some respects he seemed older, more sure, while in others . . . Sally couldn't quite figure out the difference.

Just then Ty noticed she was awake. "I was beginin' ta wonder if'n ya were goin' ta sleep all mornin'."

Sally sat up. "Ty, what . . ." she paused unsure of what to say.

With a smile, Ty reached out and gently squeezed her arm. "Everything's all right now. I reckon we'll jest keep on goin' from town ta town 'till the Good Lord tells us different. An' Sally," he added softly, "yer right, it does help ta pray."

"Oh, Ty!" Nothing else needed to be said.

That morning, for the first time since they had left their own cabin months before, Sally unwrapped the family Bible from its place on one of the packhorses and read aloud a few verses marked by their mother's hand so many years before.

In silence, Carson listened, recalling those days of long ago when Jake's Ellen would read from the Bible.

After that, everyone was more cheerful, more hopeful. They continued asking at each town, each village and each lonely farmhouse or shack, but it was always with the same unsatisfying answer: "Never heard a them." The days followed days turning into weeks, which in turn turned into months. They had left the mountains and were now in the lower desert lands heading more west than south. The year was rapidly drawing towards a close. Up in the mountains the snows of winter already held the small towns prisoner; however, down in the desert, the weather, though cooler during the night, was pleasant and the traveling was comfortable for the most part. They would have made better time if they hadn't stopped so often, but no one seemed to mind the stops.

"Ya know," Carson remarked one day after three days of only coming to one small shack at which no one was home, "I reckon we ought ta've reached the Nevada border by now."

"'Crossed it some days back," retorted Ty.

Carson snorted. "How'd ya know?"

"Jest did," Ty answered. Then, seeing his older friend's look of disbelief, he added, "Asked the last man we saw how far it were. I reckon you were already on yer horse."

"Well, I don't care if we are in Nevada or not," Sally sighed. "I just wish we'd find a town. I'm growing tired of riding day after day and not getting anywhere."

"Sure seems that way!" Ty agreed with his sister. There was not a lot of variety in the semi-arid lands they were now riding through. Plains and hills dotted with scrub trees and bushes. It was nothing like the rugged, towering mountains they had just come through nor yet like the vast expanse of prairie they had glimpsed on their ride to Fort Laramie on the eastern side of the mountain ranges.

Mile after mile the trio rode onward. Suddenly Sally screamed.

"What is it?" Ty exclaimed, half drawing his gun while Carson began scanning the nearby landscape to see what had caused Sally's fright. "Sally! What's wrong?"

Sally's lower lip was trembling and she clutched her locket. Looking up into her brother's concerned face she wailed, "Ty, tomorrow is Christmas! I don't want to spend Christmas out here in the middle of no where!"

Releasing his breath in a long sigh, Ty pushed his gun back in its holster. "Ya sure had me thinkin' somethin' was wrong, Sis."

"There is," persisted Sally. "Don't you think we can reach some town tonight?"

Ty looked over at Carson.

"I ain't sure jest how far we are from Sagebrush, but I reckon it won't hurt ta try. If'n we can get these here horses ta move faster'n a turtle." So saying, Carson nudged Flint, and the horse, not objecting to a faster gait, obliged willingly.

"There's Sagebrush," Carson called back to his companions as he reached the top of a hill and saw the few building lying before him.

"It's 'bout time," Ty called back. "I were startin' ta think the sun were goin' ta set 'fore we got there."

Already the sun was fast slipping down towards the western horizon. They were all tired, having ridden for ten days, and the last hours they had pushed their mounts on faster than usual, for the thought of spending Christmas Eve alone under the stars was not appealing.

Riding into the town, Carson and Ty kept a lookout for a hotel, but to their amazement, there wasn't one. "What's this?" Ty grumbled. "Ain't they even got a hotel or some such place for travelers?"

Carson shrugged. "I reckon maybe they don't get travelers enough ta build one. Shall we spend the night at the liv'ry?"

"Ty," Sally rode up beside her brother and touched his arm. "There's a church over there. Listen! Ty, it's a Christmas Eve service. Oh, do let's go!" Sally had pointed to a small, wooden structure, which was obviously a church, and before which several horses stood tied to the hitching posts and multiple wagons waited in the growing dusk.

Ty looked at Carson who nodded. "All right. Perhaps we can find a place ta stay too, else we're goin' ta be sleepin' outside 'gain if'n it is Christmas Eve."

The service had already started when the trio of friends slipped in the door. The room was quite full with men standing in the back, and seemingly every seat full. But, somehow one was found for Sally.

The last verse of "Silent Night" was being sung as Sally squeezed onto a bench where one of the men had given up his seat. The minister arose. He was a grey haired man, worn from years of living out in the wilderness far from the comforts of city life. But, though he looked rugged in nature, his face was kind and his smile warm and friendly.

"Dear friends," he began in a voice which reminded Sally of the wind in the pine trees which grew by their cabin, soft and soothing, yet with a feeling of power and just a touch of hidden fierceness. "Let us now read the words of St. Luke and hear the story which never grows old."

Never had Ty or Sally listened to the reading of the first Christmas with such personal interest. Before it had just been a story, now it was real, personal, for this Jesus, this One born that night so long ago, was their Savior, their Emmanuel, their Prince of Peace! Eagerly they listened to each word the old minister uttered.

"And now, friends and strangers alike, let us also remember the good news that Christ is born and share it with others as did the shepherds and let us give Him the only gift he wants: ourselves. Let us rise and sing my favorite Christmas carol, 'Joy to the World'!"

The little wooden church seemed filled to bursting with the glorious strains of Christmas cheer as everyone, young and old, man and woman, farmer, rancher, townsman and trapper, Indian and stranger joining their voices that Christmas Eve night in the little town of Sagebrush out in the middle of nowhere.

After a short but heartfelt prayer and benediction, the folks began to make their way out to their horses or wagons. Many of them stopped to shake hands with Ty, Carson or Sally and everywhere people were wishing each other a merry Christmas. As the crowd began to diminish, the old minister managed to make his way down the church to greet the three strangers who had come in.

"It was good to have you come in tonight," he said shaking hands with Carson. "I don't believe I've met you before?"

"Nope," Carson replied and then introduced himself and his companions.

"Strangers to Sagebrush? Where are you staying?"

"Well, seein' as we ain't seen a hotel, I reckon—" but Ty got no farther for the minister interrupted.

"You will stay at my house. No," he put up his hand as Ty opened his mouth to speak. "I insist. If you refuse it would be a lonely Christmas for me, for my wife passed away in the spring. So you see, you are really doing me a favor by accepting. Though," he added looking at Sally with a fatherly smile, "I wish she were here to welcome you."

After that, how could the weary travelers refuse even if they had wanted to. Sally for one, was grateful for the hospitality.

Following their guide to a pleasant house across the street, Sally remained there with their host while Carson and Ty took the horses to the livery.

Later that night, after a meal of delicious stew, when Sally had excused herself and gone to her room, the three men sat about the fire in silence.

"What brings you three out traveling on Christmas Eve?" the old minister asked at length when the silence had stretched on for some time and only the ticking of the grandfather clock was heard.

Ty had become lost in his own thoughts, staring into the flames yet seeing nothing but memories, so it was up to Carson to answer the minister. He told the story of their search to find Ty and Sally's missing sister. Of their trek to Fort Laramie where they found out the family's name and then of their stopping when Ty got shot and ending up with their arrival in that town in time for the service.

"What was the family's name?" the old minister asked.

"Westlin. Ever heard of 'em?"

The minister shook his head. "No, can't say that I have. But then, I have a hard time remembering names though faces comes easy for me. My wife now, God bless her, remembered every name she ever heard, I verily believe. But, it's growing late and you and your friend must be tired after your long trip. Suppose we turn in for the night. We've got a whole day tomorrow to talk."

Carson nodded. "Sound's mighty good ta me. Ya comin' Ty?"

When Ty didn't answer, Carson shook his arm but still Ty didn't respond. "I reckon we'll jest leave him alone. When he's ready, he'll turn in."

Leaving a lamp burning low, the minister and Carson went off to bed leaving Ty lost in memory.

The clock was striking two o'clock when Ty roused himself. All was still. Not a sound was to be heard in the streets. Only the muffled sound of someone snoring gently in the other room, the ticking of the clock and the soft, occasional crackling of the fire disturbed the peacefulness of early Christmas morning. Banking the fire and taking the lamp with him, Ty quietly made his way to his room where, after kneeling in prayer, he stretched out and promptly fell asleep.

It was shortly after breakfast, when the trio was sitting around the front room with the minister, that Sally asked, "Ty, have you checked your watch with the clock here?"

Ty shook his head. "I reckon I ought, jest ta make sure it's keepin' right time." Pulling out his watch as he spoke, he opened the case and glanced at the face with the hands moving regularly around it. After comparing it to the grandfather clock, which stood over against the wall, Ty snapped it shut and was about to slip the watch back in his pocket, when the words of the minister arrested him.

CHAPTER TWENTY-NINE

"That's an interesting watch guard you have there, Son. It looks familiar. May I see it?"

With a heart beating strangely, Ty wonderingly took the broken locket off his watch chain and handed it to the old man.

Putting on his spectacles, the minister slowly turned the locket over in his hand as he squinted at it. Holding it up to the light, he began to nod his head. "Yes," he said, almost to himself, "it sure looks like that other one. It's even broken."

"What other one?" Something seemed wrong with Ty's voice for it was strangely hoarse.

"Oh, I saw a locket just like this a couple of years ago," Reverend Benjamin remarked casually, handing the broken locket to Sally who was reaching out for it.

"Where?" demanded Ty in a voice that caused the minister to look up, startled.

"What's that? Where did I see it?" Suddenly the old man noticed the agitation, excitement and impatience on the faces of his visitors. "What's the matter?" he asked. "Is it very important where I saw the other locket?"

"Yes," Carson replied. "Ya see," when Ty remained still, "that there broken locket were Ty an' Sally's Ma's an' their missin' sister's got the other half, if'n it ain't lost."

A look of understanding as well as sympathy swept over Reverend Benjamin's face. Now he understood. "Well, let me think a minute. Hmm, I don't recall just where I was, but I do know that a young girl was wearing it."

"What did she look like?" Sally hardly dared to ask.

"She was really pretty; golden hair, rather delicate, not at all like her sisters."

"Sally," Carson interrupted, remembering the minister had said only the night before that he never forgot a face. "Show him yer picture!"

Swiftly Sally pulled the picture from its hiding place in her dress and handed it to their host.

The ticking of the clock was the only sound to be heard in the room as the minister studied the face. At last he said, "Yes, someone just like her was wearing the other half of that locket."

"Where?" Ty questioned "Where did ya see her?" He was gripping the arms of his chair and his breath was coming in gasps. Was this another clue? Miracles still happened didn't they? And on Christmas day— If only he would tell!

The old man looked perplexed. He scratched his head. "I know I'll think of it. Just a minute, I almost have it . . ."

The waiting friends sat on the edge of their seats while three pairs of eyes fastened on the rugged, wrinkled face before them.

"Yes, . . ." the minister paused. "No . . . yes, I have it. It was in Carson City."

A long sigh followed this announcement, for unknowingly, Ty, Sally and Carson had been holding their breath, waiting. "How long ago was it?" Carson asked.

"It must of been about four years ago, maybe?" The minister seemed a little unsure. "Or was it five?"

"It don't matter 'xactaly how long ago it were," Ty put in rising. "Jest long's yer sure where it were."

"Oh, I'm sure about that."

"That's the first real clue we've got since leavin' South Pass. Let's go."

"Ty," Sally asked, "Where are you going?"

Ty looked astonished, "We've got a clue now, an' I reckon we ought ta hit the trail. Let's get goin'. Carson City ain't goin' ta come ta us."

"But Ty," Sally protested. "Today is Christmas."

"Yep."

"Well, I'm not riding on today! I've been riding for days and days. Besides, one day of waiting won't make that much difference."

"She's right, Ty. Ya might's well jest sit yer self back down an' wait. I ain't goin' nowhere neither today. It ain't often ya get a place like this ta rest in fer the day."

Looking impatiently at his two companions, Ty frowned. "Ain't ya wantin' ta find her?"

"'Course we are, Ty, but we got ta get more supplies 'fore we go on."

Sally rose and, going over to her brother, placed both hands coaxingly on his arm, "Ty," she began. "We can leave in the morning, the first thing, but we really should stay here today. You know the horses will travel faster if they have a day to rest. And besides," her smile was bright but her twinkling eyes alerted Ty, "you wouldn't leave without your locket."

Ty started to turn to the minister but Sally stopped him with a little laugh.

"I have it now, Ty, and I'm not going to leave here until morning. I'll give it back now if you promise to wait until then to leave. If you won't promise—" Sally laughingly backed away from her brother with a merry toss of her head. "I'll just keep it until we do leave."

Ty tried to scowl, but finding that Sally only laughed at him, he gave up and sat back down.

"Promise?"

Ty nodded and Sally gave him back the cherished half of the locket, which he immediately placed back on his watch chain.

"Besides," Carson told him, "I reckon we ought ta plan this here next trip a might, an' since the Reverend were in Carson City, I'm thinkin' he could help us." Then, stretching out his legs and clasping his hands behind his head, he added with a chuckle as he looked at the ceiling, "It sure were right dandy a them folks ta name their city after me. An' ta think they've heard a me that far away. My! I ain't never known I were so famous. Why I reckon I must be jest as famous as, well . . . as . . ." and he ran his fingers through his beard in perplexity.

"As Kit Carson?" Ty asked dryly.

"Yep, that's it."

The front room of the parsonage rang with hearty laughter.

Later, Sally went into the kitchen and prepared such a meal that Reverend Benjamin said delightedly, "Why it sure does bring back memories of my wife. I was expecting a lonely Christmas day but you folks have brought good cheer as well as a delicious meal and I thank the Good Lord for sending you to me."

"An' we thank Him for sendin' us too," Ty replied. "If'n we weren't a come, it ain't likely we'd a gotten that there clue which has filled us with cheer." Then, with a teasing glint in his eyes, he glanced at Sally and added, "Even if'n Sally ain't wantin' ta get back on the trail."

Sally made a face as the men chuckled.

Altogether the day was full of merry talk and good cheer. Visitors dropped by to wish their pastor a merry Christmas and many brought him little gifts. Always there was a warm welcome to the three strangers and many hearty wishes for success and a pleasant journey when it was discovered that they were leaving in the morning.

"I'll jest go open the general store if'n ya need ta get ya some supplies fer the trip," the shopkeeper told them, and Carson, Sally and Ty followed him to the store.

All went to bed with the sun that night, for Carson and Sally knew that Ty would demand an early start. They were right. The sun had not yet given its first hints of dawn before Ty was up and rousing his sister and their older friend. Rapidly the trio made their preparations. The horses were brought around from the livery, saddled and bridled, the packs fastened securely around the two packhorses and a hasty breakfast partaken of. The last was done more for the sake of the old minister than for their own, for now that it was no longer Christmas Day, Sally and Carson were as anxious as Ty to be off for Carson City.

At last, just as the sun was beginning to peek over the mountains in the east, the three friends mounted their horses and bade a final farewell to their kind host.

"May our Father bless and keep you all," Reverend Benjamin prayed. "May He give you a prosperous journey and bring you swiftly to a reunion with your missing sister. Amen."

And so, Ty, Sally and their father's friend, Carson, rode out of the little town of Sagebrush towards Carson City on what they hoped would be the last leg of their journey. The morning was slightly cool, but as the sun continued to climb, the temperature rose until it was quite pleasant. The horses, eager to be off after their day of rest, moved along at a rapid, ground eating pace.

Hour after hour passed. The sun climbed higher. A gentle breeze tossed the manes of the horses and fanned the faces of the riders. After a little while, Sally took off her hat, loosened her dark hair and let the wind blow it about.

Glancing sideways at her, Ty couldn't help admiring this sister of his. Not only was she pretty, she had the undefeatable spirit of their father, for had she not been traveling far from home for nearly a year and not one word of complaint had come from her lips? True, she did grow tired as they all did, and weariness and fatigue on such a long, uncertain journey would wear on anyone, yet, Sally had met most of the troubles with a smile or at least a strong determination to beat whatever problem arose. Ty was proud to call her his sister.

It was shortly before mid-day when a horse and rider came into Sagebrush. The rider was young and both he and his horse appeared to have ridden for some time and to be tired out. Swinging out of the saddle, the stranger glanced around.

One of the men from the livery approached him and remarked, "Yer horse looks like it could do with a bit a rest an' some water."

The young stranger smiled. "I'm sure he could. I could to, but first, have there been any strangers around here lately?"

A few other men of the town had gathered around. "Well," one of them drawled, "I reckon yer a stranger."

The man smiled. "I am at that. But tell me, have two men and a woman come through this town? Recently?"

The townsfolk glanced at each other suspiciously, eyed the man's six-shooter at his side as well as his rifle in the scabbard of his saddle, and it was a few minutes before one of them answered. "What's it to ya if'n some had?"

"I need to find them."

"What fer?"

"I have some news for them." He looked around. "They were here, weren't they?"

"Well, there were two men an' a woman, but they ain't here now."

A look of keen disappointment swept over the stranger's face, and he scarcely suppressed a sigh. "How long ago did they leave, and where were they headed? Do you know?"

The men of Sagebrush eyed the young stranger closely and muttered and whispered amongst themselves. At last the man from the livery spoke up. "If'n ya want ta know 'bout them, ya ought ta talk ta the Reverend Benjamin. I reckon he'll get ya a drink too. But why n't ya leave yer horse here fer a bit of a rest while yer talkin'."

"Thanks," the young man replied, "I'll do that if someone will kindly point out the way to Reverend Benjamin's."

This was done and, as the livery man led his horse away, the stranger strode down the short street and knocked on the minister's front door. In a moment it was opened and he was let inside leaving the men of the town to gather in groups and talk, wonder and speculate about who he was and why he had come.

Nearly an hour and a half later, the stranger came out with the minister, saddled his horse, paid the livery fee and with hearty thanks to the minister, rode off following the trail of Ty, Carson and Sally.

CHAPTER THIRTY

When Carson, Ty and Sally at last decided to halt for the night, the stars were already beginning to come out and the sun was nearly gone.

"Ty," Sally remarked as she unsaddled Starlight, "we're starting to stop for the night later and later."

"That ain't it, Sis," Ty grinned at her over Par's broad back. "It's jest that the sun's takin' ta goin' ta bed earlier each night."

Sally only shook her head with a smile. It was such a relief to have Ty teasing again. She had always been able to tell when he was worried or thinking something over because his teasing stopped as did his smiles.

Hobbling the horses so they wouldn't stray far in the night as trees in the area were few and scattered, the friends built a small fire, cooked their supper and relaxed after their fast paced riding of the day.

"How long do you think it will take us to get to Carson City, Uncle Bob?"

"Well," and Carson looked thoughtful, "I reckon it'll depend on how fast we ride an' how far each day. Ain't never been there myself an' don't rightly know how far 'way it is. What da ya think, Ty?"

"Maybe a couple a weeks. I'm wonderin' what we'll find. Think it'll be the end a the journey?"

For a moment neither Sally nor Carson replied. At last Carson shook his head. "I can't say fer sure, but I got a feelin' we'll have ta go farther'n Carson City ta find her."

"What kind a feelin'?"

Shrugging, Carson gazed across the fire into the darkness. "Jest a feelin'."

No one said a word then until just as they were about to bed down for the night. Ty, whose quick ear was on the alert for signs of danger, suddenly whispered, "Listen!"

The trio about the fire froze. At first they couldn't hear anything, then the faint sound of horse's hooves moving steadily towards them came softly over the night breeze, growing more noticeable each passing minute.

"Who by thunder would be ridin' out in this country at this time a night?" grumbled Carson picking up his rifle.

"I ain't sure. Sally," Ty turned towards his sister. "Move—" but he didn't say any more for he saw that Sally was already beyond the dim glow of their small fire. Only the gleam of her six-shooter in her hand told him where she was.

Silently the three travelers waited as the unknown horse and rider continued coming closer and closer.

Suddenly a voice called out from the approaching rider. "Ty? Carson? Sally? It's Joe Fields."

"Joe!" Ty and Carson exclaimed in unison.

"Why boy, what brings ya all this way an' at night too?" Carson added more wood to the fire until it blazed up.

Ty caught hold of the horse's bridle as Joe slipped to the ground. "Where did ya come from?"

Sally said nothing, only slipped her gun back into its holster and glided into the firelight.

Joe gave a long sigh as he shook Ty's offered hand. "I must say, you three certainly know how to travel quickly! I've been on your trail for over a month. Here, Ty," and Joe turned towards his horse. "I can take care of Why-Not."

But Ty already had the saddle off the horse and now said, as he gave Joe a slight push, "I'll jest take 'im out ta the rest a the horses. Ya sit yerself down. Sally, see if'n ya can't rustle up some grub for our visitor."

Joe sat down and in another minute Sally was handing him a plate of food and Ty had returned.

"Now, what's this 'bout ya trackin' us fer over a month?" Carson demanded.

"There isn't any trouble back at your place is there?" Sally questioned in sudden alarm, fearing to hear news that the rest of the Fields were sick, dead, the house had burned or some equally dreadful story.

"No." Joe shook his head. "No trouble. I just came across some news you might want to know about so I set off for the last place Sally's letter mentioned. However, by the time I had arrived, you were long gone. Thankfully I was able to find out where you were heading and by asking at every town I came to, I managed to stay on your trail. But it wasn't until this morning when I rode into Sagebrush that I realized just how close I was to you. Having gotten your direction and destination from Reverend Benjamin, I determined to ride until I found you." Joe took another drink of coffee and sighed deeply in satisfaction. "But I must say, you certainly cover a lot of miles when you ride.

The sky was full of bright twinkling lights, and the moon, though it was only a partial one, shone brightly. The occasional stamp of one of the horses or the far off call of a coyote broke the stillness as the four friends sat around the campfire watching its flickering flames and glowing embers.

"Ya said ya had news for us," Ty reminded Joe quietly. "What news?"

"I think I've found where your sister is living."

Ty, Sally and Carson simply stared stunned at their night visitor. Had Bartram himself suddenly ridden in to their campsite with a six-shooter in each hand and his four cohorts behind him, the sight couldn't have moved them. Could Joe be right? How would he have found out? Did he know her? All these thoughts and hundreds more like them raced through the minds of the three speechless friends.

Joe simply looked at them all, then, seeing that no one seemed able to fully take in what he had just said, he slowly repeated his words, adding quietly as no one moved, "But we can talk about it in the morning." He yawned. "I'm rather tired and think I'll catch some sleep if you don't mind. Goodnight."

Those words had the effect of rousing the trio to life.

"Yer not sleepin' till ya've told us everythin' ya know!" Carson declared.

"Oh, Joe!" exclaimed Sally. "Do you know her?"

"Where is she?" Ty demanded. "For Pete's sake, tell me where she is!" Ty rose and, grasping Joe's arms, shook him slightly, his eyes alight with an eager almost frantic look, his breath coming in gasps.

Joe could feel Ty's hands shaking as he pushed them off. "Sit down, Ty, I'll tell you everything. No, Sally, I don't know her. I believe she is in Sacramento."

"Sacramento," Ty's voice was shaky. The sudden knowledge that this missing girl, this long wondered about youngest daughter of his dead father, this child who had disappeared so many years ago from Carson's care, this sister, his sister, could actually be in the next state, and not only that but in a certain city, was almost too much for Ty to take in.

"What makes ya think she's in Sacramento?" Carson asked cautiously. He saw the emotion on both Ty's and Sally's faces and, though his own heart had leaped with sudden joy at the thought of perhaps actually finding his beloved Sunshine, he hesitated to believe this sudden news.

Joe too, was watching the faces of his friends. He had a dim idea of what they must be feeling at that moment. "It's rather a long story. Do you want to hear it now or wait until morning?"

It was Sally's faint, tear-filled voice who answered. "Tell it now, Joe. Please." She placed her hand on his arm. "I couldn't sleep now if I tried."

Joe laid his hand on top of Sally's a moment and looked into her dark eyes. "All right, I will."

"It began when I rode with Jack to call on a sick man some twenty miles away in a small town. While I was waiting for Jack, I happened to be sitting near a table on which some letters had been laid. Now I don't go reading other folks' mail, but I couldn't help see the signature. It was Ellen Westlin. I immediately thought of your sister but hesitated about asking, for it seemed highly unlikely that it could be the same person or even the same family. But, as I continued to wait, the young lady of the house came in and, sitting down near me, picked up the letter and refolding it, placed it back in its envelope. It must have been the Good Lord who made me ask then about that signature. The young lady, Mary her name was, seemed quite willing to talk about her friend. She said Ellen lived in Sacramento with her family. They had only moved there four years ago from Carson City. I asked Mary how she had met Ellen, and Mary replied that it was when they were in Fort Laramie together and then their families had both headed west on the Oregon trail. I can't remember how she said they had managed to keep in touch all these years, but I do know that Ellen doesn't look like the rest of her family. Mary informed me that Ellen is light while her sisters and brother, as well as both of her parents are dark. Mary thought that was quite interesting and then asked me if I would like to see a picture of her."

Joe stopped for another drink of coffee and to collect his thoughts. As no one spoke, he continued, "Of course I said I would be glad to see a picture, and then I couldn't believe my eyes." Here he paused again. "Sally," he asked, "may I see your picture?"

Silently Sally drew the locket from her dress and held it out. Holding it so that the dim light from the fire fell on the sweet face within, Joe looked long at it. At last he handed it back.

"The face I saw looked so much like that one," and he nodded towards the locket Sally still held in her hands, "that

I almost couldn't believe it. I still wasn't completely convinced, but the more I talked with Mary or rather listened to her, the more certain I became that Miss Ellen Westlin of Sacramento, California was indeed the girl you are searching for."

"Yer certain?" Carson asked.

Joe nodded. "If I wasn't fairly certain, I never would have ridden after you. Mary wondered why I was interested, and when I told her briefly, she brought out all the letters she had received from Ellen and let me read them. In them Ellen mentions her broken locket and her wish to know where the other half is. She even drew a sketch of it in one letter. Ty, it is the exact same as yours."

Ty didn't reply but rose suddenly and moved away into the darkness. Carson too arose murmuring, "My Sunshine, oh my Sunshine. Ta think that ya are still livin'!" He stumbled off leaving Sally and Joe alone by the fire.

Sally was crying softly. The excitement and joy of this new discovery was almost more than she could take in. Her sister found! All at once she was struck with a terrible thought. "Joe! What if . . . what if that Ellen is . . . isn't our sister?"

"I've thought that too, Sally," Joe said softly. "After I first heard of her, I went home and told the family. Everyone was eager and excited, yet at the same time, there was doubt. No one wanted to raise your expectations only to have them dashed to the ground again. We spent much time in prayer over it and when Jack again when to the house, I again accompanied him as did Ma. She wanted to see the picture of Ellen as well as the locket sketch. After she saw them and had talked with Mary, she too was convinced that you all should be told of her."

CHAPTER THIRTY-ONE

"It was then that we decided I should try to find you and let you know since we didn't have any other way of reaching you."

Sally didn't say anything but sat clutching her locket.

When the morning sun dawned, everyone was eager to be off. But, where should they go? Should they go on to Carson City as they had planned, or should they find the fastest route to Sacramento?

"When I talked to the minister at Sagebrush," Joe informed them, "he told me the best way to get to Sacramento from here was to go through Carson City."

"Then that's where we'll head," Ty declared, swinging up on his horse. "But what 'bout you, Joe? I reckon it'll be mighty hard ta get back ta yer place with all the snow in them mountains."

Joe smiled. "Well, if it wouldn't put you out too much, I was thinking of going along with you. At least until Sacramento."

Ty glanced at Carson and raised his eyebrows knowingly before he replied. "I reckon since ya brought in the news, ya might's well go 'long with us 'stead a stayin' here."

"Yep," Carson added. "Ya can tell us all them things ya didn't tell last night."

Nodding his thanks, Joe turned to find out how Sally would take the news of his joining them. To his surprise, she had already mounted and was waiting for them some little distance away.

Just then she called back, "Are you all going to Carson City, or do I have to go alone?"

The three men exchanged glances and rode after her.

As the now four friends traveled that day, they went over every scrap of information that Joe could give them about Ellen Westlin. During a lull in the talk, Sally asked, "Joe, won't Mary write to Ellen and tell her there are people looking for her?"

Shaking his head, Joe replied. "We had thought of that possibility also, and when I first talked with Mary, I said I wasn't certain and to please not mention anything just in case it turned out that it wasn't the right person after all. Then, when Ma was convinced it was the girl you were searching for, she also told Mary the same thing. So, though I don't believe Mary will write anything about what has happened, I'm sure she now will be eagerly awaiting Ellen's letters with even more interest."

Carson nodded his approval. "That were a wise thing ta do, I reckon."

Many miles the travelers rode in the days which followed. Only here and there were scattered ranch houses, but mostly it was just open plains. Since there were no steep mountains to climb, thin windy trails to follow, deep ravines and gorges to cross, rushing rivers to ford or any of the other hardships or difficulties which hamper travelers in the mountains, they made good time.

At last, Carson City was reached. Locating a hotel was a simple matter in the capital city of the new state of Nevada. Once settled in, Ty and Sally, Carson and Joe gathered around a table enjoying their supper and planning their next step.

"I'm thinkin'," Carson began, "that we ought ta talk with a few folks, least ways if'n we can find any that used ta know 'em."

Ty and Joe nodded in agreement, but Sally asked, "How are we going to find someone who knew the Westlins? This isn't a small town like the ones we have been traveling through."

Looking thoughtful, Joe at last spoke, "Mr. Westlin was a lawyer. That might give us a clue as to who to ask."

"Lawyer, huh?" Carson stroked his beard. "They got themselves a courthouse, I reckon we ought ta check there first thing an' see if'n we can't find out somethin'."

And so the four travelers made their way down the streets of the city to the courthouse. Inside, they found a clerk who was willing to tell all he knew about the Westlins.

"Yes, Mr. Westlin was a lawyer here in Carson City before he moved his family to Sacramento. It was the city's loss for he was a fine man. Lovely family too. Daughters were quite charming creatures. Only one son though. Ah, well. The Westlin family was well liked by everybody that I ever talked to. I heard last week that Mr. Westlin is even richer now than he was here. And he was rich enough in Carson City, let me tell you. But he's not like the uppity-up, rich folks, if you know what I mean," and the chattering clerk raised an eyebrow and gave his visitors a knowing look.

"He seemed to like everyone; it didn't matter how rich or poor you were. I suspect he was poor once himself so he knows what it is like. Don't know where they came from. I heard it said that Mr. Westlin had a gold mine in the Dakotas before he came out here, but mind, I don't know. They were in the city before I came," the clerk jabbered on.

"Exceptional lawyer. I'd hate be arguing a case against him. Not that I'm a lawyer, you understand," the voluble clerk added hastily. "Might I ask what you were wanting to see him about?" Though he tried to hide his curiosity, it was obvious to Carson, Ty and Joe. Sally had already given up listening and was looking about them in wonder.

"Business," Ty briefly answered the clerk. "Thank ya for yer help." And, turning away from the disappointed, gossipy clerk, Ty led the others outside without another word.

"Well!" Carson exclaimed when out on the busy street once more. "I wonder if'n he knows everyone in this here city as well's he knows the Westlins!"

Joe nodded and added, "They ought to make him the town crier."

"Ty, ya think we got all we need ta know 'bout that family?"

"Yep. Think he knows where Bartram is too?" Ty scoffed.

Making their way down the street, Ty and Carson discussed in low tones what their next step should be.

"I reckon we ought ta get ta Sacramento," Carson said.

"I'd like nothin' better, only . . ." and here Ty paused significantly as they stopped in front of their hotel.

Carson sighed. "Yep, it's jest them Sierra Nevada mountains we got ta get 'cross."

Glancing back to see where Joe and Sally were, Ty lowered his voice as he replied, "Reckon I know that. If it were jest you an' me I'd say let's get goin'. But Joe, he ain't a mountain man seasoned ta the dangers a the mountains. An' Sally, she'd put up a mighty fuss if we jest talked a leavin' her behind. But there ain't no way she's crossin' them mountains in the winter." He sighed, crossed his arms and leaned against the side of the building.

For several minutes Carson too stood in thought, then all at once he straightened up. "Ty, ya jest wait with them two an' I'll be back."

"Carson, what—" Ty looked narrowly at his older friend. What did he have planned in that head of his? "Ya ain't goin' alone—"

"I said jest wait," Carson cut him short. "Best ta stay with yer sister lest ya lose her." And Carson grinned, nodding towards Joe and Sally who were standing together talking eagerly while the color came and went on Sally's cheeks.

Pushing himself away from the wall he was leaning on, Ty dropped his hands to his gun belt, tucked his thumbs in the leather strap and, after watching Carson stride away down the street, he sauntered over to his sister and Joe.

Joe turned at once to him remarking, "Well, we've reached Carson City; what are the plans for the next leg of the journey?"

Ty shrugged. "Carson's goin' ta figure somethin' out or least ways have a go at it."

"Why can't we just go on as we have been?" Sally asked.

"It's jest the Sierra Nevadas. An' winter."

For a moment Sally looked puzzled, then a look of understanding came over her, which turned into concern. "We have to wait until spring?"

Ty shrugged. "Reckon we'll find out when Carson gets back. Joe," Ty turned to him, "ya don't got ta stay 'less ya want ta."

"Then I'll stay," Joe replied lightly. "It is growing cool, shall we go in?" He had seen Sally shiver slightly.

It was late, the sun was saying goodnight to the world, and the night life in the city was beginning. Ty was pacing the room restlessly. Where had Carson gone? Why wasn't he back yet? Had something happened to him? Had Bartram—? No, Bartram didn't know Carson. But what could have happened to him?

"Ty," Sally began, her voice unsteady, "where is Uncle Bob?"

"I don't rightly know, but I'm goin' ta find 'im." Ty had strapped on his six-shooter as he talked and was reaching for his rifle when the door opened and in walked Carson.

"Oh, Uncle Bob!" cried Sally, running to him and putting her arms around his neck. "You had us worried something had happened to you."

"Ah, ain't nothin' happened ta me 'cept getting mighty twisted up in this here city. It sure were the most strangest thin' ever happened ta me. I ain't never been lost in them mountains back home nor anywheres else I've been, but put me in a city and, jumpin' horny toads, I can't find head nor tails a this place!"

"Well, ya made it back somehow," Ty remarked. "Did ya find out anythin' 'cept that ya can get lost in a city?" Ty had stood his rifle up again and was unbuckling his gun belt.

Carson looked indignant. "I weren't lost, Ty Elliot! I were jest a might . . . well, twisted up fer a spell."

Ty snorted, and Joe grinned.

"But Uncle Bob," Sally persisted dropping back into the seat she had occupied beside Joe before Carson had returned. "Did you find out how to get to Sacramento?"

"Yep. We jest ride up north ta Reno, stable the horses 'till we get back, catch the train an' ride it ta Sacramento. Ain't nothin' to it really. Least ways that's what Sheriff Benson told me. We could leave first light an' get ta Reno by dark, I reckon."

"A train? I didn't know they had trains this far west." Joe looked surprised.

"Have you ridden on one?" Sally asked him, looking half frightened at the thought.

Joe nodded. "Sure, when we lived back east. I just didn't expect to find one out here."

"What the sheriff said were that they're makin' a railroad that'll run clear from one side a the country ta the next. They ain't got it connected yet, but it sure is through them mountains. Goes clear ta San Francisco, Sheriff said."

"I never thought I'd ride on a train," Sally whispered to herself and half aloud.

"They are easier to ride than horses," Joe told her. "And faster too."

"That I'd like ta see," Carson declared.

For several minutes the room was full of talk of trains with Joe telling of his experiences as a boy and questions from Carson and Sally.

Only Ty remained silent. He had never ridden on a train either. In fact, he had never seen one though he had heard of them. Now he was going to ride across the mountains in one. The thought of not going mingled with the thoughts of how they would cross the mountains any other way. It really seemed as though this way, this riding of the steam horses was their only way to get to Sacramento, and to get to Sacramento was the one thing Ty was determined to do as quickly as possible.

Standing up, he interrupted the conversation. "I reckon we ought ta turn in if'n we're ta git up 'fore the sun."

"Then we really are going to ride on a train, Ty?" Sally had risen and grasped her brother's arm, her eyes fixed on his face.

Ty looked down at his sister. "Ya want ta?"

"I think so," she answered half timidly.

"Then I reckon we ought ta set out at first light."

It was the first light of the morning dawn when the brother and sister, Carson and Joe set off on their horses for Reno and the new railway line, which would hopefully take them to Sacramento and the Westlins, Miss Ellen in particular. This ride was colder, reminding Ty of the winter weather up in the mountains, the one large barrier between himself and what he hoped would be the end of his search.

Sally, riding beside him, pulled her shawl closer about her shoulders. "Ty, do you really think our sister will be there?" Sally asked the question hesitatingly, for she wasn't sure what Ty thought of the news, which Joe had brought. True, they were following his clue, but Ty had been rather silent about it.

Fixing his eyes on the distant mountains to his left, Ty replied slowly and quietly. "I jest ain't sure, Sally. Part a me wants ta think she's there an' yet another part says we ain't searched long enough." He turned to look at her. "I jest don't know."

It was quite late when the four travelers reached Reno and the following day, after making arrangements for the care of their horses until they should return, with Joe in the lead, Carson, Sally and Ty purchased their tickets and climbed aboard the train. The only one who had ridden on one of them before was Joe and that was many years before.

There were not many passengers riding on this train and besides three other men, the four friends were the only passengers in their car. There was only one other passenger car. As the train began moving, Sally sat rigid in her seat not sure if she should be frightened or not. She couldn't really believe that she was riding on a train. Watching the countryside move past her windows faster and faster as the train picked up speed caused her to grip the side of her seat until her knuckles turned white, yet she couldn't take her eyes away from the flying scenery which seemed to hold her fascination until a hand was placed over hers. She turned her head. Joe was watching her with a smile.

"What do you think of traveling by train now?"

"I don't think I quite know yet," she replied. "It is warmer than on horseback."

Joe laughed softly. "That's because you don't have a stove with you on Starlight to keep off the cold."

Sally glanced behind her at the stove in the middle of the car. "It would be a little large for Starlight to carry," she admitted smiling, then her smile faded. "I hope Starlight is taken care of while we're gone."

Neither Carson nor Ty spoke a word for over an hour. Though neither one would have admitted it for anything, even to themselves, this train ride was more nerve racking to them than facing the desolate, snow covered mountains on foot would have been. As they steamed around curves on the side of the mountains with sheer drops of a hundred feet or more on one side and solid rock walls on the other at paces which to them were speeds of incredible swiftness, where the cars bumped and swayed, rattled and creaked, both heartily wished they were on foot.

Ty glanced at their fellow travelers, three men of reputable looking character obviously well used to such modes of transportation, for one was reading a paper while the other two dozed.

"How can anyone sleep in such a smoky, stifling atmosphere," Ty grumbled.

Joe looked across the aisle. "It is growing smoky in here, isn't it? Perhaps I can fix the stove a bit so it won't smoke so much." So saying, he stood up and made his way down the car to the stove. After messing with a few things he came back. "The shaking of the car had shut one of the dampers. It should grow better soon."

As the hours passed, Ty and Carson gradually became more accustomed to the motion and speed of the train and were able to carry on a conversation with Joe and Sally. The uppermost thought in everyone's mind was of the family they were going to see in Sacramento; however, these thoughts were kept strictly to themselves thus, of necessity, turning their conversation to Joe's family.

Joe told everything he could think of which would interest them up to the time of his leaving and then, having only heard of his companions travels from Sally's letters until he left, he in turn questioned the trio about their experiences before he met them. He had heard a brief outline of their trip as they had ridden to Carson City, but always it had been in the evenings and never lasted long for, being tired from the day's travels, all had soon fallen asleep. Now he plied them with questions and through Carson and Sally, finally heard the whole story of 'them'. Ty refused to talk about that experience.

It was growing late when the train suddenly slackened speed and came to an abrupt stop with brakes creaking. They were in the middle of the mountains and no station or anything was to be seen out of the car windows. Nothing but trees, rocks and snow everywhere.

"Where are we?" demanded Carson starting up. "An' what in thunder did we stop fer?"

"I don't know," Joe replied slowly, peering out the windows.

The other three men in the car had been roused and were looking about them too. Ty had risen and now stood, ready for, he knew not what.

Just at that moment someone came bursting into the car. He was shivering but still managed to gasp out, "It's an avalanche!"

CHAPTER THIRTY-TWO

"The whole tracks covered up yonder for we ain't sure how many miles! We can't go on!"

"What?"

"Avalanche!"

"When did it happen?"

"Do we have ta go back ta Reno?"

The news bearer was bombarded with questions. For a moment he looked bewildered as the passengers gathered around him in excitement.

"I ain't sure what's goin' ta happen. Maybe we can go back—"

Here the arrival of another man interrupted. It was the conductor who said, "We aren't going back. Least not till we've tried to dig our way through this. Come on, we can use every one of you able bodied men. Let's get going!" Then he seemed to notice Sally for the first time. "It'd be best if you'd move up to the next car. There's another woman up there I'm told. Now let's get a move on, boys."

Rapidly the men pulled on their heavy coats, scarves and hats. Just before they left the car, Ty drew Sally to one side. "Here, keep this safe," and he pushed his watch with the precious broken locket on its guard into her hands.

Her face grew white. "Ty," she gasped, clutching his arm. "Ya think—"

"I jest don't want ta lose it in the snow." He looked directly into her eyes. "I'll be back, Sis." Then with a kiss, he left her at the door.

With her heart in her mouth she watched him wade through the snow after the other men until the train hid him from sight.

Stepping into the next car, Sally saw a woman standing with her back to her, staring out the far windows. "Can you see anything of the men?" Sally asked.

The woman turned, shaking her head. "Not any more." She sighed and her voice quivered.

"I'm Sally Elliot."

The other woman offered a small smile. "Clara Dodd. Have you traveled on this route before?"

"No, this is my first time to ever ride on a train."

"Oh." This news didn't comfort the woman and in spite of the obvious effort to control herself, the tears found a way down her cheeks.

"Why," Sally exclaimed, "what's wrong?"

"My husband is out there!" wailed the young woman bursting into sobs and sinking down into a seat.

Sally sat down beside her. "Now look here," she began knowing that giving way to emotions at such a time would only make things worse. "My only brother is out there as well as my father's best friend and . . ." she hesitated and blushed as she wondered how to label Joe. In the end she didn't say anything about him, but went on, "This is no time for tears, Mrs. Dodd; we have work to do!"

The young woman looked up. "Oh, please call me Clara," she sniffed.

"Very well, Clara," Sally smiled. "Those men are going to be needing something hot to drink after a while and something to eat. Suppose you and I try to find what we can. I know I have some cold biscuits and meat."

This was the very thing the young wife needed. Something to do and someone to direct. Clara remembered that she had coffee and a tea kettle and Sally hurried back to the other car for her food supplies. She was very thankful that Joe and Carson had insisted on bringing plenty of food along.

Together the two women went to work melting snow for the coffee and checking their food supplies.

When all was done that could be done, Sally and Clara sat down to wait. That was the hardest part of all. It was easy to imagine all sorts of terrible things happening out there in the snow, and soon young Mrs. Dodd's shoulders began to shake.

"Clara," Sally began, putting an arm around her. "When I'm worried about things I've found the best thing to do is pray. Do you want to join me?"

Silently, Clara Dodd nodded and slipping from the seat, the two young women knelt in prayer for their loved ones and the others out attempting to clear the train tracks.

Out on the mountain, the men surveyed the massive pile of snow, which lay before them. There was the engineer, conductor, fireman and a dozen passengers from the train.

"Well, it's goin' ta take some doin' ta move all this snow," the engineer shook his head. "A lot a backbreakin' work."

"How far does it go?" asked one of the passengers.

"No tellin'."

Carson and Ty had been looking on, eyeing the snow and the surrounding mountainside. On one side, about ten feet from where they were standing, was a drop off. On the other side was a snow covered slope with pine trees. It was only where the avalanche was that the one side rose in a sharp cliff.

"Anyone have any snowshoes?" Carson asked quietly.

The engineer and brakeman both had some but asked what he wanted them for.

"Jest let Ty an' me go see how far that there snow mountain goes an' if'n there's a good way ta clear it."

"We'll have to shovel it," one of the men growled. "And we'll need all hands to help."

Carson ignored him and looked at the engineer.

"You know mountains?" he asked, seeing the rough clothes and heavily bearded face of the speaker and that his companion looked about the same with the exception that his beard wasn't as long nor was it grey.

"I know 'em more'n ya know trains," was the reply.

In a few more minutes Carson and Ty were climbing the mountainside, making their way up through the trees and over towards the top of the cliff. By grabbing hold of the tree branches and using them to pull themselves on, they soon became lost to the sight of the men below. It was silent and still in the woods with the snow lying everywhere, thick and deep. Not a sound was to be heard when they paused for breath except the faint sound of the diggers below them.

Over two hours had passed before Sally and Clara heard the sounds of approaching voices. Peering out of the train car windows, they saw three men sledging through the snow, heads bent and showing by their every move the weariness which claimed them.

Clara flung open the door to the car with a little cry and pulled the first man in, clinging to his arm and half crying, half laughing. Sally knew at once that it must be her husband.

Hurrying to pour the hot coffee into mugs for the tired, nearly exhausted men, Sally then offered each one some food from their small store.

"I sure weren't expectin' this when I come back ta thaw out," one of the men commented. "I reckon this'll keep me goin' another spell."

"Yep, much obliged, ma'am.," It was the last one who had come in and who now stood up. "The others'll be wantin' a rest, let's get back out there boys,"

Mr. Dodd kissed his wife, and together the three men headed back out into the white world.

In groups of three, the weary laborers returned to the passenger car to rest, have a cup of coffee and warm up. Sally was thankful for that coffee as she watched it put new life into each of the chilled, tired workers. As group after group came with no sign of Carson, Ty or Joe, Sally began to grow slightly anxious. She was sure Uncle Bob and Ty wouldn't tire very easily for both were used to facing difficulties and hardships. But they had to come in sometime. And where was Joe? No doubt he was staying out until the other two came in.

As yet another group stumbled through the car door, Sally recognized Joe. Hurrying to him, she pulled off his wet, snow covered coat and scarf and gave him a cup of steaming coffee. Not until he had drunk that and some color had returned to his pale cheeks, did she speak.

"Where are Ty and Uncle Bob?"

Joe shook his head. "Out on the mountainside. I haven't seen them since they left."

"Left? What do you mean?" Sally sank onto a turned seat facing Joe. "Why would they leave and where did they go?"

"They went to try to find how extensive the avalanche was and they said something about finding an easier way to clear it." He shook his head. "I don't know. I thought they'd be back by now, but—" and he didn't finish.

Sally bit her lip, but rose and refilled Joe's cup. It wasn't until Joe and his two companions had disappeared into the dark night that a moan of anguish came from her tightly pressed lips.

Clara came and put her arms around her. "I'm sure they'll be back," she whispered.

Sally nodded but still continued to shake, covering her face with her hands.

"Sally," whispered Clara, "you remember what you told me, praying helps. Why don't we pray right now?"

Making no audible answer, Sally slid to her knees and buried her face in the seat of the railway car. Clara knelt beside her.

Silence reigned in that little car for several minutes. Faintly the muffled sounds of the workers farther down the line could be heard through the still, snowy night. Shining brightly from the starry heavens, the moon sent its silvery light to sparkle and gleam off the snow in such a way as would have entranced a beauty-loving person. However, no one seemed to notice it.

At last Sally, with a slight catch in her voice, broke the quiet. "Thank you, Clara. I needed that."

Clara smiled as they rose from their knees. "Do you suppose we should make more coffee?"

It was another half an hour before the soft sound of more footsteps in the snow alerted the women that some of the men were returning. The door opened and two men entered.

"Ty! Uncle Bob!" Sally rushed to them and tried to take off Ty's coat, but he pushed her away.

"Jest let me have a cup a coffee, Sis. I ain't gonna stay here long, jest need somethin' ta drink."

Clara had two cups ready and was handing one to Carson as Sally took the other and gave it to her brother.

"Did you find out anything?" ventured Sally as Ty drained his first cup and handed it back to be refilled.

He shrugged, but Carson replied, "It weren't a large avalanche an' I reckon it ain't gonna take us more'n a couple more hours ta clear them tracks. Thanks fer the coffee. Ya ready ta go, Ty?"

Ty nodded, flashed a quick smile at his sister, and the two disappeared into the night leaving Sally and Clara to wait again for the next round of tired workers.

Towards morning, as the sky was growing light, the two waiting women heard a sudden muffled shout. Eagerly they looked at each other. What did that mean? Was the snow finally cleared? Had an accident occurred? With bated breath they waited. Footsteps, hurrying ones coming nearer and nearer. Sally and Clara tried to peer out the windows but they were so fogged over that they couldn't see. Then the door into the train car burst open.

"We did it!" someone announced excitedly. "We've cleared the track!"

"How 'bout another cup a coffee."

"Yeah, that's what I need."

"I'm not driving this train without one," announced the engineer in decided tones, and Sally hurried to pour him a steaming cup.

Hurriedly draining it while the fireman and brakeman did the same, the engineer thanked the men for their hard work, and the ladies for the coffee and then added, "Well, do you all want to go on to Sacramento or shall we stay here?"

A hearty laugh filled the car and the train crew disappeared through the door and clambered aboard the engine. Soon the fire was built in the boiler and when the steam was up, the engine slowly and carefully rolled forward.

With a shriek of its whistle, a hissing of brakes and a clanging of its bell, the train pulled up at the depot in Sacramento. They had arrived at last. Ty and Sally Elliot, Bob Carson and Joe Fields gathered their belongings and climbed down off the train. The bustling, hustling crowds shoving each other here and there, the streets crowded with wagons, carriages and people, many imposing buildings lining the streets, the noise, the crowds, the clamor pressing in on the four travelers from every side, left most of them utterly bewildered and made talking nearly impossible.

Joe, having been in large cities as a boy, now took charge, and tucking Sally's hand protectively through his arm and nodding for the others to follow, led the way down a street until he stopped before one of the smaller hotels.

There they registered and were speedily settled in their rooms.

It wasn't until they had all had time to clean up a bit that they met in the hotel dining room to talk. But, as they sat around the table, no one seemed inclined to start. It was as though the thought of what lay before them in this very city was too much. Ty sat silent and grim, looking much like his father, Carson thought. Sally, too, was silent and played with the food on her plate instead of eating it.

"Well," Carson at last broke the silence, "I reckon we ought ta look up them Westlins an' find out if'n this is the end a the journey or jest another rabbit trail that leads nowhere."

Drawing a deep breath, Ty let it out slowly before nodding.

"How do we find them in such a large city?" ventured Sally, appalled at the idea of wandering the city asking for a family they didn't even know.

"Excuse me," a pleasant voice interrupted, and a gentleman at the table next to theirs lowered his paper. "I couldn't help hearing that you were looking for the Westlin family? Would that be Thomas Westlin, the lawyer, you are wanting?"

Ty glanced at Carson. He didn't remember ever hearing the name of the father. But Carson was nodding.

"That'd be the one. Ya know 'em?"

"I live right next door to them. Fine family. Their house is on the other side of town, but if it is only Mr. Westlin you are looking for, you might be able to catch him at his office tomorrow. It is only two blocks over."

The four friends exchanged rapid glances before Ty replied. "We're lookin' fer the family, if ya'd give us directions ta the house."

With a nod the gentleman quickly wrote down the directions and remarked as he handed Ty the paper, "I imagine you will find them all at home if you go this afternoon."

Thanking him, Ty, Carson, Sally and Joe rose and quickly left the room.

As they departed, the old gentleman looked after them, remarking to himself, "I don't know who they are but I like their looks. Seems to me that I've seen that girl somewhere before, and maybe the roughest of the young men. But I can't place just where. Oh well, Westlin will find out all about them if I'm not mistaken." And he returned to his paper.

"Ty," Sally whispered as she, her brother and Carson stood before a large mansion with huge pillars on the porch, wide windows and a massive knocker on the door, "I'm scared."

Ty didn't reply but swallowed hard, one hand moving up to his freshly shaven chin. His breathing was faster than normal and, though the day was chilly, he kept wiping his moist hands on his pant legs.

Even Carson looked unnerved and clearly uncomfortable. If Joe had been there he would undoubtedly have been the first to mount the imposing steps and knock on the heavy door, but he had remained behind at the hotel. This was not his sister and he didn't want to intrude.

For several minutes the trio stood looking at the house, then as though by common consent, they climbed the steps slowly and Ty knocked on the door.

Only a brief amount of time elapsed before it was opened and a lovely girl stood before them. "Yes?" she asked politely, though somewhat astonished at the evidently unexpected visitors before her.

No one answered. Instead they simply stared. The girl looked to be about sixteen with lovely, long, golden curls framing her face. Her eyes were a rich, deep blue while her smile was sweet though somewhat perplexed.

Ty's eyes swept the girl from the top of her hair to the tips of her boots, which peeped out from beneath her skirt. Then they noticed the necklace. A simple locket, but it was broken! He gave a gasp and his mouth opened as though to speak but no words came out. He drew a quick breath his eyes glued to the girl's face.

"Is there something I can do for you?" the girl asked, blushing at the stares she was receiving and evidently wondering what errand these three visitors were on.

"Who is at the door, Ellen?" a gentle voice called from somewhere in the house.

The girl turned somewhat from the doorway and replied, "I don't know, Mother."

A matronly figure now appeared beside the girl. "Are you here to see Mr. Westlin?" she asked, trying to put the strangers at ease.

This sentence, as well as the presence of the older woman, seem to restore Carson's tongue enough to murmur, "Yes, Ma'am, we've come fer that. Ain't got no 'pointment, but we've got ta see him jest soon's we can. We come a long way an'—" Carson couldn't say anymore.

The door was hospitably opened wider and the woman beckoned them in to a wide hall. "I'm sure my husband will see you. If you will follow me, I'll take you to his study."

CHAPTER THIRTY-THREE

It was a dazed group that followed Mrs. Westlin into the study of the well-known lawyer. Awed by the splendor about them but mostly made speechless by the sight of the lovely Ellen Westlin, no one spoke a word.

Mr. Westlin rose upon their entrance and placing a chair for Sally, beckoned the men to seats beside her as his wife softly left the room, closing the door quietly behind her.

"What can I do for you folks?" Mr. Westlin inquired kindly seating himself at his desk and smiling.

But for some time there was no answer. Ty struggled with the lump, which had risen in his throat, and Sally clutched her locket hardly daring to breathe. As for Carson, the thought of trying to tell this man, this wealthy, well-to-do lawyer, that the lovely girl he has called his own for over a dozen years is really the daughter of his dearest friend and the little sister of the two friends beside him seemed utterly impossible. What if it was all a mistake, he suddenly thought. Perhaps it was not the right family.

Patiently Mr. Westlin waited. His sympathies were with his three visitors, for he felt sure they were in some sort of trouble. At last he broke the silence, "If I can be of assistance to you in any way, I wish you would let me." His voice was low but there was a feeling of power when he spoke.

"Were ya . . ." Carson began and then stopped, hesitated and began again. "Did ya ever live near Lowrise Pass?"

Mr. Westlin looked a bit surprised at the question but answered readily enough. "Yes, for a little over a year. But that was a long time ago." He raised his eyebrows questioningly at his visitors.

Carson swallowed. "Could yer wife come in. I'm a thinkin' it'd be a heap easier ta talk if'n she were here." Carson spoke after trying several time in vain to say something about his Sunshine.

A bit surprised but willing to do all in his power to help his visitors, Mr. Westlin rose to comply with this unusual request. Stepping to the door, he opened it and called, "Thomas, would you please ask your mother to step into the study for a few minutes?"

The companions in the room heard a young, boyish voice answer quickly, "Yes, Papa!" and then hurrying footsteps which disappeared down the hall.

In another minute the door opened and Mrs. Westlin entered.

Rising and drawing up a chair for his wife, Mr. Westlin told her quietly, "Our visitors requested your presence, Dear. They thought it would be easier to talk."

Yet, even then no one seemed able to speak. Carson finally said, "I jest can't find a way ta say it."

"Suppose you just start at the beginning and tell us everything," the lawyer encouraged.

Carson turned to his young companion, "Ty," he prodded, "ya tell it."

Ty shook his head. "I jest—" he couldn't go any farther. The emotions stirred at the sight of that broken locket around the girl's neck were still struggling for control.

In the end it was Sally who broke the awkward pause which followed Ty's unfinished sentence. With a half sob, she slipped the locket with its precious picture off from around her neck and placed it on the desk, saying in a voice choked with tears, "Look at her. It will tell you the story, and Ty has the other half of her locket."

The Westlins looked at the picture, their eyes growing wide.

At last Mrs. Westlin turned to look closely at the three strangers and gasped out, "Who are you?" She was looking directly at Carson when she spoke.

"Bob Carson, Ma'am. Ya took care a my Sunshine when Aunt Kate were sick."

Mrs. Westlin put both hands over her mouth, her eyes filling with tears.

"And these are—?" Mr. Westlin questioned, glancing at Ty and Sally.

"She's our sister," Ty spoke huskily.

For a full ten minutes no one spoke. The Westlins, too stunned by this sudden and unexpected news to speak, could only sit half bewildered and wholly astonished. The large clock ticked the minutes slowly by.

Finally the lawyer broke the silence. "Well, I don't know what to say. Can you start at the beginning and explain how this could be possible and how you found us?"

Now that the ice was broken, so to speak, Carson told once again about his friend Jake Elliot and his Ellen, of his grief over her death when the youngest, a daughter, was born and how he had left with the two older children, Ty and Sally, leaving the baby in his care. Of the years which followed when, together with his Aunt Kate, Carson had cared for and loved the small child. Then he told of his leaving Aunt Kate and Sunshine to go trapping and coming back to an empty cabin. How he had searched for his Sunshine, but couldn't find her and at last had given up hope of ever seeing her again. "I were always half afraid when I went ta visit Jake that he'd ask 'bout her, but he never did. I'd promised ta look out fer her an' now she were gone."

Audible sniffs came from the ladies.

"I ain't never expected ta find my Sunshine, an' if it hadn't been fer Ty's determination, I don't reckon I'd a done it neither."

Mr. Westlin turned to Ty, and after clearing his throat once or twice, asked, "How did you ever find us?"

"It's a long story . . ."

Holding up his hand, Thomas Westlin excused himself a moment and went to the door of the study. "Kitty," he called, stepping out into the hall, "please excuse your mother and me to any callers and see that no one disturbs us. Now," he said, returning and drawing his chair a little closer to the others, "let's hear it."

Drawing a deep breath, Ty began.

"Pa ain't never told us 'bout our sister an' he weren't never one ta talk 'bout Ma either. Sally an' me used ta ask him 'bout her, but I reckon he jest couldn't talk a her. It weren't till last winter, when he were dyin', that he made me promise ta find her. I weren't sure jest who he meant. Then he said I was ta take care a my sisters." He sighed, recalling those days, and fell silent as he usually did when memories stirred within him.

Carson, along with Sally's help began to tell the rest of the story. Of how the only clues they had been given were the picture and the broken locket. How they had set off for Lowrise Pass hoping to find some clue, how they had traveled to Fort Laramie and to South Pass where they then headed south. Of Ty's wound, the Fields, and traveling on once again. Of the next clue found in Sagebrush by an old minister and of how Joe Fields had ridden after them with his bit of news. They told of their train ride across the Sierra Nevadas and at last of their arrival in Sacramento.

It was quite late before the story was told, for Mr. and Mrs. Westlin interrupted time and again with questions. Ty had roused from his reverie and joined in the talk.

In their turn, Carson, Ty and Sally begged to know of the Westlins and more especially of their sister.

"Ellen has been a daughter to us since the first day we took her into our house after your Aunt Kate died," Mrs. Westlin told Carson. "No one knew what had become of you; most people thought you were dead. When we left for Fort Laramie, we didn't know of any living relatives and besides, at that point, we couldn't bear the thought of letting our little Ellie go. She was always so bright and happy. And to think that at that time her own father was living as well as her own brother and sister, and we never knew it." Mrs. Westlin wiped her eyes.

"I reckon," Carson put in quietly, "If'n Jake had known Sunshine, he'd a held on ta her tight, but ya see, he jest couldn't bear the memories a his own Ellen an' so jest tried ta shut all others out."

Mr. Westlin nodded. "I can understand."

Mrs. Westlin continued, "Ellen had that broken locket when we took her in, and she's worn it ever since. She remembered somewhere that it was her mother's and has always wondered where the rest of it was and why it was broken."

Ty and Sally glanced at Carson for neither of them knew why or how it had broken.

"Her pa broke it," he said simply. "It were jest 'fore he gave me the wee mite. He broke the locket an' put the half with the chain 'round her neck an' said, 'Carson, I can't keep her. But I'm goin' ta keep jest a little part a her. Don't let her lose that locket, it were her ma's weddin' gift from me.' An' not till the day he died did I ever see his half a the locket. Then I know'd he kept it close ta his heart an' he ain't never did forget his baby girl."

By that time, Sally was openly crying on her brother's shoulder while Mrs. Westlin sat with tears streaming down her cheeks. Even the men were blinking back their emotion, for all were deeply stirred.

Dong, dong, dong. The clock began to toll the hour. Dong, dong, dong, dong. Mr. Westlin glanced up in surprise. Dong, dong, dong. "Ten o'clock!" he exclaimed. "I had no idea it was so late. And you folks have had a long tiring journey."

"But there is still so much to talk over; you will come back in the morning, won't you?" Mrs. Westlin rose. "And bring the other young man along."

"Of course they'll be back, Dear," Mr. Westlin smiled. "They haven't even been introduced to their sister."

"Oh!" Mrs. Westlin turned pale. "What are we going to tell Ellen? How—?"

Ty interrupted, "Ma'am, I ain't wantin' ta take my sister away from the only family she's ever really known."

Mr. Westlin placed his hand on Ty's shoulder. "We'll talk more about it all in the morning. I think right now everyone needs a good sleep. Miss Sally, you look exhausted. Where are you staying?"

Carson named the hotel.

"Why that is on the other side of the city." Mr. Westlin rang a bell. "I'm going to send you in our carriage. The streets aren't safe at night. Especially for ladies, even if they do wear guns," and he smiled at Sally.

A knock sounded on the door and Mr. Westlin answered it to direct his stable hand to prepare to drive his guests to their hotel.

Silently Mrs. Westlin handed Sally the picture of her mother and then, fingering Ty's broken half of the locket asked, "Ty, might I keep this tonight? It might help in breaking the news to Ellen."

Ty nodded.

As Mr. and Mrs. Westlin accompanied their guests to the front door, Ty and Sally caught a glimpse of their sister. It was only a passing one, for she was in another room with several dark haired girls and one young lad. Mr. Westlin followed them down the porch steps and helped Sally into the carriage.

"Shall I send the carriage for you in the morning?" Thomas Westlin inquired.

Carson looked puzzled. "What fer? I reckon it'll be light enough ta see by an' we ain't afraid a walkin'."

The lawyer couldn't keep from smiling. "Then I'll look forward to seeing you when you arrive. And don't forget to tell your friend he is welcome too. Good night!"

Eagerly the Westlin young ladies and smaller children crowded around their parents.

"Who were they, Papa?"

"What did they want?"

"Do we know them?"

"Why did they stay so long?"

CHAPTER THIRTY-FOUR

With a tight laugh, Mr. Westlin held up his hands. "Whoa, hold on a minute. It is long past bedtime. No questions tonight."

There was a groan from the younger ones.

"Wait until tomorrow. They are coming back and you will then know all you need to know. Now, off to bed with you. Scoot!"

Laughing and somewhat mystified, the children kissed their parents and mounted the stairs to their rooms. If Mrs. Westlin's kiss on Ellen's cheek was longer and more clinging than usual, and Mr. Westlin's embrace of her tighter than normal, no one noticed.

When alone in their own room, Thomas Westlin turned and put his arms about his wife for she was shaking. "There, there," he soothed. "It will be all right."

"But, Thomas, how are we going to tell her?"

"Remember, Sweet," Mr. Westlin whispered, "she won't be losing anyone, but gaining a brother and sister as well as a friend."

"I know."

Together they knelt in prayer.

Arriving at the hotel, Ty assisted Sally up the stairs to their rooms where they found Joe waiting up for them. He asked no questions, but watched the faces of the three companions as they entered. Sally went straight to her room and was seen no more until morning.

After several minutes of silence, Ty looked at Joe, "Yer clue were right. We found her." And then he too retired to his bed, more worn out by that half a day's talk than he had ever been after a full day of trapping or riding.

A servant answered Carson's knock the following morning and showed the visitors into the sitting room. Sally and Ty were nervous. Today for the first time they would meet their sister. As they waited in silence for they knew not what or who, a boy of about ten or eleven years of age paused in the doorway and looked at them half shyly.

"Howdy," Joe greeted him with a smile.

"Hi." The boy moved a step inside the door, his eyes roving from one face to another and lingering on the guns at their sides. "Are you trappers?" he asked at last.

Joe grinned. "Not me. I'm just a ranch hand. But," he added as the boy's face fell a little, "those two are."

The lad's eyes grew wide. "Did you ever kill a bear or a mountain lion?" he asked eagerly.

In spite of his nervousness, Ty couldn't help a chuckle. He liked this wide-eyed, eager, inquisitive boy. "Yep," he replied.

"Oh!" the word was long and drawn out and the lad drew a deep breath.

"What's yer name?" Ty asked.

"Thomas Westlin Jr.," he replied, then asked with childlike frankness, "What's yours?"

"Ty Elliot."

"Which did you shoot, a bear or a mountain lion?" was the next question.

"I've shot both."

"Thomas!" hissed the voice of an unseen speaker out in the hall.

But young Thomas only moved farther into the room with his hands shoved in his pockets and remarked coolly, "A man's got to do what he's got to do, in spite of the women folks."

Carson cleared his throat a few times and Joe turned away as if to study a painting on the wall.

"Yep," Ty agreed, "but I reckon we ain't gonna let the women worry needlessly or be bothered, eh?"

"You bet I won't let anyone bother my sisters!" exclaimed young Westlin Jr. "If anyone even tried to bother one, why I'd just—" and he doubled up his fists like a prizefighter.

Here Sally spoke soothingly, "I'm sure your sisters feel protected when you are around."

Thomas threw back his shoulders and raised his chin. "I just wish Papa would let me carry a gun."

Before anything else could be said, Mr. Westlin entered the room. "Ah, I see Thomas has made your acquaintance. Carson, Ty, Miss Sally, it is good to see you again." And the lawyer shook hands with his guests of the evening before and then turned to Joe. "And you must be the friend they talked about."

"I'm Joe Fields, sir," and Joe held out his hand.

After greeting him with a hearty shake, Mr. Westlin, dropping a hand on his son's shoulder, said, addressing Joe, "I hope you will excuse your three friends for a little while. Thomas, can I leave you to see to it that our guest is entertained until we return?"

"Of course, Papa." Thomas looked pleased with the prospect. "I'll entertain him myself."

His father raised his eyebrows and smiled. "I have no doubt of that, my son. No doubt at all."

In silence, the three travelers followed their host down the hall to the study. Upon the opening of the door, they saw Mrs. Westlin standing on the far side of the room. Beside her was Ellen.

Softly Mr. Westlin closed the door behind them all. No one spoke. Ellen stood, her face pale and her eyes full of a mixture of joy, fear, hope and sorrow. Pressing her lips tightly together, she made no sound, but dropped her eyes to the floor, only stealing a glance now and then at the strangers who had suddenly come to claim kinship with her.

It was Carson who broke the silence. Advancing a step past Ty and Sally, he looked long at the slight figure before him and then with a broken, "Sunshine, oh, my sunshine!" he crossed the room with swift strides and folded the girl in his arms.

In Ellen's mind, memories long since forgotten came flooding back and she clung to him sobbing, "Uncle Bob!" That voice, those arms, which held her now so closely, she remembered. The little cabin, the love she had felt, those happy days together; though but a wee thing then, she had never really forgotten it all; it was only new life, the busy whirl of growing up which had crowded the past until it grew dimmer and dimmer.

Now, in the fold of those strong arms, with the smell of the great outdoors on his shirt, and above all, the cherished name, it all came rushing back.

"Sunshine, I thought I had lost ya ferever! The good Lord was right kind ta me an' I reckon I ain't never can thank Him enough!"

It was some moments before Carson released Ellen and stepping back from her, raised her chin to look into her face. "Yep," he murmured after a searching look, "ya look jest like yer Ma. Sally," he called, "come show yer sister yer ma's picture."

Biting her lips, Sally moved slowly across the room, drawing out from her dress the wooden locket Ty had carved to hold the small picture. In silence the two girls looked at each other. Everything was so still that the ticking of the clock sounded strangely loud to those watching the first meeting of these sisters. At last Sally held out the locket.

"This is our mother, Ellen, and," she added, "you have her name."

Ellen had taken the picture but at Sally's words she glanced up quickly. "I do?" she whispered.

Sally nodded.

Trying to blink back the sudden rush of emotion, Ellen bent over the picture. But she couldn't see. Hot tears blinded her eyes and the faint sound of a sob reached Sally's ears.

Forgetting all about the difference in their upbringing, their difference in clothes and in practically everything else, Sally only remembered that Ellen, her own little sister, had never known their mother or their father and never would. Her tender heart went out and she held open her arms.

In an instant, Ellen had buried her face in the collar of her sister's dress and was crying with such an outbreak of tears that she could scarcely catch her breath. This was all so sudden, so unexpected. Clinging to each other, the girls cried, mingling their tears.

Of the two of them, it was Sally who gained control of her emotions first. Then she soothed and comforted Ellen, whispering tender words to her that no one else could hear.

Ty, watching it all, suddenly turned and left the room. Striding down the hall, his face set, he snatched up his hat, pulled open the front door and rushed outside. He didn't care where he went, he just had to get out. So lost in his own thoughts was he that he didn't notice the following footsteps until a hand was placed on his arm. He looked up.

Joe was beside him. He had caught a glimpse of Ty's face from the sitting room and, excusing himself to young Thomas, had followed his friend outside and down the street. "What is it, Ty?" he asked, concern in his every tone.

Ty didn't answer but continued moving rapidly down the street, his long strides covering the ground quickly. It wasn't until they had reached the edge of the city where the Sierra Nevadas could be seen in the distance that Ty halted. Breathing hard, he flung himself down on a rock, crossed his arms over his knees and buried his face in them his hat falling at his feet.

Silently Joe sat down beside him and waited.

After a while Ty's breathing slowed and, drawing a long, quivering breath, he pushed his arms up until his elbows rested on his knees but still kept his face shaded by his hands.

"Ty, is everything all right?" Joe asked quietly.

"I jest had ta get out," was the muffled response. When Joe didn't respond, Ty went on, "I reckon they think I'm a coward."

Joe snorted. "You, a coward? Hardly."

Sighing, Ty's shoulders sagged. "I jest couldn't stay there. Seein' her an' hearin' her talk was like Ma—" something choked his voice, and he couldn't finish.

Sympathetically, Joe gave his friend's arm a squeeze and remained silent.

At last Ty raised his head. "Thanks, Joe." With another sigh he picked up his hat and slapped it a few times on his leg. Then he stood up. "I reckon I ought ta go back, Sally'll be gettin' worried if'n she's noticed I ain't there."

Both men were silent as they strode back down the street until they reached the Westlin mansion. There they found young Thomas waiting for them on the porch.

"Aw, I thought you'd gone to shoot a bear," he complained.

Ty had to smile. "I'm 'fraid there ain't any bears 'round these here parts ta shoot, Tom."

Opening the door into the study, Ty found everyone still there. Seated side by side, the two sisters looked up when Ty entered. Crossing the room until he stood directly before them, Ty looked down. One dark haired, with a sturdy, outdoors, wide awake look in her dark eyes while the other was fair and small, with large blue eyes and light hair and a half shy look in her face and manners.

For one brief moment, he was silent while Ellen gazed up at him timidly. Then he spoke, "Sally, when ya was little, ya used ta ask me what Ma sounded like. Well, she sounded jest like Ellen. An' she looked jest like her too. Makes me feel like a little shaver standin' here lookin' at her."

Ellen's cheeks, which had been so pale, grew a rosy red, and she dropped her eyes.

"Yep," Ty went on, lifting his sister's face with one finger so he could look into it, "I ain't seen one yet, but I reckon when she smiles it'll be jest like Ma's, bright enough ta light a room at midnight."

As Ty had expected, his remarks called forth a small smile from his newly discovered sister while her cheeks grew even rosier. Suddenly, he stooped and kissed her.

That kiss was too much for her overwrought nerves. The tiny smile which had appeared vanished, and her pretty chin quivered. Blinking back the tears, Ellen rose abruptly and fled.

CHAPTER THIRTY-FIVE

Her mother called her and would have followed, but Mr. Westlin placed a detaining hand on her arm. "Let her go, Leah, this has been a trying morning. I think she needs time alone. And Ty," he added turning to the young man, "I don't think it was anything you said or did."

"I would have done the same, Ty," Sally added squeezing his arm and wiping her eyes.

The ticking of the clock was the only sound in the room for several minutes, then Mr. Westlin spoke. "You three have already met Thomas; are you ready to meet nearly half a dozen girls?"

Heads nodded and Carson, Ty and Sally followed the Westlins out into the hall.

"I know the children have been longing to know what this has all been about," Mrs. Westlin remarked over her shoulder. "I've heard them making guesses, but no one has come up with the right answer yet."

To say the news was a surprise would have been an understatement. The older girls recalled vaguely when Ellen came to live with them, but the younger ones, including Thomas, had never known that Ellen wasn't their true sister. Many and varied were the exclamations over it, the questions asked and answered by Carson and their father. Young

Westlin Jr. was thrilled to find out that Ty was Ellen's brother.

"That makes you my brother!" he exclaimed attempting a hand stand in his excitement.

"Thomas!" his mother reproved as he fell with a crash to the floor.

But the young lad didn't seem to hear for he immediately picked himself up and pranced about the room saying to Ty, "Now you can take me hunting! I've never had a brother before. Can we go now? I want to shoot a bear or a mountain lion! Yee-haw!" He waved his pocket handkerchief wildly as he uttered what he thought was an Indian war whoop.

"Thomas!" Mrs. Westlin shook her head and put her hands over her ears.

"All right, Son," his father said, grasping his shoulders firmly. "Settle down. You are not out in the wilderness, remember."

"But Papa," the boy persisted, "can't I go hunting now, can't I?"

Before the lawyer could reply, Ty answered in slow, quiet tones. "There ain't nothin' ta hunt in the city, Tom. Best wait till we can get out inta the hills 'less ya want ta shoot someone 'stead a somethin'."

Ty's words had the effect of calming young Thomas for the time being and the talk in the room continued.

When Kitty slipped away later to find Ellen, Sally went with her.

The next few days which followed found Ty and Sally, Carson and Joe at the Westlins' hospitable home. There they got to know the family who had taken the young motherless child in and given her a home. Ellen easily became reacquainted with Uncle Bob as she shyly called him, for her memories of him, though faint, were tender ones, and his evident delight in having her around was pleasant.

Between Ellen and Sally the friendship was immediate, and Ellen enjoyed having another sister about. Even if Sally was used to the wild and rugged life in the mountains with their dangers and hardships, she soon felt at ease in the Westlin mansion. From her Ellen learned about their father and of the life in the little log cabin in the mountains.

Of all the travelers, it was with Ty that Ellen became shy. Never would she remain in the same room alone with him, which wasn't difficult, for Thomas Jr. was Ty's constant shadow. When the family went out to church or some other place, Ellen ignored Ty's existence. She wouldn't admit it even to her sisters, but she was ashamed of Ty's rough clothes and evident look of a trapper or mountain man. His speech, too, was cause for embarrassment and she was half afraid of him. Never had she seen the tender side of Ty, for always others were about. Sally could have told her, but she didn't ask.

Though she didn't say anything, Sally rather guessed what was going on in her new sister's mind in regards to Ty. "If she only knew what he was really like out in the vast wilds of his country and not shut up here in the busy city with nothing to occupy his time," she would murmur to herself as she watched them both, "then she would love him. She couldn't help it."

One evening, as Joe and Ty lingered out on the hotel porch after Sally and Carson had retired to their rooms, Joe said, "Ty."

"Yep," Ty replied glancing at the young man leaning on a pillar.

"Maybe I shouldn't be saying this right now, but I wanted you to know——" he paused and wiped his forehead with the sleeve of his shirt though the evening was still chilly.

Ty grinned in the dark. He had a fairly good idea of what Joe was talking about, but he waited in silence for him to continue.

"Oh, I'm no good at beating around the bush, Ty. I'll just out and say it. Ty, I want to marry your sister."

Hiding a smile, Ty replied casually, "I reckon ya'll have ta talk that over with Mr. Westlin."

Joe whirled around. "What for?" he demanded.

"Ellen is more his daughter than my sister it seems, so it would only be fair—"

Joe interrupted, "Ellen? It's Sally I want to marry! Didn't you know it?" Joe sounded surprised and slightly bewildered.

Chuckling, Ty replied, "I've known that since 'fore we left yer folks' house last summer. Why da ya think I were in sech a hurry ta leave? I've jest been waitin' now fer ya ta do somethin' 'bout it."

"You knew? Then why did you say . . ." Joe let his sentence die on the air and gripped Ty's offered hand. "You sure had me there for a minute, Ty. Why didn't you give a fellow a hint that you knew about it?"

Ty shrugged, still with a grin on his face. "Ya think I were goin' ta help ya out with stealin' my sister?"

"I thought it would be the only way to get you to come back to the ranch and visit now and then," Joe retorted. Now that he was certain of winning Sally, for he had no doubts about her, he felt lighthearted and willing to joke.

Chuckling, Ty clapped him on the shoulder then turned and went inside, leaving Joe to rejoice alone out in the dark.

Though Ty had known it was coming, still it took some getting used to. Sally's marriage would leave him alone. What would he do then? He lay for a long time that night pondering and puzzling. At last, reminding himself that he would never be truly alone, he turned over and was soon snoring.

Before noon of the following day, Sally was the happiest girl in the city while Joe never stopped smiling. Ellen was thrilled with the idea of Sally marrying Joe for she greatly admired him. His speech was polished as were his manners and even if he did wear rougher clothes than most young men of her acquaintance, he was still a gentleman. The Westlin girls, too, shared in the excitement.

Standing at the door to her father's study, Ellen knocked softly. It was late afternoon, and he was home from the office. On being cordially invited to enter, she slipped in, closing the door behind her.

Mr. Westlin smiled when he saw her, pushed away his papers and leaned back in his chair. "What can I do for you, Dear? Or did you come to help me?"

She smiled slightly. Often she had taken dictation for her father, for he said she had a remarkably clear hand. "Papa," Ellen began, "will you—" she paused and slowly drew something small from her pocket. "Will you fix my locket?" her voice was tremulous and she held out the broken half, which Ty had faithfully carried on his watch guard during his search.

Taking the broken piece in his hand, Mr. Westlin looked first at it and then at his daughter's face. He had not been blind to Ellen's rejection of her brother. Though he understood somewhat of how difficult it must be to suddenly adjust to having an older brother, he still couldn't understand why it was taking Ellen so long to get to know him.

At last, in a gentle voice he handed back the locket and said, "Ask Ty to fix it." Looking keenly at her, he saw a flush creep up her cheeks, and she dropped her eyes.

There was a moment of silence before Ellen slowly turned to leave the room. At the door, her father's voice caused her to pause with one hand on the door handle and glance back.

"Ellen, Ty would do almost anything for you, if you would let him."

Softly she slipped out of the study and went up to her room without a word. She didn't want to ask Ty to fix her locket. What would people say if they knew she was the youngest sister of a rough trapper from the mountains? The words her father had spoken echoed in her mind. Would Ty really do anything for her? She wasn't so sure. Wrapping the locket back in her handkerchief she slipped it back in her pocket. Then, putting on her cloak and hat, for though spring was coming, it was still quite chilly at times, she slipped down the stairs and out the door without attracting anyone's attention. She had to think things out.

Striding down the street with thumbs tucked in his gun belt, Ty looked at the many buildings around him and sighed for the wide open places where nothing was taller than him except the trees and the mountains. How he longed to get back out to those wild lands of his where he could trap and hunt to his heart's delight once more, where he could sleep out under the stars or in a log cabin, and the only neighbors nearby were the wild animals with an occasional Indian or fellow trapper. Away where a person could hear himself think. But spring had not yet come and so he had to wait.

It was at that moment that he suddenly became aware of a voice nearby. Two voices in fact. One sounded like that of his new sister while the other was a man's voice. Curiously, Ty wondered what Ellen was doing so far from home. As he listened, he noticed that the tone of his sister's voice seemed indignant and almost frightened. Moving closer quickly yet quietly, Ty approached a sheltered little park. There he could see without being seen. Ellen was standing facing the bushes behind which Ty was watching and, with his back to him, stood a man. Ty had no idea who it was, but his keen ear could now make out Ellen's words spoken in a protesting, appealing manner.

"Please, Mr. Bernard, Papa doesn't want me to have anything to do with you, and I don't either, so kindly have the goodness to step aside and let me pass."

Then the stranger's voice answered, sweetly, smoothly, too smoothly Ty thought. "Come now, Miss Ellen, I know you love me."

"I do not!"

"They always protest when it is the truth," the man purred. "Just one little kiss, my sweet."

"Unhand me! Leave me alone. No! I will not kiss you." Ellen's voice was shaking as she drew back a step and Ty's jaw tightened.

"Then I'll have to take one."

"Leave her alone!" A stern voice interrupted the man as he made a move to take his coveted kiss. Ty, with brows drawn and eyes flashing now stood behind the man.

Slowly the man turned with a snarling, "Leave us be."

Then Ty saw his face. "Bartram!"

Quick as a flash the outlaw's gun was in his hand.

CHAPTER THIRTY-SIX

Ty realized instantly that a shoot-out might mean injury or even death for his sister. Like a rattlesnake when he strikes, Ty's left hand had caught the barrel of Bartram's gun even as he pulled it from its holster and, with a mighty twist, he wrenched it from his hand and flung it aside before Bartram had time to pull the trigger. Just then Bartram's left fist connected with Ty's jaw splitting his lip and causing him to stagger, but he remained on his feet.

Moving quickly to one side, he struck his opponent on the eye. With a snarl of rage Bartram became a wildcat. His heavy fists swung wildly only to be blocked by Ty's skillful maneuverings. At last Ty managed to land another blow to the outlaw's face, this time resulting in a bloody nose for the villain. Furious by this added pain, Bartram pressed forward, but Ty moved away. With a cool head and the knowledge that if he were to let down his guard even for a split second, Bartram would finish him, Ty watched his chances.

Slowly the seconds ticked by with no visible advantage to either opponent. It wasn't until Ty's quick ears caught the sound of the outlaw's labored breathing that he began to press the attack. Those years of outdoor work and living now showed themselves in Ty's favor. They had toughened him. Moving about quickly and lightly, he rained blows down on Bartram, sometimes receiving blows in return, but mostly moving aside or blocking them.

Beginning to grow desperate, for he saw that in another few moments Ty would have him, the wanted outlaw reached down to draw his other gun. That was his undoing for, as he lowered his guard, Ty sent a blow with all his weight behind it above Bartram's right ear. Then, without a pause, his left fist connected so solidly with the villain's jaw, that his head jerked back and he fell in a senseless heap on the ground.

Ty drew a long, deep breath and looked down at the inert figure at his feet. Hearing a slight sound a few steps away, he glanced over to Ellen and saw his sister, with face as white as her collar pressing her hands over her mouth, her eyes wide with fear. "Ya all right Ellie?" Ty asked, stepping over Bartram's still form and moving to her side.

She nodded, starting a little at the pet name of her girlhood.

Seeing that she was not hurt, only frightened by the fight, Ty returned to his fallen foe. Swiftly he bound Bartram's hands behind him, rolled him over and pulled out his other pistol. "I don't reckon he'll be needin' these where he's goin'," and he retrieved the first one from a nearby bush where it had been kicked in the scuffle. Stuffing the two guns in his own belt he glanced around.

Ellen was still standing where she had been when the fight had started only now she was shaking. Never had she seen such a sight as that fight had been.

Pulling off his coat, Ty placed it gently around his young sister's shoulders. "I'll take ya home, Ellie, but I've got ta take that low-down skunk ta the sheriff soon's I see ya ta the door."

Ellen shook her head. "I'll . . . go with you to the sheriff, Ty. It's on the way." Lifting her eyes from the quiet form of the man she had known as Bernard, she noticed Ty's face had blood on it. "Ty, you're hurt!" There was concern in her voice.

"Ain't much. Jest a few cuts. Ya needn't fret 'bout it," and he tried to smile though his split lip made it somewhat difficult.

Bartram stirred a little and Ty nudged him with the toe of his boot. "Come on, Bartram, I reckon the sheriff'll be interested in seein' ya."

Glaring up at his conqueror, the wanted outlaw growled. "We'll get you yet, Ty Elliot. Mason'll be hunting you down like a fox in the hen house."

Ellen gasped, but Ty snorted. "I ain't likely ta believe that, Bartram, 'cause I took them four rat-snakes ta the lockup myself an' I reckon the U.S. Marshall had 'em swingin' long time 'fore this. Now, on yer feet. I ain't wastin' no more time on ya." With no gentle hand, Ty grasped Bartram's shirt and jerked him to his feet. "An' no tryin' ta slip away." As Ty spoke he drew his own six-shooter and cocked it.

Bartram heard the soft click and knew Ty meant every word he said.

Moving softly up beside her brother, Ellen slipped her hand through his arm. Her face, still pale, held a look of admiration that would have warmed Ty's heart had he seen it. As it was, however, his attention was focused on the man before him.

Down the street the three marched. Ellen, holding Ty's rough coat about her with one hand while clinging to her brother's arm with the other, Ty, face grim and with marks of the recent fight on it, kept his gun in Bartram's ribs as that fellow stumbled along, one eye black and closed, nose bloodied and a look of mingled anger and defeat on his face.

It only took a short time before they reached the sheriff's door. Ty opened it and shoved his prisoner inside. Ellen stepped through the door and then Ty followed.

Sheriff Jones and two of his deputies looked up in surprise as the unlikely trio appeared before them.

"Miss Westlin," the sheriff exclaimed starting up from his desk.

"Sheriff Jones, this is my brother, Ty Elliot. He has a scoundrel for you to lock up."

It was Ty's turn to look surprised. Never had he expected this sister to introduce him as her brother. Had she really accepted him as part of the family? Sheriff Jones was waiting for him to speak.

"Sheriff, I'd like ya ta meet Outlaw Bartram. Yer paper yonder," and Ty nodded his head towards the wanted list tacked up on the wall, "says ya want 'im."

"Bartram!" exclaimed Sheriff Jones and his deputies simultaneously. "Where in the world—? How did you ever—?"

"Well, I reckon if'n ya don't want him . . ." Ty interrupted the wide-eyed lawmen.

"Want him! Why there's a three hundred dollar reward for his capture! Take him and lock him up!" the sheriff ordered, and his deputies hurried to obey.

"There'll be a reward coming to you, sir," Sheriff Jones said, shaking Ty's hand as the deputies led Bartram away to lock him securely in a jail cell. "How ever did you find him? I see from the looks of your face that it wasn't easy bringing him in. He's a tough coyote. What's the story?" and the sheriff leaned against the wall regarding the young man before him with intense interest.

Ty really didn't feel like talking, but as he pulled out the outlaw's guns from his belt and placed them on the desk he said, "He insulted my sister an' I knocked him out."

The sheriff laughed. "I reckon there was a little more to it than that, but I have enough to keep that stage robber behind bars until the marshall gets here. I'll wire him at once. When you feel more like talking, I wish you'd let me hear the rest of the story. I have a feeling it'd be worth listening to."

"May we go home now, Sheriff?" Ellen pleaded, anxiously watching Ty's face.

"Of course, of course," the sheriff agreed adding as Ty and Ellen stepped through the door, "What did you say your name was, sir?"

Before Ty could reply, Ellen answered for him, "He is Ty Elliot, my brother."

Leaving a thoroughly puzzled sheriff to wonder how the beautiful Miss Westlin came to have such a brother, Ty and Ellen started on their way home.

Ellen insisted on giving Ty back his coat but still clung to his arm. Neither one said a word on the way back to the Westlin mansion.

In the front hall Thomas Jr. met them. His eyes grew wide as he saw the blood on Ty's face. "Did you meet a bear?" he inquired eagerly.

"Rather like one," muttered Ty in tones too low for the boy to catch.

Ellen answered, "No, Thomas, it was an outlaw."

"An outlaw!" the boy breathed. Then suddenly he found his voice and dashed off down the hall shouting, "Papa! Ty fought an outlaw! Mama, come see! Sally, Joe! He really did, Ellen said so."

Ty shook his head. "I reckon I ought ta take 'im huntin' soon."

"Come in here," Ellen urged, drawing him into the library where he sank into the nearest chair and tried to smile.

"I reckon I ain't a pretty sight, best let me go wash up a might."

Before Ellen could reply, the door into the library was flung open and Sally rushed in followed by Joe and Carson at her heels.

"Oh, Ty!" Sally exclaimed dropping down on the floor beside his chair. "You're hurt."

"Who was it, Ty?" Carson asked. "It weren't—"

"Yep," Ty answered his unfinished sentence. "Bartram."

Sally gasped. "How did it happen? How did you find him? Where is he? Ty, what happened?"

"Give him a chance to answer, Sally," Joe soothed.

"Oh, Papa!" Ellen turned to her father and clung to him. "He tried to kiss me! And then he fought him and I thought he would be killed and he knocked him down and—" Ellen ended with a burst of tears.

The arm about her waist tightened and her father's voice was almost stern. "Who tried to kiss you?" Then it softened. "Ellen, you are making no sense. Which he is who?"

"Well, Ty," Carson began, "I reckon it's up ta ya ta tell us what happened. Yer sister ain't likely ta speak plainly 'bout it, bein' as she's rather winded."

Ty remained silent a few minutes with his eyes closed. He hated talking about the fights he was in, but he realized that this was a story that would have to be told.

Mr. Westlin had requested a basin of warm water and when it arrived, Sally gently began washing the blood from her brother's face. Besides the split lip and a few cuts and bruises there didn't appear to be much damage.

At last he opened his eyes and looked at the eager, excited, expectant faces about him and he gave a lopsided grin. "Ain't much to it, like I done told the sheriff. I heard Bartram insultin' Ellie, an' when I ordered him ta stop he turned an' I saw who it were. He tried ta draw on me an' after I took the gun away, we had a bout with our fists. He's in the lock up now. I reckon that's the last we'll see a him," and Ty pushed Sally's hands away from his face with a soft, "I'm all right."

Young Thomas wasn't satisfied with the story. "But who won?"

"I don't reckon I'd be here if'n he had," Ty replied.

Then Ellen, recovered from her fright, began the tale again, only this time with more detail. Her powers as a story teller were wonderful and everyone sat or stood in silence as she recounted the entire event. Only Ty was restless, and he would have slipped from the room had there been a chance to do so.

Later, after Ty had been praised and thanked, and finally left alone to his intense relief, Ellen slipped in silently and drawing a low stool sat down before her brother's chair.

He gave her a welcome smile.

"Ty," she asked somewhat timidly, for when the excitement of the fight had worn off, she again turned shy, "would you . . ." She paused and her voice became a mere whisper. "Would you fix my locket?" Opening her hand, she held out the broken half.

CHAPTER THIRTY-SEVEN

Ty gazed down into that sweet face before him and smiled. "Yep," was all he said, but he took the locket and looked at it.

Ellen leaned against his knee and watched him. Those strong hands, which had knocked the outlaw down and could handle a gun with ease, were also skillful in the tiny details. Neither one spoke until at last, after so many years, the two halves of the locket once more were made into one.

"Thank you," Ellen murmured as Ty clasped the delicate chain about the white throat. Giving a long sigh, Ellen rested her head on Ty's knee and let him stroke her long golden hair.

"Tell me about Ma, Ty, please?"

In low, quiet tones, Ty began. And for a long time they sat there together, that brother and sister so long unknown to each other, Ty telling about their mother and then of their father. The room grew dim but neither one noticed. They had so much to learn and so little time, for the days would go by swiftly and soon it would be spring when Ty would head back to his beloved wilderness and mountains.

And so the days passed by. The air grew warmer. Spring was coming. The Westlins dreaded the upcoming separation, which they knew would take place. Ty had taken Thomas Jr. out of the city several times and instructed him in horseback riding and the use of a gun, much to the boy's great delight. Joe and Sally were looking forward to their approaching wedding, and, though the Westlins urged it, they refused to be married in Sacramento.

"No," Sally would say when urged. "The first real mother I can remember was Mrs. Fields and there I will be married."

As spring became more apparent, Ty and Carson became increasingly restless. Finally plans were made. At the pressing invitation of the Fields as well as the passionate plea from Ellen, Mr. Westlin agreed to accompany Carson, Ty, Sally and Joe at least as far as the Fields' home and to take Ellen and Thomas Jr. along. Young Thomas was wild with excitement and planned day and night what he would do if the train was held up, they were attacked by Indians, or if a bear or mountain lion should suddenly appear. Ty merely grinned when Sally or Ellen begged him to try to curb the boys enthusiasm.

Ty received the three hundred dollar reward money for capturing Bartram and tucked it away for a later time.

As the train pulled away from the Sacramento station to cross the Sierra Nevada mountain range heading for Reno, the seven travelers settled themselves down in relative silence, each thinking about what lay before them. Even Thomas Westlin Jr. was quiet, not, however, from thinking about what lay ahead, but wondering if those men who were talking in low tones several seats before him were planning on robbing the train.

The train ride through the mountains was swifter than the previous one the four friends had taken and this time they were not held up by an avalanche. Arriving in Reno, the party headed for the stables where they had left their horses before moving on to Sacramento. After the long rest, the horses were anxious to be out and ridden again. Mr. Westlin declined the offer of a horse and instead purchased tickets for himself, the two ladies and Thomas on the stagecoach. Young Thomas begged to be allowed to ride with the men and to his delight, was given Sally's mount, she being the best suited for a young and inexperienced rider.

"Don't ya worry none, 'bout young Tom," Ty told Mr. Westlin in undertones as Sally was helping the boy saddle and mount Starlight. "I'll keep my eyes on him an' I reckon it won't be long 'fore he's askin' ta ride in the stage."

Mr. Westlin smiled. "I'm not worried, Ty. I know you'll look out for the lad. But don't count on getting rid of him to the stagecoach any time soon. If I know my son, and I think I do, he'll ride in that saddle until he drops."

Grinning, Ty turned to Ellen who was never very far from his side since they left Sacramento. "When Tom drops from the saddle, ya goin ta ride Starlight instead?"

Raising her eyebrows with a look of doubt, the girl shook her head. "I wouldn't even last half a day, I'm afraid."

"We'll get ya used ta the saddle once we get ta the Fields," Ty promised her, turning to mount Par. "We'll see ya folks at the first stopping place."

"Ty, wait," Ellen called as Ty turned his mount's head to join the other three riders.

He paused and Ellen stepped over to him. "I was going to wait to give this to you, but—" and she placed a small package in his hand.

When the wrappings came off, there lay in his hand a watch guard shaped much like the broken locket his father had given him. On it was painted a small miniature of Ellen and Sally. For a moment, Ty couldn't speak. Then, with a tender smile, he swung off Par, wrapped his arms about his sister and kissed her tenderly. "I'll wear it always, Ellie," he whispered slipping the guard with its doubly sweet picture onto the chain of his watch and glancing about for Sally.

Leaving Thomas and Starlight with Carson and Joe, Sally had seen Ellen and Ty and guessing what was going on, came over. Ty gave her a brotherly kiss and then, vaulting into the saddle, rode off after the three riders, waving his hat and calling back over his shoulder, "See ya soon!"

Traveling day after day, it wasn't long before the travelers all reached the small town closest to the Fields ranch where Mr. Fields waited to greet them with the wagon. Thomas Jr. had managed to ride on horseback for the first two days, but after that, Carson, Joe and Ty rode alone each with a horse behind them.

Sally, Ty and Carson's welcome back to the hospitable home of the Fields was warm. Sally especially was embraced tenderly by Mrs. Fields while Joe was greeted by much hand shaking and back slapping from his brothers, Jack and Jed, and from the ranch hands. Mr. Westlin immediately developed a liking for this family and he and Mr. Fields found much in common. Ellen was quiet, taking in everything she saw with wonder. Everyone liked her.

As for Tom, as Thomas Jr. now insisted that he be called since he was out of the city, his enthusiasm knew no bounds. His days began at sunrise and ended only after the sun had disappeared and everyone else was retiring. He rode horses with the men, helped round up cattle and went hunting with Ty.

The day of Joe and Sally's wedding was beautiful. The sun was shining brightly while white fluffy clouds dotted the sky. Everywhere the grass was green and late spring flowers were blooming. Standing out in the yard with everyone else, Ty watched with a strange feeling tugging at his heart. Sally was gone from him. She would no more be in the little cabin when he came home hungry and tired from hunting or trapping. All these years she had been his companion until he had to leave for two years with Carson, and now, . . . He tried to swallow the lump in his throat, but it refused to leave. Having kissed the bride and shaken hands with the groom, Ty strode away and was seen no more the rest of the day.

When he returned at dusk, his face was peaceful and his smile bright. Out there alone with his God he had found peace.

For several weeks following the wedding, Ty's party remained as guests at the Fields', helping out with the cattle or in the house, but at last Ty announced his intention of returning to Mel's Ridge and his own cabin.

"Papa," Ellen begged, "I want to see the cabin and . . ." her voice broke, "Pa's grave." She looked up pleadingly, her eyes full of unshed tears.

"It's a long journey, darling," her father told her.

"I know, but—" she didn't finish but her eyes spoke for her.

Drawing a deep breath, Mr. Westlin turned to Ty, "Well, Ty, what would you think of some visitors?"

A slow smile spread across Ty's face. "I were tryin' ta get up courage ta ask ya ta come out."

Tom held his breath. Would his father really say they could go with Ty?

Mr. Westlin was looking at his daughter. She was so young and sheltered, yet he knew she came from the same hearty stock as did Ty and Sally. At last he spoke. "All right. We'll go."

Tom let out a yell so loud that Mrs. Fields dropped a stitch in her knitting.

"Joe," Sally whispered, wrapping her arms about her husband's neck, "couldn't we go too? I want to see Pa's grave and the cabin once more."

Joe kissed the ruby lips so near his own. "If Ty doesn't mind more company."

Of course Ty didn't mind and in three days the party set out, all on horseback, for Ty had snorted at the idea of a wagon. "We'd have ta leave it someplace," he had said. "'Cause there ain't no roads ta get ta Mel's Ridge 'less we go the long way, an' I aim ta get back jest soon's I can."

It was late afternoon. Smoke came from the chimney of the little log cabin in the woods a couple of miles from Mel's Ridge. Lights filtered through the windows and the stamp and occasional whicker of a horse in the barn could be heard. Birds sang in the lofty branches of the tall, straight pine trees. In one tree, a squirrel chattered about his neighbor's doings and scolded the young boy who sat below on the ground looking up at him.

Inside the cabin, Sally was busy preparing the evening meal over the fire just as she used to do. Joe was bringing more wood in while Mr. Westlin wandered about, recalling the few years he had spent out in the wilds before moving his family.

Carson was in the barn, tending to the horses. "I know this ain't 'xactly a large barn like yer used ta," he told the animals, "but I reckon it'll have ta work. Tomorra we can turn ya out ta graze some, but it'd be a whole heap safer fer ya ta sleep here tonight. 'Sides, some a us men folks'll be here ta keep ya company if'n it rains."

Out in the woods, Ty was leading Ellen slowly through the trees. At last they stopped before a low mound of earth. There was no marker, but Ty had notched a tree before leaving the grave that snowy winter day. Now in silence the brother and sister stood gazing down at the last earthly resting place of their father.

"Pa," Ty spoke quietly, dropping to his knees, "I done it. I found my sister jest like I promised ya I would, an' I brought her to ya. She's all right."

With tears streaming down her cheeks, Ellen knelt beside Ty. "Oh, Pa! I'm here. I wish I could have known you and Ma, but I'll never forget you. Thank you for sending Ty to find me. I—" and she broke down completely.

Gently Ty wrapped his arms around her and said, "We're all home Pa, me, Sally an' Ellen. Home together at last."

In the course of time, Mr. Westlin took his son, Tom, and daughter, Ellen, back to Sacramento. Joe and his wife returned to the Fields' to set up a home of their own while Carson returned to his trapping and hunting with renewed zeal, for now his desire to find his Sunshine had been satisfied. As for Ty, to Sally's great satisfaction, he was elected the first sheriff of Mel's Ridge and faithfully served the people there for many years.

Rebekah A. Morris

ABOUT THE AUTHOR

Rebekah A. Morris is a homeschool graduate who has a love for writing. She is the author of dozens of short stories and poems. After six years of loving labor, her first book, <u>Home Fires of the Great War</u>, came out in March, 2011. Currently Rebekah has two books of short stories publish as well as the first two books in her <u>Triple Creek Ranch</u> series. Every Friday her blog <u>www.rsreadingroom.blogspot.com</u> is updated with her work. In addition to her own writing, Rebekah enjoys sharing her passion for writing with her students.

Made in the USA
Coppell, TX
27 September 2022

83665749R00174